Grace

Another Homecoming

JANETTE OKE
T. DAVIS BUNN

Another Homecoming

BETHANY HOUSE PUBLISHERS
MINNEAPOLIS, MINNESOTA 55438

Published by Bethany House Publishers
A Ministry of Bethany Fellowship, Inc.
11300 Hampshire Avenue South
Minneapolis, Minnesota 55438

Printed in the United States of America.

Library of Congress Cataloging-in-Publication Data

Oke, Janette, 1935–
    Another homecoming / by Janette Oke and T. Davis Bunn.
      p. cm.
ISBN 1–55661–978–2 (cloth)
ISBN 1–55661–934–0 (paperback)
ISBN 1–55661–979–0 (large print)
ISBN 1–55661–980–4 (audio book)
    I. Bunn, T. Davis, 1952–   . II. Title.
PR9199.3.O38A82   1997
813'.54—dc21

                                                         97–4669
                                                          CIP

Dedicated to
all those who have helped and
prayed us through this creative process,
with our heartfelt gratitude.

The first fiction collaboration between novelists Janette Oke and T. Davis Bunn resulted in a delightful story set in North Carolina in the early 1900s, *Return to Harmony*.

This second joint effort, *Another Homecoming*, unfolds with World War II. Characters come to life through heartbreak and hope and discovery. Once again, the complementary strengths and creativity of these two gifted writers provide a compelling reading experience.

Janette Oke and her husband, Edward, live in Calgary, Alberta, where she writes her well-loved stories and enjoys her grandchildren. Davis Bunn and his wife, Isabella, make their home near Oxford, England, where he continues his award-winning research and writing.

Books by T. Davis Bunn

The Quilt
The Gift
The Messenger
The Music Box

*Another Homecoming**
The Presence
Promises to Keep
*Return to Harmony**
Riders of the Pale Horse

THE PRICELESS COLLECTION
Secret Treasures of Eastern Europe

1. *Florian's Gate*
2. *The Amber Room*
3. *Winter Palace*

RENDEZVOUS WITH DESTINY

1. *Rhineland Inheritance*
2. *Gibraltar Passage*
3. *Sahara Crosswind*
4. *Berlin Encounter*
5. *Istanbul Express*

*with Janette Oke

9701

Books by Janette Oke

*Another Homecoming**
Janette Oke's Reflections on the Christmas Story
Nana's Gift
The Red Geranium
*Return to Harmony**

SEASONS OF THE HEART

Once Upon a Summer *Winter Is Not Forever*
The Winds of Autumn *Spring's Gentle Promise*

LOVE COMES SOFTLY

Love Comes Softly *Love's Unending Legacy*
Love's Enduring Promise *Love's Unfolding Dream*
Love's Long Journey *Love Takes Wing*
Love's Abiding Joy *Love Finds a Home*

CANADIAN WEST

When Calls the Heart *When Breaks the Dawn*
When Comes the Spring *When Hope Springs New*

WOMEN OF THE WEST

The Calling of Emily Evans *A Bride for Donnigan*
Julia's Last Hope *Heart of the Wilderness*
Roses for Mama *Too Long a Stranger*
A Woman Named Damaris *The Bluebird and the Sparrow*
They Called Her Mrs. Doc *A Gown of Spanish Lace*
The Measure of a Heart *Drums of Change*

DEVOTIONALS

The Father Who Calls *Father of My Heart*
The Father of Love *Faithful Father*

———

Janette Oke: A Heart for the Prairie
Biography of Janette Oke by Laurel Oke Logan

The Oke Family Cookbook
by Barbara Oke and Deborah Oke

*with T. Davis Bunn

CHAPTER ONE

THE BALTIMORE TRAIN STATION was awash in khaki. Soldiers crowded every nook and cranny, their faces taut with the excitement of travel and adventure and war. Uncle Sam pointed fiercely at them from every wall, exhorting them to go and do their duty.

She was one of a thousand weeping women that day, her quiet misery a single drop in an ocean of noisy chaos. Martha clung to her husband, feeling his strength as he held her close, so tight she could scarcely breathe. "Take care, my love," he said to her ear, having nearly to shout just to be heard. "I'll be back soon."

"But what if—" The question she had dared not voice during their nine short weeks of marriage now was cut off by his lips finding hers with urgent passion. Even here, amid the tumult of a world going to war, with the tooting whistles and the blaring brass bands and the shrilly, excited kids, Martha felt herself once again overwhelmed by Harry's kiss. It had been that way since the very first time. Before, really, though she could not have explained how, even to herself. Back when Harry had simply been the young boy who had returned from boot camp a man, back when they were walking out to picture shows and taking ices beneath the softly greening trees of spring, back when she felt her heart first begin to sing with love. Even then she knew that if ever he kissed her, even just once, she would be lost forever to loving him.

Harry released her, and the world jarred back into painful focus. "Don't even think it," he ordered. "Just remember, I'll be back soon as I can. With the good old US of A in it now, we'll have them Krauts ducking for cover in no time flat."

His jaunty strength and confidence was overpowering. She managed a wobbly smile and a nod. But the tears kept coming. He was leaving and going off to war. And what if—

The whistle shrilled another time and was joined by a single, impatient chuff from the distant engine. The soldiers who were not already on board surged forward. Martha's sob was lost in the khaki tide that plucked Harry from her embrace.

This time he did not return to her and silence her fears with his lips. This time he shouldered his kit and turned just long enough to give her a grand flashing smile and blow her a kiss. This time her arms reached out, but he was not there to fill them. She could only stand, one in an endless line of weeping mothers and wives and lovers and children. They watched as their men raced for the slowly moving train, flinging their bags and then themselves into the doorways. They saw the men fight for a crack of space to stick out heads and one arm and shout farewells. Martha's last image of Harry's departure was of a train smothered in smoke and made even more blurry by her tears, a train that had grown a thousand arms of its own.

There were three enemies in Harry Grimes' war—the Germans, the heat, and the desert.

Harry tried not to show his discomfort. He was a master sergeant, after all, and Sergeant Grimes had a reputation for not showing anything. But as far as he was concerned, the desert was a lot harder to take than the Germans. He had seen the Jerries only twice during recent skirmishes. But Harry was surrounded by the desert night and day.

He stretched out in the trench, the camouflage netting overhead offering a hint of shade. Though it filtered out the worst of the blistering sun, it also kept out any breeze, trapping the heat and turning the trench into an oven. He looked up and noted the sun slowly sinking toward the ochre hills. He glanced at his watch, then held it to his ear. Even when he heard the ticking he had trouble believing it was keeping proper time.

"Aye, the last two hours are the longest, and the last five minutes longer still." The boy with the British accent to his left was named Harry as well, which was good enough for a laugh now that Sergeant Grimes had been tested under fire and found acceptable. The Brits were a scrawny lot, mostly wiry and small, but they fought as if the world's future depended on them alone.

Harry Grimes asked, "You really think we'll find them this time?"

"Not a doubt, Yank. They're out there. They're ready, and *they'll* find *us*," he corrected. Harry the Brit was only eighteen, three years younger than Harry Grimes. But he had been fighting in Montgomery's North Africa Campaign for ten long months. His face was a taut mask tainted by sun and war and desert sand. His eyes looked a thousand years old. "Old Rommel's a wily foe. He's kept shifting and turning and running back and forth until he has us right where he wants us. Now he'll be on us like a pack of wild dogs."

"Ease up, Harry, yer a right one with the gloom and doom." The man farther to their left was a heavyset Londoner with a cockney accent so thick Harry Grimes could hardly understand him. "Pay the bloke no mind, Yank. All them Lancashire lads've got porridge between their ears."

"Aye, wait 'til you've been out here long as me, then we'll see how you hold up, sitting here on Rommel's flank."

" 'Ang on, let me go find Monty, tell 'im me mate's got word on how to fix the Jerries up proper."

Harry Grimes slid farther along the trench and shut his ears. The grousing would go on for as long as they were forced to sit and wait. That much was the same here, but not much else. He had been assigned liaison duty with the Brits, and he felt like the proverbial fish out of water—a fish in the desert, no less. But the Brits had been here for a year already and had learned the lessons of desert warfare the hard way. The Americans were just getting started, and everything was in chaos—no surprise, given the speed with which their army had been plucked together.

Harry pulled pad and pencil from his pocket. He had been working on this particular letter to Martha for almost a month. But he never had been much with writing. Besides, there was so little he wanted to say—could say—from such a dislocated distance. The fact that he was thrilled to bits that Martha's pregnancy was going well had been good for a paragraph. Harry desperately wanted that child. The thought of being a father fueled his homesickness. Home to Martha, home to a son. Or a daughter. It really didn't matter one way or the other to Harry.

The fact that he was to become a father made this war even more important. He wanted a safe world for his child. Sure, it would be harder moving from base to base with a family in tow. But many men did it. It gave added stability to army life. And Martha was so excited. He could feel her anticipation even across the miles. It flowed from every line of her letters, and she said it gave her something to look forward to in his absence. "A little bundle of you," she called the child she carried, but he knew it was not just him. The new baby would be a part of each of them.

He had been totally unprepared for his inner excitement at the news of the coming baby and wished with all his being that he could be there with Martha to share their joy.

Martha's letters were full of bittersweet anticipation. She looked forward to the coming child. Yet she so longed for him to be there with her. It didn't seem right that she had to face each day alone. Harry sighed and tapped his pencil. Even though he felt so deeply, he found no way to put the words on the stiff, trench-dirtied paper.

The stuff the Brits called chow had made for another couple of sentences. But there was little else to report except the heat and the dust and the waiting. He didn't want to talk about this second world war. Days and weeks of endless boredom were followed by seconds of noise and terror so fierce he felt as though he had been permanently wounded down deep, where only he could see the scars.

He had come from the wrong side of the tracks, raised in a home without a father and with a mother turned shadowy by hardship and hard work. In high school, girls like Martha had seemed as far away as the moon. He had joined the army because it had been a way out. He had not minded the drill and the marching and the training at all. In fact, Harry had loved everything about the army. The order and the discipline had been reassuring. At long last, Harry Grimes had found himself a home. He had been sure nothing would make him happier than spending the remainder of his days wearing khaki.

Then the Japs had attacked Pearl Harbor and America entered the war. Suddenly Harry Grimes was being hailed as a visionary, one of the few who had seen the coming tide of events and had signed up before any draft notices were sent out. He had already learned the army's lesson of keeping his lip buttoned, and so said nothing to the contrary when they awarded him with stripes and a medal and orders to help train the newly drafted recruits.

He gladly would have spent the entire war as a drill sergeant, but word came of the battalions they were sending to fight Rommel in North Africa, wherever that was, and Harry found himself volunteered. He did not think he would mind.

And then there was Martha. She was the best thing that had ever happened to him. Along with the army. So if he could get this North Africa stint safely behind him, he would go back to Martha and the baby, and he would cheerfully drill soldiers the rest of his life.

A whistle sounded far down the line. One shrill blast, then nothing except the sound of the wind. Harry the Brit hissed at him, "It's time, Yank. Get your kit together."

Harry Grimes buttoned the letter into his left pants pocket. He checked his pack for water and ammo, then slid the greasy rag over his gun a final time. There was nothing worse for fouling a gun than this desert silt. It was so fine it worked into everything, his water, his food, his—

"Good luck, matey," whispered Harry the Brit, then scrambled out.

"Never fear, Yank." The Londoner jumped up from the trench alongside Harry. As they hustled across the baked desert sand, he hissed, "The Krauts're long gone. We'll just reccy over the other side of those hills, then be back in time for another fine breakfast of eggs and tea and sand."

Harry started to speak, but another whistle sounded. This one was much louder and did not stop. Instead it grew more shrill and closer. Then a roar of noise and light and dust and pain blacked out his world.

Dr. Howard Austin raced up the stairs and into the little apartment, not even bothering to knock. "I came as soon as I heard, Martha. Is it . . ."

He stopped midway across the floor. The yellow telegram lay on the floor at her feet, telling him the news was true. Her motions halting and uncertain, she looked toward him. But her eyes did not see him. Her face was void of expression.

"Oh, Martha." Howard walked over and scooped up the telegram to stare at its message. Somehow the words, pasted on the flimsy sheet, looked even more cold and impersonal in their long lines of capital letters that spelled out such devastating information: WE REGRET TO INFORM YOU THAT YOUR HUSBAND MASTER SERGEANT HARRY GRIMES IS MISSING IN ACTION AND PRESUMED DEAD STOP

"They came in a big brown car," Martha said from her place on the worn davenport, her tone as blank as her face. "Two of them. With medals and uniforms and salutes. One of them was older. He looked like he had done this a thousand times. I felt sorry for him. Can you imagine? They bring me this news, and I'm feeling bad for him."

"Because you've got a heart of gold," Howard Austin replied. He pulled a chair over close and seated himself. "It does say 'presumed,' you know," he said gently, knowing even as he said the word that its tiny offering of hope had already been snatched away from her.

"They told me—" She stopped, her face a bewildered mask, then started again. "They said that battle in North Africa was so . . . was so awful that there wouldn't be any survivors." Howard had to lean forward to catch her last words, barely a whisper. He had heard the news reports and knew the officers were correct in not leaving her with false hope.

"Is there anything I can do?" he asked. "Anyone I can call?"

"I don't have anyone, you know that." A single tear trickled down her cheek. She did not bother to wipe it away. Her unseeing gaze returned to the window. "I'm all alone in the world now." Her voice sounded drained of all energy. All feeling.

Howard started to protest, to tell her that she could always count on him. But he couldn't honestly say that. Just that morning he had received his own induction papers. Every glance at the yellow telegram in his hand left him chilled to the bone. "Anything at all," he repeated. "Isn't there something?"

"I don't know." For the first time Martha seemed to find the strength to bring the world into focus. She turned to look at Howard with eyes so full of haunting pain and fear that his heart twisted. "I'm eighteen years old. I have nobody in the world." She crossed her arms over her distended belly. Martha was a small woman, and the child was scarcely three weeks away from term. Even seated as she was, her lightly boned frame seemed scarcely able to support the load. "What am I going to do, Howard? How will I take care of this baby?" Now her tears fell freely, as though she were weeping on behalf of her unborn child who would never know a father's love.

The deliberate way she pronounced the last sentence left him unable to draw on his doctor's training or his usual good cheer. Howard leaned back in his chair and studied this stoically calm woman. And woman she was, no matter how few the number of years she could claim. Her marriage and pregnancy and now the loss of her husband had left little of the child he had known for most of her life.

A few years apart in age, they had been raised on the same Baltimore street, in a section of the city that had been almost entirely Irish in their youth. Now it was much more cosmopolitan. To Howard it seemed as though while he had been away at college and then medical school, other parts of the world had invaded and taken over their old neighborhood. And during that same six-year stretch, knock-kneed little Martha O'Leary had grown into a willowy young lady, lost both her parents, fallen in love with a man from a different social class, a soldier, and wed. Howard could not help but wonder how things might have been had he stayed in Baltimore as his mother had wished and attended a local college.

"What am I going to do?" Martha was asking again. Her quiet voice held to a single note, droning out words heavy with feeling.

"Martha," Howard started, then hesitated. Suddenly he found himself taken by a desire to ask her to wait for him, to let him send her money until he could return from his own army stint. But something held him back. How could he say such words the same day she had learned about her husband? It was impossible. And what if he didn't return? Howard Austin felt as though his heart was humming with the tension of not being able to say what he wanted, while his country pressured him to leave and prepare for war. He swallowed hard and said, "Wait a few days—maybe something will turn up for you." He hoped the words didn't sound as empty to her as they did to him.

"I know what I have to do."

Something in Martha's voice filled Howard with apprehension as he looked at her across his desk. She had come in for a final examination before her baby's delivery. He watched the play of emotions across her delicate girl-woman features, deep pain and sorrow along with determination.

"I want you to find a family who will adopt my baby."

Howard's breath left him as if he'd been struck in the stomach. "You don't really mean that, Martha."

"You said you would help me, Howard." Her voice was pleading.

"Wouldn't it be better—well, a child would be such comfort to you now."

"And wouldn't that be a fine, selfish reason to deny my baby a decent chance at life?" Martha rose from the chair, easing herself up in careful stages. She walked over to the office window and traced one finger along the trail left by gently falling rain. Her other hand caressed the baby. "I couldn't do that, Howard."

There was no anger to her tone, nothing he could hang an argument on. His heart ached for her and the unborn child. It was at times like this that he wished he did not care for his patients as much as he did. Being colder would have made him a much better doctor. And his personal feelings for her made it even worse. "If you say so. But I still think—"

"A good home," she said and turned back to him. For an instant her features crumpled despite her resolve. Howard watched as she swallowed and seemed to gulp away the tears, making a huge effort to regain control—not for herself, but for her child. "A mother and a father who can give everything my baby deserves to receive."

"Sergeant, hello, can you hear me?"

The voice was as soft as the light. He struggled to open his eyes. He looked up at a golden haze. Strange how the light could be so brilliant and so soft at the same time.

"Can you hear me, Sergeant?"

He licked dry lips. A hand slid beneath his head, lifted, and a cup touched his mouth. When he had sipped a few mouthfuls, the hand lowered him back to the pillow. A voice said, "There, is that better?"

A tent. His eyes focused enough for him to see that he was lying in a tent. The sun struck the canvas overhead and turned it into a sheet of brilliant gold. He turned his head and saw that a nurse was seated beside his bed. She smiled at him. "Nice to have you back among the living, Sergeant."

She kept calling him "Sergeant." Was that his name? He could not think. His mind felt so foggy. And there was something about the way she spoke, something strange.

"You're in a British field hospital. You've been wounded." The nurse hesitated a moment, then continued, "Nod your head if you can understand what I'm saying, Sergeant."

He nodded his head, though he could make little sense from her words. They seemed to dance through his mind and then disappear before he could lay hold of them. Strange how he could hear her and understand her, and at the same time understand nothing at all.

"You lost your identification in the battle. We don't know who you are. There seems to be no record of you." When he did not respond, she raised her voice. "Can you tell me your name? What regiment are you from?"

A dull drumbeat sounded at the very back of his consciousness. Steadily it grew louder, until he realized it was not a sound at all, but rather a pain. A dull agony that beat to the steady rhythm of his heart.

Another voice approached the end of his bed, one that spoke with authority. "Any word who he is?"

"Not yet, doctor. He seems to just come and go."

"Just as well." The deep voice spoke with clipped brusqueness. "No need to have him awake enough to feel his leg."

His leg. As though the words were a cue, he felt the dull beat of pain center down to his left leg. It did not hurt too badly yet. But there was something about the pain that scared him, even in his confused state. As though the pain was only the slightest hint of what was to come.

The terse voice demanded, "Any word from HQ?"

"Yessir. Still no idea who he is."

"Well, let's see what we can do about this leg. There probably was a letter in his back pocket, but the scraps that are left don't tell us anything. We can worry about his identity later." The deep voice drew nearer. "Help me shift his bandages so I can have a look."

Harry felt movements around him. Then the pain focused. It became not just a feeling, but a white-hot light. He groaned.

"How long has it been since his last injection, nurse?"

"Just under two hours."

"Well, no need to chafe him any more than necessary. Hurry and give him the morphine before we go any further."

Hurry. *Harry*. The pain shot through the fog in his mind, bringing every thought into crystal clarity. Perhaps that was his name. But maybe it was the name of someone else, another friend out there in the heat and the dust and the war. He wanted to speak, to ask if he was the Harry or the other guy. Then he felt the needle's jab, and soon a new wave of confusion swept through him. He did not mind. The pain receded with the sound of his heart, until it was nothing more than a shadow on the distant horizon of his consciousness.

The last words he heard were, "Now let's see if we can save this leg."

The administrator of Baltimore General Hospital stepped into Dr. Howard Austin's office. "Got a minute?"

"No." He did not want to be disturbed. Packing up and preparing for his departure was harder than Howard Austin had expected.

But the administrator did not move. His normally unflappable calm had deserted him. "I told you, leave all that. We'll just lock the office up and hold it for your return."

Howard finally said the words that surrounded him, clawing at his throat until it was hard to breathe. "And what if I don't come back?"

Instead of arguing, the administrator slumped in defeat. "Howard, this is a terrible time to be asking, but I need a favor."

"You are joking."

"I wish I were."

"My train leaves in exactly"—he glanced at his watch, then continued—"four hours."

But the administrator still did not budge. "You know the baby you delivered yesterday morning."

"The Grimes girl?" His attention finally shifted to the man standing in his doorway. "What about her?"

"We've been in contact for quite some time with a couple who wants to adopt a baby girl." It was the administrator's turn to avoid Howard's gaze. "They want to speak with the doctor in charge of the birth and prenatal care. They insist on it."

His movements stilled, Howard demanded, "What are you *not* telling me?"

"This couple," the administrator said, with a sigh, "they're, well . . ."

"Rich," Howard guessed, his tone flat.

"You know we urgently require donors to keep going and buy new equipment," the administrator replied, his voice rising defensively. "They've offered to help build our new wing if we find them a proper baby."

A *proper* baby.

"How much?"

"Half a million dollars," the administrator replied, awe-struck. "No strings attached."

Right, no strings—but a baby.

Howard rose to his feet and started toward the door. Despite all he faced, he very much wanted to meet this pair. He had a deep feeling of obligation to Martha and her baby. The baby she had refused to see. She knew that once her eyes settled on her baby girl, she would never be strong enough to carry out her resolve. It would be so much easier for her to know that her child had been well placed. "Where are they?"

The hospital entrance was a product of a bygone era, a tall, swooping dome of brick, crowned by brass lights. The floors were marble and worn into soft waves. The wooden walls probably had once been very grand, but now looked faded and in dire need of varnish. Howard was halfway down the stairs when he drew to a halt, his attention caught by the Rolls Royce automobile. Just outside the glass-topped entrance doors, a uniformed chauffeur stood patiently beside the long, low-slung vehicle.

The administrator backed up a step to ask nervously, "What's the matter?"

"Nothing." Howard started forward once more. "Let's get this over with."

He passed through the long corridor too quickly, granting him little time to form some kind of picture of what this couple might be like. Old? Young? Dark? Fair? Tall? Short? Just where was he sending Martha's little girl?

The administrator pushed open a door, and Howard found himself face-to-face with the prospective parents. One quick sweep was enough to work a knot in his stomach. The woman was as erect and cold as the Statue of Liberty. She stood by her husband's side, gazing at the baby with an expression of utter bafflement. The husband was big and gray and hearty, his face creased by unbounded joy as he cradled the little one in clumsy yet gentle arms.

At the sound of their footsteps, the woman stiffened even further. "Lawrence."

"What, oh—excellent." The big man took a step forward. "You the doctor?"

"That's right. Howard Austin."

"I'm Lawrence Rothmore. This is my wife, Abigail."

"Charmed." The woman's single word was as cool as her demeanor. As she adjusted the mink stole draped about her neck, the double strand of pearls was fully revealed and the diamond on her finger glinted in the light. "Don't you think we should speak with the doctor alone, dear?"

"Sure, sure." He gave the administrator a hearty smile. "You don't mind if we have a quiet chat with the doc here, do you? Sorry, doc, I've forgotten your name already."

"Austin. Howard Austin."

"No, no, of course not." The administrator gave the couple a little half-bow, followed by a look of genuine entreaty to Howard. Then he backed from the room. "I'll just be in my office."

The woman turned her full attention on Howard. "Doctor, can you assure us this is a proper baby?"

The directness took his breath away. "I beg your pardon?"

"Proper," the woman repeated, drawing out the word in an exaggerated fashion. "A proper baby. Not one from—well, pardon me, doctor, but we don't know a thing about the family, do we?"

"Abigail," her husband said. But the word did not carry heat. His attention remained focused upon the tiny child in his arms. "The administrator has already told us—"

"The administrator wants our money," she replied crisply. "There is absolutely nothing wrong with wanting to know that our baby is healthy and comes from parents who aren't, well, deranged or anything."

Howard Austin's sudden anger brought a grating depth to his voice. "The baby's mother is one of the finest women I have ever known."

Abigail Rothmore faltered momentarily under the doctor's glare but managed to draw herself together to demand, "And the father?"

"Sergeant Harry Grimes," Howard Austin began, and then stopped. He had broken one of the primary rules governing adoption, which was to never let the adopting couple know the names of the parents.

"Yes, doctor?"

Howard Austin sighed. Put it up to the day's stress and strain. "He was killed on the North African front."

"Hey, that's tough." The gentleman lifted his graying head at the news. He was an older man, and probably had twenty years on his society wife. Genuine sympathy shone from his face. "How is the mother holding up?"

"Not well." There was a sincerity to the gentleman that the woman lacked. Howard focused his attention on Lawrence Rothmore. It was easier than allowing himself to think of Martha Grimes, lying upstairs in a private room. She had been moved out of the obstetrics wing, where her sobs had been upsetting the other mothers and newborn babies. "Not well at all. She's young and doesn't feel that she can take care of the child on her own. But that doesn't make it any easier to give Katie up for adoption."

"Hey, I'm sorry to hear that." The man had the gruff voice of a hale and hearty type, big across the shoulders and a paunch from good living. "Think maybe we could help out?"

"I'm sorry," Abigail interrupted. "Did you say the child's name is Katie?"

"It's nice of you to offer," Howard responded to the husband, "but actually I was breaking the law in mentioning the father's name. Besides, she'll hopefully have a war pension coming to her." He then turned to Abigail and continued, "Katherine is the name given by the birth mother. But you have the right to change that if you wish. Just as the child's birth certificate will list you as the actual parents."

Both adults showed genuine relief. Lawrence Rothmore spoke first. "I'd sure like Katie to think of us as her real parents."

The man, Howard noticed, had an unhealthy flush to his complexion. Too much rich food, high blood pressure, and not enough exercise. Definitely a heart patient in the making. "That is entirely your choice."

"Let me just be perfectly clear on this point," the woman said, her cool aloofness fully restored. "You are saying that there is no chance that some pestering journalist might ferret out details sometime in the future?"

"None at all," Howard replied, understanding her perfectly. "If you want to claim to all the world that you have borne this child, that is your decision."

"It's just like Randolf told us. The secret lives and dies with us," Lawrence concluded. He added for the doctor's benefit, "Randolf Crawley, he's our lawyer. My wife's cousin. Getting on in years, but sharp as they come."

Abigail fingered her pearls and murmured, "I still say we would be better off selecting a proper male heir."

"We've been through all that," Lawrence said, hugging the baby closer to his chest. "If you want to adopt a second child—"

"Simply out of the question." Abigail's tone closed that door permanently.

"I want a baby daughter." There was a sudden power to his voice, a revealing of the force that had carried him to the top. "And that's final."

Abigail opened her mouth, must have thought better of it, and changed tack. "Very well," she said. "But this name, Katie, simply won't do. I mean, really, it's just too—well, too ordinary."

As swiftly as the man's power had been revealed, it vanished. Lawrence Rothmore's attention returned to the little bundle sleeping in his arms, and his features softened. "What did you have in mind?"

"Kyle," Abigail announced. "It was my maternal grandmother's name, as you know. And Elizabeth from my mother."

"Kyle Elizabeth Rothmore." He nodded his head. "Sounds good to me."

Howard Austin glanced at his watch and gave a start. Where had the time gone? "If you'll just step into the administrator's office, he will have the papers ready for you to sign."

"Yeah, he mentioned you were off today for a year's duty." Lawrence Rothmore allowed himself to be ushered across the foyer. "Any idea where?"

"Three months' surgical duty on a hospital boat—after that is anybody's guess."

"Well, good luck to you, doc. And thanks. Thanks a million."

Or half a million. Howard accepted the man's hand, while he returned the woman's perfunctory nod. He then raced back up the stairs. But instead of heading for his office and the pile of unfinished paper work, he continued up to where Martha Grimes lay on the third-floor private wing. It was the least he could do, a last gift to a woman for whom he wished he could do more. A lot more.

Perhaps it would help her to know that little Kyle Rothmore was going to receive everything that Martha herself could not give.

CHAPTER TWO

"NOW, BERTIE, DON'T YOU DARE drop them."

"No, Miss Kyle, I wouldn't dream of it." Bertrand Ames shut the manor's tall oak door, which was difficult given the load he carried, and turned sideways to make sure Kyle Rothmore, nearly three, was coping with the broad flagstone stairs. Her two teddies kept her from seeing the steps. "You be careful, now," he cautioned in return.

If anyone had ever suggested to Bertrand Ames that his job would include responsibility for the well-being of a Raggedy Ann doll, three stuffed bunny rabbits, and an enormous pink elephant, he would have turned in his resignation on the spot. But here he was, taking the curving front steps very slowly, so as to be there in case his small charge lost her balance. The doll and stuffed animals were crammed together in a colorful bundle up against the chest of his immaculate uniform.

And then Jim, the head gardener, chose that moment to come around the corner of the house. As with all the servants, Jim answered directly to Bertrand Ames. Jim was a fine gardener but an impossible man to deal with. He had an acid wit and complained with every breath he drew. It did not help that Bertrand and his wife were, like all the staff, relatively new to the Rothmore household. For some unknown reason, the entire household staff had been fired and new people hired three years ago. He and his wife had come shortly after that. At times

Bertrand still felt as though he were struggling to establish his authority and position.

It would not do at all for the gardener to go back to the kitchen and start making caustic remarks at Bertrand's expense. Dignity was a vital part of his position.

Bertrand wore three hats within the Rothmore household— butler, chauffeur, and head of the household staff. He managed the tasks by rising before dawn, working hard all day, and keeping himself aloof from the other staff. His habitual expression was a disapproving frown. As Jim walked toward them, Bertrand prepared a frosty response to any remarks about his unusual bundle.

But Jim did not pay him any mind at all. Instead he doffed his ancient cap and gave a creaky bow. "Morning, Miss Kyle. Great day for going out and about."

"I'm taking Mr. and Mrs. Teddy for a drive," she announced.

"Now ain't that a grand thing." He hustled over to the gleaming Rolls and opened the front door.

"Bertie has all their friends so they won't get lonely," Kyle continued.

Bertrand winced at the announcement. Only Maggie, his wife and the Rothmores' head chef, called him Bertie. But like all the servants, Maggie's heart had long been lost to the charms of this child. Their own children were long gone, grown up and off leading their own lives.

Bertrand readied his coolest voice, preparing for the snide comment on his nickname Jim was bound to offer. But to his surprise, the gardener only nodded and agreed. "Always a good thing to have your friends around."

Bertrand stepped forward and began settling his load onto the front seat's posh leather. Kyle handed him the teddies. "Thank you, Bertie."

The gardener had eyes only for the little girl. He asked eagerly, "Anything I can do, Miss Kyle?"

She gave that one careful thought. "They might get a little cold."

"There's a lap blanket in the trunk," Bertrand said cautiously, handing him the key.

"Right you are." The old man scurried around, came swiftly back with the checkered alpaca cover. "Want me to set it in place?"

Bertrand reached over. "I'll take that, thank you."

"I was the one got it out."

"That will do, James." There was a momentary tug of war before seniority won out and Bertrand had the privilege of tucking the blanket around the row of fuzzy passengers. He backed out and straightened. "Will that do, Miss Kyle?"

Inspecting the arrangement meant climbing onto the Rolls' running board and peering inside. The action hiked her little skirt up high enough to reveal the row of blue ribbons in her pantaloons, ones that matched the pair in her honey-colored hair. "Does Mrs. Teddy have room to breathe?"

The question required both Jim and Bertrand to fit in around Kyle. They gave the passengers a careful examination before Bertrand repositioned the pink elephant over closer to his seat. Then he solemnly proclaimed, "I feel certain Mrs. Teddy will be most comfortable, Miss Kyle."

"Yep," Jim agreed. "Looks mighty fine to me." He retreated, waited until Kyle had climbed down and straightened her skirt, then asked, "Seems I've heard talk about some big day coming up, Miss Kyle?"

"My birthday," she announced proudly. "Mama says we're gonna have a party."

Bertrand started to dismiss the gardener but was held back by the gleam in the man's eyes. There was a genuine affection in Jim's tone as he said, "A party. Now ain't that nice. Think maybe it'd be a garden party?"

When Kyle seemed perplexed by that question, Bertrand found himself offering, "Perhaps if the weather is nice."

"Then you oughtta come out and show me where you'll have your guests," Jim said eagerly. "Maybe I can put some pretty flowers around, dress things up a little."

Bertrand was hard pressed not to smile. The gardener had

a thousand excuses for avoiding any extra work. But the little child had this effect on the entire household. There was something special about Kyle, as though a glorious light shone from her heart, even at this early age, something so special that it lit up the lives of everyone around her. Everyone, that is, except for—

"Ah, good, there you are. For once you're ready on time." Abigail Rothmore carefully swept down the steps on her high heels. "James, I noticed the flowers in the front hall are wilting."

"We were just talking about that very thing, Mrs. Rothmore." The gardener shifted over far enough to block Bertrand from view as the butler ducked into the front seat and flipped the blanket up and over the stuffed animals. "I believe the roses are ready."

She dismissed him with a flick of her gloved hand and inspected her little girl. "Turn around and let me see you, child. Well, it appears you've managed to keep yourself clean for once. Very well, Bertrand, you may open the door."

"Yes, madam." He bowed lower than necessary, the only way he could hide the glint of anger as he saw the child freeze under her mother's austere gaze. When they were both settled, he shut the door and found himself facing the gardener. Jim was still watching Kyle through the car window. He caught Bertrand's eye and gave a slight grimace before turning away.

Bertrand walked around to his door, reflecting that he and Maggie had only two reasons to put up with Abigail Rothmore, and those were her husband and her daughter.

Before he even started the car, Abigail was off on her usual litany of instructions. "Sit up, child. Straighten your dress. And just look at your hair. How on earth do you manage to—"

"Where to, madam?" Bertrand asked, putting a bit more bark into his voice than necessary.

"What? Oh, the dance academy, of course. It's Thursday." But his question had the desired effect and deflected Abigail from further berating the little girl.

"I don't like ballet," Kyle said very softly. "It makes my toes hurt."

"If I've told you once, I've told you a thousand times, dance will teach you both proper posture and an appreciation of music. Besides, it will introduce you to our kind of people."

"I don't have any friends there," Kyle quietly persisted.

"Of course you do. I just heard that the Crawleys' lovely daughter is being sent there as well. She will make an excellent friend."

"I don't like Emily Crawley," Kyle said. Her voice was so quiet as to almost go without noticing. "She's mean to me."

"Nonsense. Emily Crawley comes from one of the finest families in Chevy Chase. Not to mention the fact that her father sits on the Rothmore board. Even if the idea of him having a daughter at his age is positively scandalous." Impatiently Abigail tapped her fingers upon the polished burl of her armrest. "Bertrand, I have a luncheon in town. You shall need to drop me off, go back and pick up Kyle, and bring her home on your own."

"Very good, Mrs. Rothmore." At least there was that to look forward to. Kyle liked to sit up front with him, hugging one of her animals and asking all the questions that she kept to herself whenever her mother was around. Bertrand had never known another child of her age to be so bright and inquisitive.

And yet nothing could please her mother. "Nanny says you have finally managed to learn all your alphabet."

"Yes, Mother." A hint of eagerness. "Can I 'cite them?"

"Recite, child, recite. You really must practice your elocution. And no, it is quite enough to hear a positive report from Nanny for a change."

Bertrand clenched down hard on his irritation as he observed the little girl through his rearview mirror. Kyle gave a little frustrated kick, then commented, "I wish I could have a baby brother."

Abigail gave her daughter a look of genuine horror. "Where on earth did you come up with such a notion?"

"Maggie says her daughter's just had a new baby. A little boy. Can we, Mama? Please?"

"Absolutely not. Out of the question. As if you were not already more than I can manage. Oh, do stop swinging your legs,

Kyle. Can't you be still for an instant?"

Bertrand's heart lurched as he watched her subside into a shadow of the bright little thing who had chattered with them earlier. But Abigail was not finished. "Really, you must stop treating the staff like they were family. It just isn't proper to call the cook by her first name."

"But she's . . . she's my very best friend," Kyle protested.

"Don't talk nonsense. Help are not friends. You are a privileged young lady, and you must learn to act the part. I don't see why it is so much to ask, expecting you to be at least a little grateful for everything that has been given to you."

"Thank you, Mama," Kyle said dully.

"That's better." Abigail Rothmore adjusted the fold of her skirt. The diamonds in her bracelet caught the sunlight and shimmered little rainbows round the car's interior. "Now if only you could learn how to behave in a way that reflects your social standing and family position, I will be satisfied."

Kyle's chin quivered a moment, but she brought it under control. When her mother's attention was caught by something outside her window, Kyle gave her eyes a swift little wipe. She raised her gaze, and Bertrand attempted all the warmth he could manage into the smile he gave her through the rearview mirror. Then and there he decided he would treat her to her favorite snack, a chocolate malted milk and a box of animal crackers. They would stop by the sweetshop on the way home, no matter what Maggie might say about the child's appetite being ruined. He would give anything to see the little girl smile again.

Howard Austin removed the stethoscope from his neck and fitted it into his black carrying bag. He forced a cheery tone. "Fit as a fiddle, heart big as a mule's. Nothing's going to keep our Harry down for long. I want you to start walking with just one cane—see how far you can make it."

Harry gave a silent nod, the expression on his face not changing. When he had first arrived home, he had been wasted down to skin and bones, but now he was beginning to put on weight. His leg was mending well. But nothing could be done about the eyes that looked empty of everything, or the flat, toneless voice that expressed the few words he chose to say. At the moment, he chose not to speak at all.

As Howard backed toward the doorway, he tried to find some cheerful note to end the visit. He could only think of the news that was on everyone's mind that summer. "Looks like we've got the Japs on the run once and for all. Can't be long now."

Harry looked up from his chair. It was placed just beneath the bedroom window so as to catch whatever breeze the sultry day might bring. Sunlight falling through the lace curtains turned his face into stark lines and shadows. The words he spoke now carried deep feeling. "Wish I were over there with them, Doc. That's where I belong. The army's the only thing I ever found worth doing."

"Where you belong is right here with your family," Howard responded, feeling his smile was as false as his hearty tone.

"America's finest hour," Harry mumbled, as though the doctor had not spoken at all. "And here I am, trapped in this chair with a gimp leg."

"You've done your part," Howard insisted stoutly, more because Martha was standing there beside him than because he thought the words might do some good. "Now you're home, where a lot of our boys wish they could be. And your leg was saved. Count your lucky stars, Harry."

When Harry did not respond, Howard started down the hall, saying to Martha as he passed, "There's no need to see me to the door."

But Martha Grimes pushed one hand into the small of her back, making her belly protrude even further, and moved slowly along behind him. Still a small woman, she was carrying this second baby very low. Two weeks until term, and he wondered if her size indicated twins. Only when the screen door had shut behind them did she speak. "He's not getting any better."

"Of course he is."

"Even when one of his old buddies comes by, all Harry does is sit around. There's no fire left."

"Just give it time, Martha."

"And when he does talk, it's about the army. How much he misses it. How he hates his leg. How his wound has kept him from staying with the one profession he'd ever like. That's his name for it, his profession." She sighed deeply and absently rubbed the curve of her belly with her other hand, as though able to adjust the load she bore. "Talking like the army was a calling, like being a doctor or something important."

"It is important—or was," Howard Austin replied quietly. "At least to Harry."

"He's been mourning the loss for way too long as it is." Her hand kept moving, as though she sought comfort from the child she carried. "I just don't know how much more I can endure, Howard."

"Be patient," Howard said, the words coming automatically. He seemed to be saying them a lot these days. "Be strong. He'll come around."

Instead of arguing, Martha carefully examined his face. "You've changed too, Howard. You look the same as before you left, except for some new lines on your face. But your eyes—they look a hundred years old."

He did not try to deny it. From somewhere down the street, a radio blared out a marching tune. Another house was full of revelry, and at five o'clock in the afternoon. It seemed as though Baltimore had been one vast party ever since the Germans had surrendered three months earlier. "He's been through a lot, Martha. It will take him time to come around. The scars on the outside are easy to see. They'll always be there, I'm sorry to say. The ones on the inside, who knows how long . . ." Howard let his voice trail off. Martha did not need to hear all the details.

Howard found himself recalling the one time Harry had let down his barriers since returning from North Africa. Frustration and anger and bitterness had poured forth from the lips of a broken man. Howard had stood helpless and silent, listening to heartrending accusations directed at Martha for giving away his child. He wanted their daughter, he had shouted over and over. He wanted his baby back. Harry had wept with uncontrollable sobs when Howard had told him firmly that there was no way to undo what had been done. It had been an ugly scene, one that had left Howard with nightmares.

Harry had never spoken of his lost child again.

"He just sits there and stares at nothing," Martha went on, almost to herself. "For hours on end, he won't say a word."

The thousand-yard stare. That was the name Howard had heard. He had seen a lot of that during his time at the military hospital. And a lot of other things he would rather forget. He pushed away the memories that suddenly began crowding forward and produced a tight grin. "This is something, isn't it, how I've gotten back in time to deliver your second baby?"

But Martha did not respond as he had hoped. She brushed away a wisp of hair matted to her forehead, her face flushed from the exertion of bearing such a heavy load. "Tell me the truth, Howard. Will my Harry ever come back to me?"

Howard fought back a sudden longing to reach forward and take her into his arms. He had thought he was over his yearning for her. After all, he had returned to find that Harry Grimes had not been killed. Upon hearing the news about Harry's return, Howard Austin had stamped down tight on his dismay, locking away his feelings for Martha along with all the other emotions the war had left as a legacy, things he never wanted to think of or feel again.

But here he was, caught flat-footed and openhearted by a single look.

"Martha," he sighed, wishing for all that was impossible to have. "I can't lie to you."

"That's why I'm asking," she responded, her tone as quiet as his. "I need somebody I know will always tell me the truth."

"The truth," Howard said quietly, his heart aching. Once again he was glad he had not poured out his feelings to Martha before he left, and that he had held to a friendly tone in his few letters. He had wanted to wait and confess his love for her face-to-face. He had owed it to her, if for no other reason than because she had already lost one man to the war, or so he had thought. Now his disappointment was an acrid twisting to his heart, but at least it was private, something he had shared with no one. "The truth is, your husband is home."

"Is he?"

"He has returned with his body relatively intact. His mind is okay, as far as I can tell."

"It doesn't seem that way to me."

I care too much. The accusation had been leveled at him time after time on the front. Other doctors had taken him aside and told him repeatedly that if he did not grow a tougher hide around his heart, he would not survive. Howard drew himself up. "Martha, Harry was a man made for soldiering. You've told me that yourself. And now he's got to learn to accept that there are other occupations for him than the army. He needs to count his blessings, find a job, raise his family. Having a new baby will help bring him around."

The dark brown eyes did not waver in their careful inspection of his face. Martha asked quietly, "What about my needs, Howard? I lost my husband and then my baby. I spent almost a year mourning the pair of them, thinking my husband was lying dead some place with a strange-sounding name."

"El Alamein," Howard said quietly. "A lot of good men didn't come back from there, Martha. You should count your blessings."

"Blessings." Her mouth pinched down, as though she had tasted something bitter. "What about my baby girl? I dream about her, you know. After all this time, I wake up and wonder where she is, and I feel like my heart is going to break."

"Blessings, like the child you're bearing," Howard plowed on determinedly. He fought down the urge to tell her about Harry's bitterness over losing the baby girl. It would serve no purpose, other than perhaps ease his own nights. "Blessings, like having your husband home from the war."

She stared hard at him, the gaze carrying the force her words did not. "Tell me where my baby is, Howard. I'm begging you."

"For the last time, Martha, I can't. And even if I could, it wouldn't do you any good. The child is theirs. And that's final." He tipped his hat to her and turned for the steps. "I'll see you in a day or so. Call me if anything changes."

Briskly Howard started down the sidewalk, pausing for a final wave before turning the corner. Up where the street joined a main thoroughfare, a young man hawked papers, shouting more news about the war. Howard tuned him out, the action having become automatic.

I care too much, Howard repeated to himself as his shoulders slumped in defeat. It was a flaw he really had to overcome.

CHAPTER THREE

KYLE RACED AROUND THE CORNER, one hand holding her leather satchel, the other her hat. Her long dark blond hair and the cap's blue ribbons flew out behind her as she hurried toward the car. Her brown eyes sparkled with anticipation.

The chauffeur stood stiffly at attention as he waited for her, his face set in downward sloping lines. "I'm sorry, Bertie," she said breathlessly, "but Miss Pincushion made me stay after class again."

Bertrand opened the front passenger door. He could not keep an aggrieved tone from his voice as he said, "I do wish you would permit me to wait for you in front of the school, Miss Kyle."

At the sight of the front door open and waiting, Kyle gave off a little exclamation of delight, swiftly stifled. She gave the empty rear seat a quick glance, then asked, "Where's Mother?"

"Mrs. Rothmore felt it necessary to remain behind and prepare for her charity function this afternoon," Bertrand replied stiffly.

"Oh, Bertie, don't be like that." Kyle slid into the seat and straightened the blue skirt of her school uniform. When Bertrand shut her door and started around the car, she allowed herself a smile. Mother couldn't come after all. The day was already wonderful and would soon be even better. A lunch with her father, all to herself, was one of her favorite things in the world.

When the chauffeur opened his door and climbed in, Kyle gave him a look of utter appeal. "Bertie, I've told you how the other girls make fun of me when they see you waiting out front." Further protest was diverted when she glanced at the little round clock set in the burl dash. "Oh, look. You'll have to hurry. Daddy doesn't like to be kept waiting."

"I am well aware of your father's attitude toward time," Bertrand replied. "And I am certain that the young ladies of St. Albans have seen a chauffeur before."

"Now you sound just like Miss Pincushion." Miss Pincus taught eighth-grade math at the exclusive St. Albans Preparatory School, and she was the bane of Kyle's existence. "Not in a *Rolls*. And not the way you wait for me."

"And just what, pray tell," Bertrand demanded, "is the matter with the way in which I wait for you?"

"Oh, you know. Standing there by the door with your gloves and hat and everything. You look like a soldier at attention."

"I merely intend to show proper respect."

"You look like you're waiting for . . . for a princess." Kyle laughed, a musical sound. Then she confessed, "I don't like the other girls to know, that's all."

"There are many wealthy young ladies at St. Albans, Miss Kyle. And if memory serves me correctly, young Miss Emily Crawley is collected in a Rolls."

"But the other girls are nicer, the ones that aren't so, you know, well off." She avoided the additional point, which was that Emily Crawley and her cold, aloof ways frightened her. "If they see you . . . well, I'm afraid they won't like me."

"Anyone in her right mind would like you," Bertrand responded reverently.

"The others don't. The ones Mother says I need to socialize with. They don't like how I talk to . . . to everyone." The tone dropped as she added the word Emily Crawley used most often to describe her. "They call me *common*."

"They wouldn't dare," Bertrand said hotly. "Not if you allowed me to meet you out front like you should."

She gave him a smile that carried warmth and appreciation,

then changed the conversation by reaching into her satchel. "Look what I made for Maggie's birthday."

Bertrand slowed long enough to glance over. What he saw caused him to turn the car to the side of the road and stop. "Kyle, what can I say? It's lovely."

Neither of them noted that he had not included "miss" with her name, a misdemeanor that would have brought Kyle's mother to the point of banishing him forever. "It's a watercolor of 'The Praying Hands,'" Kyle explained. "It's Maggie's favorite."

"Twelve years old, and already you're a marvel." Bertrand's heart nearly burst with pride. "Maggie is going to love this."

"I'm thirteen—remember?" The young girl's face shone with delight. "You really think she will?"

"I know so. I've been wondering what to get her myself, and now I know. I will arrange to have this framed."

Kyle drew up her shoulders in pleasure. "We'll be giving her something together."

"Indeed we will." They shared a smile until Bertrand glanced at the clock and jerked upright. "I've forgotten the time. We're already late."

But Kyle did not look worried. Carefully she replaced the painting into her satchel, then leaned back with another smile. "Lunch with Daddy, all by myself. Then I can be in his office all afternoon. And guess what? *I Love Lucy* comes on tonight."

Her sigh of pleasure warmed Bertrand's heart. "I'm certain your favorite program does not come on until tomorrow," he said as he watched her from the corner of his eye.

Kyle frowned, ran through the days of the week on her fingers, then caught sight of Bertrand's teasing glance. "Oh, you."

"Here's your father's street, Miss Kyle," Bertrand said, returning to formality. "Perhaps you should think about—"

But before he finished, Kyle took a quick glance around, then in a flash was over the seat into the rear. She settled back, then leaned forward to snatch up her hat. A few seconds of straightening her clothes and hair, putting the hat on and her face into proper lines, and the car slowed to a halt.

As Kyle waited calmly as Bertrand cut the motor and came around to open her door, she caught sight of her father. He was standing just inside the Rothmore building's brass-lined glass doors, talking to someone she vaguely recognized. Then she saw what he was holding as he stood grinning and waiting for her to alight. Kyle's breath came out in a gasp, and she scrambled out the door Bertrand held for her, positively at odds with what her mother would have called ladylike behavior.

She ran to her father. "You got it! Oh, Daddy, it's *beautiful*!" she exclaimed.

"A Schwinn," Lawrence Rothmore declared proudly. "Won't be released until next summer, but a buddy in their head office wrangled this one for me. Get a load of those white side-walls, will you."

"And colored tassels, and I love the silver and blue," she enthused. "Oh, Daddy, can we take it for a ride?"

"Later, my daughter," he said, putting his arm around her shoulder as he motioned Bertrand forward. "Put this in the trunk, will you?"

"Very good, sir."

Kyle watched as the bicycle was wheeled away. "Promise you'll ride with me, Daddy?"

"Soon as I get home." He waved forward a young man who hovered just out of range. "You remember Randolf Crawley, don't you?"

Kyle stopped watching intently as Bertrand maneuvered the bicycle around to the back of the car and turned back to her father. As she had been taught, she lifted her skirt lightly and gave a graceful curtsey. "Good day, Mr. Crawley."

"Call me Randolf, please." Her father's associate sounded surprisingly friendly to Kyle's way of thinking. "There's not that much difference in age between us."

She looked curiously at him. His hair was a shiny blond, combed up and back in careful folds. His chin was cleft, his nose straight and long, his teeth perfect. Randolf Crawley was ancient as far as Kyle was concerned. At least twenty-four or five. "There isn't?" she asked frankly.

Her father patted the younger man on the shoulder. "Randolf's going to become my protégé. It's your mother's idea. He's got a law degree from Yale, and insurance law's becoming trickier by the minute. Besides that, I'm not getting any younger, and I need a pair of strong shoulders and a good mind to carry some of the load. Abigail thinks he's perfect for the position."

Kyle had not understood all of what was just said. But she did not like any suggestion that her father was not well. And she *really* did not like the way that man was smiling at her. "You're fit as a fiddle, Daddy. That's what you're always saying."

Lawrence Rothmore's laugh was as big as the rest of him. But nothing could disguise the sudden flush that crept into his face as he stopped and the heavy breaths that followed. "My little lady. Loyal to the end," he puffed.

"I am pleased to see my young sister becoming friends with you, Kyle," Randolf commented. "She talks about you quite a bit."

"How nice." Kyle used the phrase she heard her mother say whenever she was displeased but didn't wish to show it. In truth, Kyle was uncomfortable around Emily Crawley. She was as beautiful as her older brother was handsome. Emily was leader of the group of wealthier girls at St. Albans, and this group was the biggest reason Kyle did not feel like she belonged. The Crawleys were her mother's distant relatives, and Emily seemed to have Abigail's ability to make Kyle feel as though she did not measure up, could never be as correct and superior as she was supposed to be.

Kyle felt she had been polite to Randolf Crawley long enough. "Where are we having lunch, Daddy?"

"The boardroom, where else?" Dining in the boardroom was one of their little rituals, whenever they had a time alone. "I believe I heard the chef say he had managed to make your favorite dessert."

"I bet it's banana cream pie!"

Lawrence squeezed his daughter's shoulder and said to Randolf Crawley, "You've never seen anything like it," he boasted. "All my little lady has to do is smile, and she could get the Statue of Liberty to lend her the torch."

"I don't doubt it for a minute," Randolf agreed. "I've heard Emily say something about Kyle's friendliness."

But Lawrence had already turned away. "Come on, princess. On to the top."

He handed over a key to Kyle, a ritual they had played out from when she was a tiny girl. There was a private elevator for members of the board. Her father had let her operate it since she had been old enough to reach up on her tiptoes and fit the key into the special hole. Kyle stepped into the wood-paneled elevator, and as the polished doors closed she caught a final glimpse of Randolf's smile directed at her. She wondered why it made her uneasy.

As though reading her mind, Lawrence asked, "So what do you think of my new protégé?"

"I think he's—well, he reminds me of his sister," she said, speaking her mind as was only possible when she and her father were alone.

Lawrence chuckled fondly. "He's going to be the youngest member of our board before long, taking over the seat from his father. When I was just starting out, old Crawley helped bankroll me. His father and your mother's grandfather were brothers, but I suppose you know that. He probably did it out of family loyalty, but he's done well by it. Very well. He has ten percent of the company stock and a permanent seat on our board."

Kyle did not ask him to explain what all that meant. She had no interest in Randolf Crawley. Instead she announced, "Maggie's kitty had six babies."

"Is that a fact." He regarded her fondly. "Don't I recall your naming that cat Benjamin?"

She nodded. "Yes, that was back when I was too young to know better. So now she's called Ben-Hur." When her father laughed again, she worked up nerve to ask, "Daddy, do you think I could have one of the kitties?"

"No pets, my love. We've already been through that with your mother when Jim's golden retriever had puppies."

"Oh, Daddy, *please*. They're such precious little white fluff-balls."

"No pets," he repeated, his tone regretful but firm. "Your mother's really put her foot down on that. I'm sorry, princess." He steered the subject back around with, "She thinks very highly of young Randolf." He hesitated a moment, then added, "She says it would be a good idea if you were to get to know him."

Kyle looked up at her father in utter bafflement. "But why, Daddy?"

For some reason, the question made him laugh a third time. He stroked her fine silky hair once more as the elevator doors opened before them. "Why indeed, my princess. Why indeed."

Joel Grimes sat on the parlor floor, his birthday present opened in front of him. Light from the setting sun spilled through the louvered windows, framing him in sharp lines of gold and shadow. He unfolded the large page of plans, being as careful as he could. It was important not to grow impatient, even now when he was so excited he could hardly sit still. Experience had taught him that the plans would be opened time and time again, and the crease-lines needed to be followed very carefully, because when the paper became old it would easily tear. And it was always in the creases that there was some important connection he couldn't figure out without the plans. So he unfolded the white paper, big as a road map, very carefully, noting how the folds went so he would know how to put it back later.

Beside him was the magnifying glass Dr. Austin, his parents' friend, had given him for his last birthday. Save his eyes from squinting over those tiny lines, was what the doctor had said. And now he had a brand-new tube of epoxy glue that was from Grandma. And a new razor blade in the little metal holder that his father had brought him from the tool shop. His mother always left the room when he started working with the blade. She was back in the kitchen now, preparing his tenth birthday dinner. Which meant he only had a few minutes left to look over the plans.

Joel's father sat on the other side of the small front parlor in their Riverdale home. Joel had been born in Baltimore, but the family had moved the fifteen miles south soon after. This was the only home Joel had ever known. He sat on the floor and watched his father listening to news over the radio. The announcer was talking about something called the Cold War. And some man called Nikita Kruschev. Whenever the news started on about those things, his father would always clam up and lean over, his face so tight he looked hungry.

His father was quiet most of the time. He would come home from work, sit there in the front room, and say hardly a word. His distant gaze suggested he saw another world, one that really was just for him, one where Joel had no part at all. It made him feel so small, being in the room with his father and knowing that the man did not see him or even realize he was there.

There was something which lurked deep inside his father, something frightening. Joel had seen it surface that very morning when his father had stomped out on the back porch and argued with the milkman. The veins had stood out on his father's forehead and neck like whipcords. His voice had sounded like an angry lash. All over a missing pint of milk. Joel had sat with his breakfast cereal and known with wisdom far beyond his ten years that it was more than milk that made his father so angry.

Sometimes, though, his father roused himself, and he would look at Joel and say something. Joel's whole world seemed to light up when it happened.

The announcer started talking about baseball, and his father cut off the radio. Washington's baseball team, the Senators, was at the bottom of the rankings, and Baltimore wasn't doing much better. The only time his father was interested in baseball was when the Yankees or the Red Sox were in town.

His father turned to him, watching him cut the first balsam piece free of the wood strip. "What you got there, sport?"

"A B–29 Superfortress," Joel replied with a grin. His father knew that. An illustration of the plane in all its glory was on the box front, flying through a sky filled with dark gray flak clouds, its machine guns spouting flames.

"Ain't that something," his father said calmly. "How many does that make now?"

"Eleven." The gift had been from both his parents, but Joel knew his mother had saved from her household money to buy it. Even so, his father recognized the plane. His father knew all about planes. He worked as a mechanic at the Baltimore airport. It was one of the few subjects that would occasionally light up his eyes, especially if he was talking about military planes.

"I had two more," Joel explained, "but I messed them up and so they don't count. But that was when I was little."

"Listen to this guy. Ten years old and he's not little any-more." His face's deep creases tightened slightly, as close as Harry Grimes ever came to a smile. "Can you understand the instructions, son?"

"I think so." It was so rare to have his father actually say the word "son," that Joel knew a little thrill. In a sudden rush of insight, he picked up the plans and crossed the room. "I've read them, but I'm not sure I get what to do first." The large sheet rustled as he spread it on the small table by his father's chair. He pointed at a paragraph above the first drawing and asked, "Will you explain that to me?"

"Why, sure." Harry spread the plans smooth, squinted, and slowly began to read and comment. Joel listened carefully, but in truth he didn't need help. Joel wanted a reason to stand near his father. Most of the time it seemed as though his father had an invisible barrier around him, keeping everyone from coming close, even his own son. Joel hesitated, then reached up and put his hand on his father's shoulder. It felt hard as a rock. He moved a little closer so he could lean against his father's arm.

His mother chose that moment to walk into the room. When Joel looked over at her, she appeared to be holding her breath. Her face ran as if it were made of wax, just melting into soft, sad lines. It was so strange to stand there, leaning against his father, feeling so happy and so sad at the same time. His mother struggled to make a little smile for him, then turned and silently left the room.

When his father stopped his explanation of the paragraph, he sat and examined the plans for a while. Joel remained content to stand there and lean against him. Harry pointed at the turrets appearing on the drawing's underside and tail and asked, "How are you supposed to make these?"

Eagerly Joel leaped for the box, pulled aside the balsam strips intended to form the plane itself, and came up with an oddly shaped piece. It looked like a slender tree sprouting rigid gray fruit. "They made them out of plastic, Pop."

"Well, ain't that something. Here, let me have a look." Harry's strong fingers moved across the pieces, comparing them to the scale drawings. "Getting more complicated all the time, aren't they?"

"Sure are."

"Good training for a mechanic. You aiming on coming over, working on the planes with your old man?"

"That sounds great, Pop." But in truth, Joel had no idea what he wanted to do when he grew up. Whenever he thought about the future, it all felt flat to him, as though there was something important he was missing. It was the same way his family was. Everything seeming to be in order, but something was missing. He knew it in his heart.

Harry let the plans slide from his lap. Joel knelt and began the folding process. Then Harry said, "Yeah, the Superfortress and the B–17, they made all the difference. We ruled the skies after that. Had 'em on the run." He was silent a moment longer, then asked, "You heard about the new one?"

"You told me about it, remember?" The other night, the paper had printed an article on the new army bomber. "The YB–52 Stratosphere. That's what they called it."

"You sure got some memory, sport." Harry reached over and tousled his son's hair. "Mind like that, you'll go a long way."

The moment was so special, Joel decided to risk it. He kept his head bowed over the plans as he asked, "Pop, can I get me a puppy? Bobby Benson's spaniel, she had six pups. Please, Pop. They're the cutest—"

"No pets," Harry Grimes said. More than the words cut off Joel's pleadings. The cold grating sound was back in his father's voice.

Joel felt his heart fall to his stomach in fear that he had ruined the rest of his birthday. That his father would sit over to one side of the table, staring out the back window, saying nothing to anybody the whole time. Meals like that were excruciating.

Steps scraped up their front porch, and a heavy voice said through the doorway, "Are we late? We better not be. I get cranky if I don't get my share of the birthday cake."

"Haven't even got started," Harry replied. "Come on in, Howard."

Dr. Howard Austin stepped through the door, followed by his wife, Carol. The Austins had also moved down from Baltimore, and Dr. Austin ran a very successful family practice. Joel found himself thinking as always how incredible it was, the similarity between Carol Austin and his own mother. They could have been sisters. They even had the same soft, sad smile. Dr. Austin demanded, "Hey, it's the birthday boy. What you got there?"

"A model of the Superfortress," Harry replied for him. To Joel's enormous relief, the coldness was gone from Harry's voice as he rose and limped over. Favoring his left leg, Harry picked up the model box and showed it to the doctor. "Get a load of all those pieces. Some are made of plastic. It even says how many on the front cover. Look at that—two hundred and seventy-three pieces. Worse than the real thing."

"And he puts them together with the precision of a surgeon," Howard agreed. "I've seen those others he's got strung up in his room. They look like they're ready to take off and fly away, all on their own. How you doing, Joel?"

"Fine, sir."

"Happy birthday, Joel," Carol said. Even her voice had the quietly resigned tones of his mother. She handed over a smaller box. "I hope we got what you wanted."

"Gee, thanks, Mrs. Austin." Joel made swift work of the wrapping. "An acrylic paint set. It's perfect. Thanks a lot."

"Thank your mom. She's the one who told Carol what to get." Howard shifted his bulk as Joel's mother entered the room. "And here's the little lady now."

Martha Grimes stood for a moment in the doorway, her face soft and unreadable as her eyes drifted over the scene. Joel seemed to be able to stand there beside her and see what she was observing. Her husband stood smiling, the model box in his hands, her best friends smiling in return. They looked like a regular family. It happened so seldom, it was worth remembering. Finally his mother said, "To the table, everybody. The food is getting cold."

CHAPTER FOUR

KYLE STOLE DOWN THE SERVANTS' STAIRWELL at the back of the Rothmore mansion. She had been ordered to appear for her mother's inspection, but first she felt the need to check with Maggie. Quietly she pushed open the door and waited for Maggie's head to lift. "How do I look?"

Maggie offered her a small, wistful smile but did not speak. Kyle prompted, "Well?"

"I was just wishing you didn't have to grow up so fast, is all."

"Oh, Maggie." Kyle moved quickly to hug the older woman. "I don't know what I'd do without you."

"Look at what you've done now—you've gotten flour on your pretty dress front. Brush it off. There, that's better." Maggie's eyes were as quietly happy as her voice. "I can scarcely believe my little darling Kyle is already fifteen years old."

"Sixteen in eight months. Say it that way. It sounds better."

"Just look at you, standing there in your lovely blue silk dress, high-heel pumps, and with your grandmother's pearls."

"It scares me to wear the pearls. I'm so afraid they'll break and spill all over the floor," Kyle confessed quietly. She cast a rapid glance at the door to the front rooms, then added, "But Mother wants me to wear them tonight."

"Then there's no use complaining, now, is there?" Maggie's voice turned brisk. "Besides, this is a formal do, and you might

51

as well get used to dressing the part."

"Emily Crawley is coming tonight," Kyle sighed. "Mother invited her. She told Randolf the invitation came from me, but Emily knows how likely that is," she added darkly.

"That's quite enough, Kyle."

"Anyway, Mother says I could learn a lot from Emily. I don't see what."

"Miss Emily is a . . . a very lovely young lady," Maggie replied carefully.

"But she's not very nice. At least not to anybody who doesn't have as much money as she does. And she only speaks to me when she wants something."

Maggie coughed discreetly, then reminded her, "The Crawleys are an important family, and Emily's brother sits on your father's board now that his father has retired."

"I know, I know. Mother's telling me that every time I turn around. But that's *business*. What has business to do with friendships?" She looked appealingly at the older woman. "Mother keeps bringing Randolf's name up and encouraging me to be friendly with him. But what on earth for?"

"There are some answers that you will simply have to obtain from your mother," Maggie replied firmly.

But Kyle was too distracted to notice the warning. She lowered her voice and whispered, "It scares me."

"Who, young Mr. Randolf?"

"No—well, yes . . . sort of, I guess."

"Which is it, young lady?"

Kyle leaned back and settled her hands on the big kitchen's wood-block central table, then remembered how she was dressed. Hastily she dusted the flour off her hands, checked the back of her dress, and said quietly, "I'm frightened by how Mother won't tell me what she means. It's like she's planning something about . . . about me. And Randolf knows, and maybe Daddy, but nobody will tell me."

"Oh, child," Maggie sighed, wiping her hands on her apron. "I love you like I do my own, and that's the honest truth. But all I can advise you about such things as this is to pray for strength, pray for protection, and pray for God's will."

"That's the same thing Bertie told me," Kyle said, searching Maggie's face.

"My husband is a wise man and a good Christian, if I do say so myself."

"I try to pray. Sometimes, anyway."

"And have you been reading the Bible I gave you?"

"I tried. But I don't think I understood very much of it. Mother says that the pastor will explain such things at church and not to worry about it."

Maggie's chin jutted out and she took a deep breath. "How about coming back to my little sitting room and reading there? Maybe I can help you with some parts you don't understand."

"Thank you, Maggie." But the offer did not brighten Kyle's mood. "It still doesn't help me know what they've got planned."

"Talking to God and reading His word to us will bring you peace," Maggie replied stoutly. "Try it and see."

Kyle avoided replying by leaning forward and kissing Maggie's cheek. Then she turned and quietly left the kitchen.

Abigail Rothmore frowned as she stood before the antique mahogany sideboard at the library's entrance. On the wall rose a full-length portrait of her in a gilded frame, wearing a ball gown by the nation's most famous artist. At least he had been the most popular society artist when the portrait was done. Now that his star was waning, she had wanted to move the portrait to the back stairway, but naturally Lawrence would not hear of it. He was so provincial when it came to such matters.

Idly she rearranged a spray of pink roses arrayed in a silver tureen. But her thoughts were not on the flowers, nor the painting, nor even the coming party. Her thoughts were on Kyle.

The girl was growing up, at least in some respects. Physically she was becoming quite a fetching young lady, though at times

Abigail had difficulty admitting it, even to herself. The presence of a daughter approaching womanhood only accentuated Abigail's own age. Just the other day, one of her charity friends remarked on how well Abigail was managing to hide the years.

But why couldn't Kyle grow up emotionally, Abigail fumed. She was such a child when it came to things that mattered. She made friends with the servants, of all things! Kyle smiled and charmed everyone who did not matter, and avoided even speaking to those who did. She cared nothing about clothes. She hated attending charity functions. She yawned through her classes in etiquette. She—

Stifling back a cry, Abigail dropped the rose. She had been so caught up in her concerns about Kyle that she did not realize how hard she had been gripping the thorny stem. Abigail turned and inspected her reflection in the tall side mirror. Her own smooth, blond, patrician beauty had enough characteristics mirrored in Kyle that no one had ever questioned their relationship. And Lawrence and Abigail had traveled enough during those early years of marriage that the appearance of the little baby fifteen years ago had not caused questions or comment.

Abigail sighed and impatiently turned away from the mirror. Emily Crawley, now, she would have been the perfect daughter. *She looks, acts, and thinks like I do* was Abigail's bittersweet conclusion. Which was hardly surprising, given the fact that Emily's and Abigail's grandfathers had been brothers. Which made them second cousins—such a cold way to describe a bond that went far beyond mere ancestral ties. If only she could mold Kyle into the proper kind of daughter.

It was a good thing that Abigail had inherited her grandfather's ambition. Lawrence had not made such a bad job of his insurance company, but he did not have that nearly ruthless instinct required to transform his middling-size business into a national power. No, her husband unfortunately shared his daughter's softness, which was remarkable, given their utterly unconnected backgrounds.

Abigail was all too familiar with the threat of softness. Her own father had been a weak, ineffectual man. Kind to his family, but weak. And it had cost their family everything. Her father had taken over a thriving business established by her grandfather and driven it into the dust.

Abigail moved closer to the sideboard and picked up the little silver bell. There was one in every room of the house, and all the servants knew the immediate summons of its ring. The bells were available for all the family, but Abigail was the only one who ever rang them. Lawrence preferred to call out his requests, and Kyle . . . well, Kyle would just do the task herself. As though the silly girl was concerned not to trouble the servants with extra work.

The doors to the main hall opened, and the maid curtsied. "You rang, ma'am?"

"Has my daughter finished dressing?"

The woman hesitated an instant before replying. "I haven't seen her, ma'am."

Which was probably a safe way for the maid to avoid saying that Kyle was back in the kitchen, against Abigail's express orders, talking with that chef again. It was only because Lawrence had put his foot down that the woman and her know-it-all husband were still in the household. "Never mind that now," she said crossly, speaking her thoughts out loud. "Go tell my husband I need to speak with him. Privately. And at once, before the guests arrive."

"Yes, ma'am." The maid quietly shut the door behind her.

Randolf Crawley. Yes. Here was a man who shared her ambition and her drive. Pity he was twenty years younger than she. The two of them would have made a formidable team. But that was impossible. No, what needed to be done was to make the proper arrangements, so that at least the next generation would rise to the ranks of *true* power. It was not that Abigail was after more money. She already had more than she would ever be able to spend. It was the power to shape and control people's lives, to bend them to her will, to see them bow and scrape and acknowledge her as the leader she had been born to be.

It was her destiny to rule.

Kyle entered the grand formal hallway at the front of the house, then stopped. Voices resounded in the distance. Loud voices. Hesitantly she walked forward, not because she wanted to, but because of her mother's orders to present herself before the guests arrived.

The closer she drew to the tall double doors leading to the library, the more it seemed as though the entire house was holding its breath. Even through the stout oak portals, Abigail's voice sounded very angry. "I simply cannot fathom why on earth you would invite that—that *boy* into our home!"

"Kenneth Adams is twenty-five years old, hardly a boy. As a matter of fact, he's only two years younger than Crawley." Lawrence Rothmore's voice sounded both tired and stubborn. "And he is more mature than some men twice his age."

"And just what is that supposed to mean?"

"Nothing, Abigail. I am simply trying to end this silly discussion."

"Silly, is it? You are choosing to bring a common office worker into my house, and you call it silly?"

"His father is a respected pastor. Ken graduated with honors from Princeton at the age of twenty, played quarterback on their varsity squad, and has been an exemplary employee of ours for almost five years now. I hardly call that common. To be honest, I am amazed that my choice of an assistant can leave you feeling so . . . so threatened."

"Threatened? Me?" Abigail's laugh sounded brittle. "Don't be absurd."

"Like it or not, he is my new personal assistant. You're always telling me I need to slow—"

"What's the matter with Randolf?"

"Young Crawley? You know quite well, Abigail, Crawley's father has retired. Randolf has been appointed to take his seat on the board. I can hardly expect our newest board member to run my errands, now, can I?"

There was a moment's hesitation before Abigail changed tack with, "In any case, you must admit this Kenneth person is a poor substitute for the real thing."

Kyle knew her mother, should she open the door, would be furious to find her listening there. But she could not move. She felt glued to the spot. Though her name had not been mentioned even once, she had the feeling that this entire quarrel had something to do with her. Something bad.

Her father's voice rose a notch. "What on earth are you talking about?"

"You know very well what I mean. You're always forming these absurd attachments with protégés. We should have had a son, just like I said."

Kyle stiffened. A son! She had always dreamed of having a baby brother. But her mother had never allowed her to even mention it. Kyle could scarcely believe her ears. Her mother had wanted a son?

Her father's astounded laugh rang through the closed doors. "Like *you* said? In case you have forgotten, Abigail, *I* was the one who begged you for a son after Kyle—"

"Don't be petty. I meant *instead* of—"

"That is more than enough." A new tone had entered her father's voice. A dangerous coldness. "I want no more of that. Not ever."

Clearly Abigail realized she had gone too far, for her voice took on a conciliatory note. "But to invite him into our house, especially tonight when so much hangs upon—"

"Our daughter is just fifteen years old." A trace of anger grated in Lawrence's voice.

"And growing up fast," Abigail retorted.

"That's right, she is." Behind the closed doors, Kyle was able to visualize her father's determined strength in standing up for her. "Which means that in time she will grow into handling her own affairs."

"Oh, really, Lawrence." Scorn dripped from Abigail's voice. "She doesn't have the faintest inkling of how to handle relationships *or* money. Do you know, I have even had to stop her allowance. She has the absurd tendency of giving it away to the first poor person who comes into sight."

"There's nothing wrong with a little charity," Lawrence said, but a note of doubt had crept into his tone.

"Let us be realistic, please. It is high time this issue be settled in everyone's mind. Which makes it even more bizarre that you would even dream of inviting this other young man—"

"The matter is closed," Lawrence replied stonily.

Her father's heavy footsteps started toward the library doors, with Abigail's continuing argument in close pursuit. Kyle inched her way along the dark paneling, then flew up the stairs.

Once in her own bedroom, she shut her door on the words that seemed to have followed her. She turned on the radio and waited impatiently as it warmed up to the strains of the new hit song, "Only You." Shakily she seated herself at her little vanity and studied her reflection. She was certainly not pretty, not like Emily Crawley, who had even the oldest boys stopping to watch as she walked by. Kyle's nose turned upward slightly, almost like a miniature ski jump. She always felt that her shoulder-length hair was too thick, even after she had brushed and brushed until her arm ached. And it seemed such a strange color—not brown and not blond, just a sort of butterscotch.

Whenever Kyle examined her reflection, like now, she felt as though her mother's disapproving gaze was there as well, pointing out all her flaws. Large eyes stared back at her from a face that was shaped like a reversed teardrop, descending from a broad forehead to a pointy chin, which of course made her mouth look even bigger than it really was. Especially tonight, when her mother had personally selected an odd peach shade of lipstick, then had made her paint her fingernails so they matched. It was almost as though Abigail wanted to make her look years older than she was. Even the dress had been personally selected, and Kyle was wearing Gran's pearls for the very first time.

Some girls would have been pleased with the chance to seem older and mature. Not Kyle. What with the constant lessons in etiquette and speech and dance and on and on and on, Kyle felt she was constantly on display. Constantly being prepared for something, being formed into an ornament to be polished and set upon a mantelpiece. Kyle picked up her brush with a sigh. No, growing older held nothing for her but a vague foreboding. As Kyle brushed with swift, hard strokes, her mind went back over the quarrel. What had her mother meant when she said "instead"? Instead of what?

The doorbell rang. Before the chimes were silenced, Kyle had stood, turned off her radio, and started for the bedroom door. Her mother would scold if she was not there to greet their guests. Besides, her mother would never dream of continuing an argument in public. Abigail always presented her loveliest smile to the outside world when she was angry. As Kyle hesitantly moved down the stairs, she wondered if perhaps that was why she herself smiled so seldom. Her mother made the act seem like a lie.

As she entered the living room, Randolf Crawley approached. Inwardly she quailed that he, the last person she wished to see, should quite naturally be the first guest to arrive.

"Kyle, good evening." He flashed a smile. "How beautiful you look."

"Thank you, Mr. Crawley," she said, feeling her mother's eyes upon her. "How are you tonight?"

"You really must call me Randolf, please." He tugged on the starched cuffs to his shirt, pulling them down below the sleeves of his tuxedo so that the heavy gold cufflinks glinted in the chandelier's light. "We're almost family, you know." He laughed at his own quip, then added, "I suppose you've heard the news. Father has retired, and I have taken over his place on the board."

"Yes. Congratulations." Kyle managed the words with a courteous smile, though she felt little interest in the man's promotion.

Randolf's gray eyes swept over her form. "You look truly spectacular," he said warmly. "That blue in your dress complements your hair beautifully." He didn't seem to notice her blush of embarrassment. "Let's see, you must be seventeen, isn't that right?"

"Fifteen," Kyle corrected. She felt terribly uncomfortable and out of place. "Just barely fifteen."

"Of course. She's the same age as me, aren't you, dear Kyle?" Emily Crawley moved up beside them, her eyes appraising Kyle from top to toe. "I must say, you have made quite an effort tonight."

Kyle tried to put a little brightness into her voice as she asked, "How are you, Emily?"

"Oh, almost as bored as you, I imagine," the girl replied, giving her sleek blond hair a pretty toss. But she did not look bored. Not at all. She surveyed the rapidly filling room with shining eyes. "Why on earth my brother wanted me to accompany him tonight, when there's nobody but old fuddy-duddies around, I shall never know."

"Almost the entire Rothmore board is here tonight," Randolf replied. "Not to mention Senator Allenby over there." He gave Kyle another look and a little bow. "If you ladies will excuse me, I must go and say hello."

Emily watched her older brother walk away, then said, "Isn't it exciting, how this is all working out? In just a couple of years, we will be sisters."

Kyle stared at her. "What are you talking about?"

Emily Crawley had the ability to look particularly beautiful when amazed. "Don't tell me you don't know."

"Know what?"

Emily lifted her perfect little chin and let out a peal of laughter. "Kyle Rothmore, you are positively too droll!" She regarded Kyle with eager eyes. "Think about it for a moment, my little innocent sister-to-be. How your mother has been urging you to come and spend time with my family—at my house with my dear older brother. Pushing you to attend certain meetings, making certain you are seated next to each other. Doesn't she speak of him a great deal?"

Kyle took a step back in genuine horror. "Not Randolf. No, I, it's . . ."

"Whyever not?" Emily followed her, stepping closer, her gaze eager to observe every shred of Kyle's reaction. "Randolf is a prize, don't you think?"

With great effort Kyle struggled for the most polite reaction possible. "But he's so . . . so *old*."

"Dear Randolf is hardly *that* ancient, although I do admit he's getting a bit long in the tooth." Emily's laugh was shrill. "But never mind. In ten years or so age won't matter hardly at all, will it?"

"I didn't, I never . . ."

"Yes, imagine, me being the one to break the news. Isn't that positively delicious?" Emily studied Kyle's face and showed a moment's disappointment that there was no further reaction. She pressed, "I've heard it said that Randolf is one of Washington's most eligible bachelors. You must be *so* excited."

"Yes," Kyle said quietly. She had quickly determined to keep everything she was thinking from showing. Especially here. "Well, if you will excuse me, I must greet our other guests."

Emily's obvious frustration gave Kyle the strength to turn and walk to her father. He reached out an arm to encircle her as he proudly introduced her to the people standing nearby. Kyle forced herself to smile and make all the expected responses. She continued on around the room, speaking to everyone in turn, doing it so well that even her mother stopped her to say how nice it was to see Kyle making an effort. Just how much effort Abigail would never know.

Even though Kyle tried to concentrate on the guests' conversations, her thoughts were constantly turning to Emily's words. *Randolf.* She was to be traded for a union between two powerful families? She felt as if there were a ball of ice where her heart should have been. As she continued about the room, she glanced over to where her father stood laughing with his group of cronies. Surely he had not been a part of this plan, surely not. It hurt more than she could bear to think otherwise.

Then her father broke away from the group and hurried across the room to the door. She watched as he walked up to a newcomer, a young man with dark hair and a grave, hesitant air. Lawrence's arm circled the young man's shoulders as he led him into the room to begin introducing him around. A brief moment of attention was granted his arrival, but as soon as Lawrence was pulled elsewhere, the young man was left standing alone.

Kyle felt drawn to him and to his slightly bewildered demeanor. He looked no more comfortable with the gathering than she did. Kyle imagined herself seeing the grand chamber through his eyes, the curved ceiling almost three stories high, the four grand chandeliers lighting yards of polished wood and precious carpets, the glittering people, the servants in their best uniforms, the sparkling platters and crystal.

As she started across the room, suddenly Emily was at her elbow. "That's the plebe Randolf was telling me about, isn't he, the one your father has pulled up from the masses to stand at his beck and call?"

"He's to be Father's new assistant," Kyle commented mildly.

"Doesn't he look so utterly ordinary," Emily remarked. "I suppose it will be my duty to have him escort me into dinner. No doubt he will bore me to tears with a discussion of actuary tables and the like."

Kyle ended further comments by walking away. She approached the young man, reached out her hand, and said, "Good evening, I am Kyle Rothmore."

"Kenneth Adams." He had a charming smile. "Mr. Rothmore mentioned that he had a daughter. I am very happy to meet you."

The familiar courtesy was spoken with a natural sincerity. Kyle found herself drawn to this pleasant young man. Before she could think of something else to say, Bertrand appeared in the doorway to announce, "Ladies and gentlemen, dinner is served."

"May I take your arm?" Kyle whispered to Kenneth.

"I'm sorry, I didn't—"

"Quickly, please." She was so startled by her boldness that

she could scarcely breathe. She reached for his extended elbow, then motioned him toward the dining room.

Four faces confronted them in quick succession. Randolf was halfway across the room and headed toward her when he stopped abruptly. He looked shocked, but swiftly gathered himself. He gave Kyle a formal smile and a slight bow before casting a wrathful glance at Kenneth. Emily was moving their way as well, and showed genuine astonishment at Kyle's maneuver.

The next face Kyle caught sight of was her mother's. Abigail's gaze burned so fiercely Kyle had to turn away. She had never dared to deliberately cross her mother before. The realization of what she was doing left her knees weak.

"Well, look at this, would you." Lawrence Rothmore's ruddy features beamed with genuine pride. "Leave it to my daughter to make our newest guest feel right at home."

That's right, Kyle thought silently. The perspective her father placed upon her actions granted Kyle the strength to straighten her shoulders. *I'd do anything for you, Daddy.*

As she thought the words, Kyle knew they were true. If her father wanted her, *needed* her to marry Randolf Crawley, the reasons did not really matter. Then and there, Kyle knew that if her father asked, she would do it. Even though the thought alone was enough to send ice water through her veins, she would do it for her father.

Lawrence's breath wheezed noisily as he beamed at them both. "Not many people are lucky enough . . ." He broke off to cough. Beads of perspiration spotted his forehead.

"Are you all right, Daddy?"

He waved away her concern. "Working too hard. That's why I need myself a young man—borrow his legs." Lawrence straightened, pulled a spotless handkerchief from his pocket, wiped his brow, then signaled a hovering Bertrand over. "Go out there and rearrange the place cards so these two young people can sit together."

The butler whispered discreetly, "But Mrs. Rothmore specifically ordered—"

"Go ahead and do it." His voice was strong enough to be

heard by both Randolf and Abigail. "Make it snappy—people are coming in."

"Right away, sir."

Kyle reached for her father's arm. "Shouldn't you lie down?"

"I'm fine, little princess, don't you fret." He gave her a look of such love and pride that she put aside her fears. "Now you two go and enjoy yourselves."

Kyle led Kenneth over to where Bertrand was holding out her chair. As she settled herself, Bertrand leaned down to whisper, "Well done."

Before she could ask him what he meant, her mother entered the chamber upon the arm of the senator. Abigail's glance flitted over Kyle as if she were not even there. Kyle dropped her gaze to her lap.

"It was very kind of you to accompany me," Kenneth said, obviously uncertain of what was taking place.

But Kyle was not about to go into that. He was an employee of her father, she reminded herself, someone her mother would have referred to as the "office help." As the guests settled around the great oval table, beneath a gilded chandelier from a castle in France, Kyle sought a suitable subject. "What do you do for my father, Mr. Adams?"

"Anything he wants me to. And please call me Kenneth." His smile, warm and broad, creased his features, accenting the vigor and strength of his face. His eyes were dark green, full of life and curiosity. "Right now I am head of his investigating services. I'm responsible for making sure insurance claims are genuine. And sometimes I have to hunt down people to whom claims have been assigned." He glanced down as a flat bowl rimmed in gold was placed before him, then soup was ladled in. "But I shouldn't bore you with business."

"Lobster bisque," Kyle said, not needing to even look at her own bowl. Her mother always arranged for every formal dinner to start with the same dish. Kyle found it rather rich for her own tastes. She went on, "Maggie says there's almost a whole cup of cream in each bowl."

"Maggie is the cook?"

"That's right." Kyle hesitated, then ventured, "And my friend."

"Sounds like a smart woman," Kenneth said, glancing about the room.

Again there was the sense of seeing the chamber through his eyes. She looked around with him, taking in the men in their tuxedos and the women in their gowns and jewels. She saw the fancy Wedgwood china and the polished silver and all the fine possessions standing upon the antique sideboards. She felt as though she were seeing everything for the first time. She also understood the expression on his face. Sometimes she did not feel as if she belonged here either.

"Pick up the round spoon," Kyle murmured quietly. "Do what I do. Just raise it up and touch it to your lips. That way you won't look impolite."

"You don't like it?"

Kyle decided to confess what she had not told another soul, not even Maggie, for fear of hurting her feelings. "Melted shrimp ice cream would taste better."

When Kenneth laughed out loud, several faces turned their way. Kyle decided to deflect the attention by turning to her other neighbor, one of Rothmore's senior board members, and asking about his family. But in truth her mind remained on the young man seated to her other side.

She waited until the second course was set in front of them before turning back. Kenneth met her with another of his appealing smiles and said, "Tell me about yourself."

"Me?"

"Sure. What do you like? Do you ever listen to rock and roll?"

Kyle felt uncertain how to respond. She had never had a dinner guest at one of her mother's events speak *with* her. Everyone politely spoke *down* to her, doing their duty, until they were allowed to turn away and discuss something that really interested them. Kyle decided to risk more honesty. "Sometimes. I'm not sure I like it, though."

"Yeah, there's a lot of strangeness out there. But some of it is powerful." Kenneth ate his filet mignon with gusto. " 'See You Later, Alligator'—have you heard that one yet?"

"Yes." Kyle was unsure what to think now. He looked like an adult, or sort of. He certainly carried himself like one. But adults weren't supposed to be interested in this music. Or were they?

"Then there's 'Que Sera.' I think it's a terrific way to think about the future."

Her eyes widened as she nodded. She had heard the song for the first time the week before.

He smiled his thanks as his plate was removed. "But it's too bad the singer didn't point out that confidence in God is the way to accept each day as it comes."

The informal yet intimate way he spoke of God reminded her of Maggie. "Maybe that's not what the singer had in mind," she ventured in response.

"Well, she should have." He gave her another smile. "Only way to make a philosophy like that really work."

When Kyle did not respond, he gave a little shrug and asked, "Have you been reading about Grace Kelly's wedding plans?"

It was the perfect question. "Oh yes, isn't it wonderful? Princess Grace, that's what she's going to be called. It's like out of a fairy tale."

"It sure will be something," Kenneth agreed.

"She's going to keep her American citizenship. I saw it on television last week."

"That's right," he nodded, his smile flashing.

"I wish I could see it. Don't you?" Then Kyle met her mother's gaze from across the table, and she felt her enthusiasm fade into a chill of apprehension. She dropped her eyes back to her plate, her appetite gone.

Kenneth asked, "Is something the matter?"

"No, everything's fine," she murmured. She was always doing the wrong thing, talking to the wrong person. She was supposed to keep the proper distance from people like Kenneth. She shivered as she pictured the coming confrontation with her mother.

Kyle leaned forward and glanced at where her father sat at the head of the table. He was laughing at something the senator's wife was saying. Would he really ask her to marry Randolf Crawley?

She risked another glance at her mother. The afternoon's discussion between her parents came back to Kyle's mind. Once again, she found herself wondering what on earth her mother had meant. *Instead* of what?

CHAPTER FIVE

JOEL LAY IN BED, unable to sleep. The moon was high and bright in the clear night sky, and silver light shimmered across his little upstairs room. The house's second floor he had to himself. Well, almost. His father did not like stairs, so his parents slept in the converted back parlor. There were four rooms downstairs, and two upstairs under the eaves. Joel had one. The other was called the guest room, which was strange, because his family never had guests. Gramma Grimes lived only fifteen miles away, and they didn't see much of anybody else except Doc Austin, and he lived just up the road.

His mother had placed frilly pink touches in the guest room that had no guests, items that Joel thought would have looked better in a baby's room. She went in at least once a week to tidy up. She would sit on the room's little bed for a while and stare out the window with a faraway look in her eyes. And when she came back downstairs, her eyes sometimes looked puffy and red and her voice was distant. Often she avoided other family members for a time. It puzzled Joel.

Once in the middle of the night he had thought he heard sobbing. Troubled, he had crept quietly across the little hall that joined the two rooms and peeked through the door. The light from the streetlamp spilled through the room and out into the hallway, touching as it passed the pink cushions on the perfectly made bed. He had expected to find his mother weeping, but to his surprise and bewilderment, it was his father who sat in the chair by the bed, his face in his hands, his shoulders shaking. His father never climbed the stairs. Never. What would bring him to the guest room in the middle of the night? Joel had had a difficult time returning to sleep and had shivered under the warmth of his comforter. But though he had wondered, he had never dared to voice the questions that troubled him so.

Joel now lay and listened to his heart. It was pounding overloud again. But it did that now and then. Usually Joel ignored the occasional pains and the odd sounds his heart sometimes made. But tonight every rapid beat seemed etched in absolute clarity.

He craned his head and through the screened window watched the stars wink at him. Down below, a solitary car drove by, its passage disturbing the crickets and wind and night owls, but only for a moment.

He glanced at the ticking clock. The hands seemed stuck in place. He rolled over, closed his eyes, and finally drifted off.

The whistle of an early bird jerked him back from sleep. He reached for the clock. His alarm was set to go off in twenty minutes. He tried to lie there, but the anticipation was too great. Finally he rose and slipped into his clothes, tiptoed down the stairs, grabbed the sandwich and apple he had set out the night before, then quietly left the house.

The early dawn was a gentle wash across the sky, the light beginning to dim the stars. The April morning was chilly enough for him to see his breath, but Joel was too excited to feel the cold. The moon was a lustrous circle in the west. As he stood on the corner and ate his sandwich, he imagined that the man in the moon was smiling down on him.

Right on time, the square van chugged down the street and stopped in front of him. A cigar-chomping man stuck his head out of the van's side door and demanded, "Are you, hang on a second, I got your name somewhere. Yeah, here it is. You Joel Grimes?"

"Yessir. Good morning, sir."

"You don't gotta 'sir' me, kid." He slid a thick work-gloved hand under the tightly wrapped wire and tossed the bundle out of the van. It landed at Joel's feet with a heavy thunk. "You bring pliers?"

"Nossir, I didn't—"

"Here, use mine today. Snip the wire and peel it back, careful, otherwise it'll jab you like a knife. That's it. How old are you, kid?"

"Thirteen, sir. Almost fourteen."

The man studied Joel for a moment, as though deciding whether to challenge his statement of age. Joel knew that he was smaller than other boys of thirteen. In fact, that was one of the reasons why his father had agreed to the paper route. "Might build some muscle, put some meat on those bones," he had said. Any reason was good enough for Joel. He wanted the route.

Joel was relieved when the man finally gave a curt nod and returned to his previous argument. "I told you, you don't need to say sir to—"

"Lay off the kid already," the driver called from his place in the front of the van. "Nothing the matter with manners." The driver was as heavyset as the first man, but his features were bright and smiling. "Thirteen's pretty young for a route all your own. Think you can handle it?"

"Yessir, I sure hope so," Joel replied, handing back the pliers.

"Sunday's the worst," the first man allowed. "Gotta remember to put a magazine and comics into each paper—they come separate. And don't try to carry them all. Find some place to stash them where they won't be seen from the road, otherwise some wise guy'll come by and steal a couple."

"I'll remember that," Joel said, breathless with the fact that it was really and truly happening. "Thanks."

"Don't mention it." The gruff man pointed a gloved thumb at his chest. "Name's Hank. The smart aleck up there driving is Julius."

"Nice meeting you, sir."

"Likewise, kid. And good luck." Hank pounded the side panel, and with a gust of black smoke the van pulled away.

For a moment Joel stood there, taking it in. The dawn was his and his alone. Finally he hefted half the bundle and carried the papers behind the nearby hedge. The others he coiled using the bag of rubber bands he had brought, then set the awkward rolls into his bike baskets. He had two of them now, one in front of the handlebars and the other over his back tire. He had borrowed money from his mom for them, promising to pay it back from his first paycheck.

In the days leading up to this moment, Joel had done his best to prepare. He had mapped out his route and discovered that it was split in two, with the collection point set almost in the middle. He had spoken to the young man whose route he was taking over, a friend of Doc Austin's who was headed for medical school up north. The young man had described the difficult people, especially the ones who called and complained to the paper's circulation office. They were the ones who could cost him his job. Joel had also called the office himself, though the act had scared him.

Joel mounted his bike and moved out on the route he had already committed to memory. A lot of his tosses didn't land right, which meant stopping his bike and walking up the lawn, sometimes hunting through bushes, pulling out the paper, wiping it clean, and setting it on the front porch. Then he came to the first problem house, an old man who complained his papers were being stolen. Quietly Joel climbed the stairs, opened the screen door, and slipped the paper down where it couldn't be seen from outside.

Another block included the house of old Mrs. Drummond; he already knew about her from Doc Austin. She was not a complainer, but her arthritis was so bad that walking to the edge of her porch was very difficult for her. Joel did what Doc Austin had suggested, which was to slide her paper through her mail slot. As he walked back to his bike, he remembered what else Doc Austin had said, how the woman amazed him with her cheerfulness, how despite her pain she met each day with a smile and a prayer. Doc Austin said he could never understand how someone so afflicted could hold on to faith. Joel wondered what that meant, "hold on to faith." But he didn't ask.

Joel finished the route's first half and hurried back for the second load. His tires whispered down the empty street, and his speed blew up a gentle breeze. He pulled the papers from behind the hedge and began rolling them up. As he bundled them into the rubber bands, he wondered what it was about some people that made them believe in God like that. His parents never talked about religion. Never. His father worked almost every Sunday because he picked up time and a half for weekend work. Joel had seen people going to church, all dressed up and looking stiff and formal. To him it seemed like a strange way to spend a Sunday.

Joel began the second sweep, not bothered by how long it was taking him. He was ready to spend as much time as it took in the beginning, determined to get things right. Besides, he loved having the morning to himself. As he biked down one quiet street after another, his thoughts stood out fresh and clean in the quiet air, and he could think clearly about things. It was even better than being alone in his small upstairs room, working over a new model plane at the desk beneath the window.

His teachers at school said he was too quiet for his own good. He had overheard one of his teachers tell another that his withdrawn nature was a sign Joel did not feel things. Joel did not agree with that at all. As far as he was concerned, he felt things too much.

He finished the route, almost sad that it was done. But school would start soon, so he gathered up the wire and the scraps of paper and started home. As he did, he thought about the call he had made to the newspaper office. The woman had been astonished to hear from him. She had dug up the complaints and read them over the phone to Joel. She said it was the first time she had ever been called for this information by a new paper boy, and that she was going to mention his name to her boss. Joel felt anew the glow over that and resolved that everything was going to go well. There would be no complaints on his route. Not one.

When he turned onto his street, for some reason Joel found himself thinking about old Mrs. Drummond. Strange how she could be so sick and still be happy. Joel parked his bike on the front walk and wished there was some way he could make his parents happy. He'd give anything to have people speak about them the way Doc Austin had talked about the elderly lady.

CHAPTER SIX

MARTHA STARED WITH UNSEEING EYES out her kitchen window. The morning sun had pushed up to a sitting position and was taking stock of the brand-new day. Seeming pleased with what it saw, it rose on the eastern horizon to flex its muscles of warmth. But Martha had no interest in the day's beauty. She seldom did. From her place by the sink she turned back to her morning duties. Joel would soon be home from his paper route. Already the smell of breakfast coffee wafted on the morning air. It was her way of getting her day going. It was also the silent signal that drew Harry from his bed to dress for another day of work. A day he never seemed to look forward to with any kind of anticipation. And his mood splashed over on Martha, burdening her with the same sense of resignation.

Martha saw Harry exit the bedroom, still tucking in his shirt and stifling a yawn. She turned away from him in pretense of stirring the morning porridge. Joel would be hungry and perhaps just a bit chilled. The sun had not yet warmed the outside world.

Silently, Harry poured himself a cup of coffee and took it outside to the back porch. The sun struck there first and warmed their postage-stamp backyard before the rest of the house. Harry had come and gone before Martha had time to sense the mood of the morning. Would he be simply taciturn, or would he be surly and quick to criticize? Joel usually returned from his morn-

74

ing route seeking for the signs that would give him the same information. He would stop by the porch, eyes quickly flicking over his father's face.

A sudden thought pulsed through Martha: *Joel's getting so tall. He's growing up—my little boy.*

The thought caught her totally off guard. She'd had no intention of starting her day with maudlin thinking. She had no intention of thinking at all. She did not like to think. She found it far too painful.

She tried to force her attention back to the softly bubbling porridge. She nearly swished the steamy contents from the pot with her vigorous stirring. But even with the increased activity she could not divert her thoughts. *I should have two of them. He should not have been an only child. My little girl—my Katie . . .*

In those chance moments when she did consciously think of her vanished daughter, she was amazed and devastated anew at how deeply the loss still hurt. Martha had been so certain that the passing of time would dim the pain of her heart, ease the emptiness of her arms. But the agony remained so intense it was a physical wound. Her tightened heart seemed to pinch against her rib cage. Her arms literally ached with the absence of a bundle of life, even years after she knew that the little bundle had grown to girlhood. Her throat constricted so she could hardly swallow back the threatening tears.

At such times Martha became even darker of mood than her husband. Even more testy and cutting. It was her only line of defense.

"He's late again," she heard her own harsh voice chiding her absent son. "How on earth am I supposed to have breakfast ready when he won't hold to a proper schedule?"

From the back porch, Harry spoke his first words of the morning. "Sounds like you're riding the boy pretty hard."

She turned to where he sat at the back table and through the open door gave him a hard, cold look. There was no use trying to explain to Harry that it wasn't the time that bothered her. Not the time at all.

It was the high chair tucked away in the pantry—though why

she kept it there since Joel had outgrown it, she would not have been able to explain. The high chair that first should have held a baby girl. The high chair that should have been pushed up close to the table, holding another chortling infant thumping an impatient spoon as she waited for her morning porridge.

But Martha could not put her deep feelings into words. She could scarcely form coherent thoughts. At such times the pain was so gripping that she felt she would smother with its force.

She sighed hard, pushing the thoughts and the feelings away as she would a lingering nightmare. "Never mind," she said dully. "I'll make do. That's what I'm best at, I suppose. Making do with what I have."

After a year of delivering papers, the work had become routine, the time cut by two-thirds. By now his bicycle seemed like an extension of himself. Had he been given to whistling, Joel might have sent a quivering tune into the stillness of the spring morning. There was a song running through his mind in time to his pumping legs, "Oh Yes, I'm the Great Pretender." It already felt like the song was written for him. But Joel made no sound. He had spent his years learning to hide all emotions.

He tossed out the last few papers, his arm cocking and throwing in smooth, automatic sweeps, the papers landing perfectly on the front porches. A year of biking through every kind of weather had brought him a very special knowledge of his little town.

Riverdale was located midway between Baltimore and Washington and had no historical past or town center. It had probably begun as an intersection of Kenilworth Avenue and Riverdale Road, then sprawled out to take over adjoining farmland. Now it was the center of a postwar building boom. Hundreds and hundreds of square saltbox houses lined consecutively numbered streets. With time, the houses became different; people added on summer terraces and winter sun-rooms and patios. The white clapboard exteriors were trimmed with different colored paints. A bush sprouted, another hedge was cut back. But there remained a sameness to the streets and the houses and the neighborhoods.

It was a family town, set in the Maryland countryside about twenty miles north of Washington, D.C. Many were second-generation folk, brimming with the memories of grandparents and great-grandparents having arrived from the old countries to make a new life.

In Riverdale it was probably best to be Irish and have an Irish-sounding name. Joel Grimes was close enough to fit in, though his own ancestors had come from Germany, at least those he knew about. Fathers mostly had jobs the kids could understand. They clerked in hardware stores, fitted pipes, worked at gas stations, put out fires. Some traveled to the iron and steel works in southwest Baltimore, willing to put up with the long commute to give their families a better place to live. The mothers mostly stayed home to mind the children. Laundry hung out behind the homes, and fences were places for neighbors to lean on and gossip.

Joel left his bike on his front walk and picked up his last paper. His father was working the middle shift, which meant Harry left the house after Joel did. Joel usually scanned the paper before he got home and tried to find something in it to talk about. It was a way of testing the waters, passing over some bit of information, seeing if his father felt like talking. Most mornings Harry replied with a grunt, but occasionally his father would continue the conversation. Those days, Joel felt as though he had won a secret battle.

Joel entered the house and heard his mother moving about the kitchen, preparing their breakfast. He gave her cheek a quick kiss as he passed, and she responded with her quiet little smile. Everything was the same, just another morning in their silent house. Yet for some unexplainable reason Joel had the feeling that something was different. Something very big. Maybe even something good.

When Joel entered the kitchen he could see his father out on the back veranda, a steaming cup of coffee on the small table at his elbow, the latest issue of *Argosy* magazine opened in his lap. Harry read *Argosy* and the paper, nothing else. He called *Argosy* the only real man's magazine.

Joel set the paper down on the table and pushed open the screened veranda door. "Pop, did you hear? The Fairey Delta 2, a British plane, it's set a new speed record. One thousand, one hundred and thirty-two miles per hour."

A frown furrowed Harry's forehead until the eyebrows met. "I don't need to know anything about a Limey plane."

Usually a response like that was enough to push Joel back inside. But today the feeling of something important happening kept him there, fishing for whatever it might be. "But, Pop, you're always saying the Brits were good fighters."

His father slapped down the magazine and rattled the paper open. The tall sheets hid his scowl. "Maybe so, but mark my words, the good old US of A will have that record back in a jiffy."

Joel returned to the kitchen, wondering why he still felt a sense of specialness to the day. He slid into his customary place at the kitchen table, where his mother had already placed a steaming bowl of oatmeal. Joel felt her hand brush against his shoulder as she put two slices of buttered toast at the side of his plate. It was so rare, a touch like that, it seemed as though it was intended to confirm that the day was indeed unique. He nearly started whistling.

He left for school without hearing a single sharp word, a single whiff of discontent. Surely this day held something good in store.

But when he came around the final corner, and his school stood just ahead, the song in his heart was squelched as completely as the one on his lips. Before him, almost blocking the concrete path leading to the building, was a cluster of boys. As soon as he saw them, Joel knew they were up to no good. His stomach knotted in response to the sight, and for one awful moment he feared they were waiting for him.

He wanted to stop, to run, to fly. But he did none of those things, though he could not understand why. His steps faltered, but something kept him going, walking toward them, his whole body tensed in anticipation of what might come.

To this point he had avoided the nasty gang that teased and tormented other kids. They loved to prey on the smaller, the quieter, the more introspective, the loners. Joel was all of those things and would have made good prey. By dodging them at every opportunity and ignoring them whenever they were close, he had so far managed to escape notice. But now he was walking directly toward them, for reasons he could not fully understand. He steeled himself, hoping with all his heart that whatever was drawing their attention would continue to hold their focus.

They were laughing, the kind that rang with a hateful sound. Joel knew it was not shared mirth over some boyish joke. Nor was it good-natured banter. It had a bitter quality. One that left a bad taste in Joel's mouth and formed a knot in the pit of his stomach.

"Hey, farmer," Joel heard one of the larger boys jeer. "Where'd you come from?"

"Looks like he crawled out of a haystack," said their leader. Herman Gadsby was a red-faced bully, a slow-moving football player with a misshapen nose. "Either that or from under some rock."

The laughter rose like a dark ominous wave. "What do you think we oughtta do with him?"

It was then that Joel spotted the object of their ridicule. A boy stood almost surrounded by the crowd. His dark suspendered pants met a simple blue shirt. A black felt hat was pulled down, almost covering the squared haircut. A battered tin pail was clasped tightly in a white-knuckled hand.

Joel had never seen the boy before. For a moment he wished he was not seeing him now. He did not like the feel in the air. All the bullies wore their hair in elaborate pompadours, with the hair in back slicked into flat ducktails. Most kids knew to disappear whenever guys with hairstyles like that came into view. Obviously this guy didn't know any better.

Joel had no idea what to do. He stood quietly, licking dry lips, working to swallow saliva that wasn't there. He felt tension crawl up his spine like a garter snake shivering through meadow grasses. Clammy moistness dampened his hands.

Deliverance came with the loud donging of the school bell. The tangle of boys unravelled and spilled toward the schoolhouse steps at about the same rate that the knot in Joel's stomach unwound.

The next thing he knew, he was staring into a pair of solemn gray eyes. Neither boy spoke a word. They just stood there, measuring each other. In the background the bell stopped ringing, and the silence fell in around them like a living thing. It stirred something in Joel, that silence.

Together they turned and moved toward the red brick school. If they were late for class, there would be trouble. Their steps quickened, and side by side they hurried off to join the clatter as students pressed down the dusty, dark-paneled halls. Joel stopped only long enough to hastily toss his cap toward his assigned wall hook. He saw the boy remove his black hat and look about for a place to deposit it.

"There." Joel pointed at an empty spare peg, and the black felt settled with a gentle rocking motion. The two boys surged ahead to pass through the classroom door, just as Mr. Murdoch stretched out a hand to close it against latecomers.

Joel slid into his assigned seat. The new boy stood silently by the door. As Mr. Murdoch turned to address the new student and assign him a place, the two boys' eyes connected. Some sort of communication passed between them, though Joel was not sure about the message.

It seemed like the most natural thing in the world to fall into step with each other after school. They walked in silence for a moment before Joel finally asked, "Want to go to the soda fountain?" Instantly he regretted it, for this young man in his strange clothes would not be comfortable there. But the fountain in People's drugstore was a gathering point for almost the entire school.

"No, I think," the boy said. He had an accent as strange as his clothes.

Joel thought a moment, then asked, "Want to go see my model planes?"

That met with instant approval. "Yes. I will like to."

Simon was the boy's name. Simon Miller. After giving his name to the teacher at the beginning of class, he had said scarcely a word the entire day. Yet both times the teacher had called on him, Simon had offered the correct answer without hesitation. Joel had spent much of the day observing Simon out of the corner of his eye. There was an unusual stillness about him, attentive yet reserved.

"What are you doing here?" Joel asked. "I mean, it seems kinda funny, starting school a month before the year's over."

"My father has diabetes. Last year they took his leg from— here." He pointed to a spot just above his own knee. "They gave him a make-pretend leg, but sometimes it hurts much." There was a calm acceptance to the way Simon spoke. "Now there are more problems yet, circulation this time. He has to come down and be near the hospital."

Despite the matter-of-fact way Simon spoke, Joel could not help but feel a lance of sympathetic understanding. "Hey, that's tough. My dad has a problem with his leg, too."

"He is diabetic?"

"No. He got hurt in the war."

"I am sorry. Hard it is to see much suffering."

"How come you talk like that? You sound like you're reading off a page."

"I am Pennsylvania Dutch," Simon said simply, as though that was all the explanation required.

"A what?"

"Pennsylvania Dutch. Cherman. You have never heard of us?"

"I don't think so."

"Papa will explain. He calls us the people apart." Simon grinned at the thought. "You think I talk funny, you wait. Papa did not learn English until he was a full-grown man. He talks English fine, but he thinks Cherman."

Further questions were cut off by turning onto Joel's street. He knew a moment's qualm. His father should still be at work. He rarely came home from the middle shift before six. But what would Simon think of his home or his mother? He had never brought a friend home before. Joel's pace slowed as he reflected how odd it was to have suggested this stranger accompany him home.

"Something is the matter, Choel?"

"No." He hoped he was telling the truth and led Simon up the walk to his front door. Cautiously he opened the door and called out, "Mom?"

The house was silent in reply. Joel gave a relieved sigh and said, "She must be at the market. Come on."

He led Simon up the stairs and into his bedroom. The boy followed him into the room, holding his hat before him with both hands. Joel saw him looking around and said, "Just drop it on the bed."

Carefully Simon set down his black felt hat and took off his coat. His eyes grew large as they took in every aspect of the display—from the suspended airplanes that gently fluttered near the ceiling to the simple shelves lined with painstakingly constructed models. "Ach—so nice," exclaimed the boy.

Joel grinned, his eyes following the eyes of his guest. It was the first time that he enjoyed pride in sharing his hours of work.

"Ach, they are some beautiful! Never have I seen anything like this!"

"They're models. I made them myself. I've got a paper route. Most of the money goes into my savings. I need to save all I can, if I'm going to go to college. But I buy some models, too."

"They are some beautiful." Simon lowered himself to the

floor rug and let his eyes wander up and over each plane above his head.

Joel squatted down beside him. It was the first chance he had to closely examine Simon's clothes. The shirt had neither collar nor cuffs. The fabric was coarse, the stitching broad and even. Even the suspenders looked homemade, fastened to the trousers by pairs of buttons. "Does your mother make all your clothes?"

Simon nodded, his eyes still focused on the planes. "We do not buy from the store anything we wear, except the shoes."

"Why not?"

"It is the Mennonite way," Simon said simply.

"Mennonite?"

Simon nodded. "That is what we are."

"I thought you said you were Pennsylvania Dutch—or German or something."

Simon lowered his gaze and laughed good-naturedly. "Pennsylvania Dutch—yes. That is our background. Cherman—that is our tongue. Mennonite—that is our belief—our faith—our whole way of life."

Joel frowned. It seemed a lot to keep track of. He really couldn't understand it all.

They sat there for quite a while as Joel explained about the models and how one had to have the sheet of instructions and carefully unfold it so that the creases would not be damaged, and then follow each step, using the sharp razor blade to shape each section from the paper-thin balsam wood. Later came the gluing and finally the painting and decals. Simon listened with the same quiet attention he had shown in class.

Finally he rose reluctantly to his feet. "I must go. I have chores, and Mother will worry."

"Okay. I'll walk you home." Joel led his new friend back downstairs, then together they started down the street. As they walked, Joel found a strange sense of pressure building up inside his chest. As though all the thoughts and feelings he kept hidden from all the world suddenly demanded release. He found himself saying quietly, "My father isn't happy."

Simon stopped at the corner. His face seemed to mirror

Joel's own sorrow. Joel had never before known this in someone his own age. Doc Austin could do it from time to time, sharing the hurt even though something in his gaze said he did not really want to. But Simon just stood and listened and *absorbed*. The pressure continued to build inside Joel, as though all the words and feelings he had tried not to think of must suddenly come out.

"He was injured in the war, like I said. He had to leave the army, and he wanted to stay in. I *think* he wanted to, anyway. He doesn't ever talk about it. But there are a lot of little things."

"Signs," Simon offered. "You watch and see them."

Joel nodded, wondering at how it was possible to be so comfortable with someone he hardly knew. "I guess a lot of what he thinks is about what he never had."

Simon nodded slowly, as though something this important needed to be taken down deep inside. They walked down several more blocks before he finally said, "The book of your name says it is only in the day of the Lord that all God's purposes for man will come true."

The strange words were so confusing that Joel did not know which question to ask first. "Which book?"

The question stopped Simon a second time. "It is in the English as well as the Cherman. Your Bible must say it."

"*My* Bible? I don't have a Bible."

"Well . . . your Family Bible. Your father must read—"

"He never reads it."

The words astounded Simon. He stared at Joel for a moment before he spoke. He sounded puzzled. "You have a name like Choel and your folks did not choose it from the Bible?"

"Joel was my grandfather's name. I'm named after him." The boy thought a moment. "I think there's a Bible in the house somewhere. But I've never seen anybody reading it."

Simon seemed at a loss to know what to say. Finally he turned and pointed. "This is my house, Choel. I will not give you welcome now, because Mama is still making empty the packing crates. But come home with me soon next week."

"Sure, that'd be swell."

"You will come and have dinner with us," Simon said, almost as though he was talking to himself. "You will speak with Papa over all these things. He will know what to say."

That night Joel lay on his bed, utterly tired, yet not ready to sleep. He felt as though he were floating on a cloud. The day had been so good, better than any day he could remember in a long while. And yet there was nothing really grand, no tremendous earth-shattering event. It was just that he had made a new friend. Someone utterly different from anyone Joel had ever known. And something more. Joel laced his fingers behind his head and smiled up at the unseen ceiling. There was definitely something more to this strange young man. Something very, very good.

CHAPTER SEVEN

MAKING HERSELF ENTER THE CHURCH for her father's funeral was the hardest thing Kyle had ever done.

It was not all the eyes watching her, although there must have been a thousand people facing her as she moved forward. It was not that the family came in last or that her mother had organized a little procession up the church's central aisle. Nor was it the heat, though the July morning was sweltering and its warmth was trapped by her veil and made each breath steamy. It was not even the coffin with its beloved contents that left her feeling so helpless as she slowly walked alongside her mother.

What filled her with dread was all that lay beyond this day and this ritual. The prospect of a life without her father's booming laugh, his hearty voice, and his love left her legs so weak they felt scarcely able to carry her.

The relatives followed behind them, a procession made up mostly of people Kyle had only seen once or twice before in her life. At the news of her father's heart attack, however, they had started showing up, as though word had been passed by telepathy. But even as they had pressed her hand or hugged her close, they had remained strangers.

The whole church was full of strangers. Kyle kept glancing through her dark veil, searching for a familiar face. Occasionally she caught sight of someone she recognized from one of their many dinners, or one of her visits downtown. But most of them she had never seen before.

The church was huge, the grandest in all Washington, D.C. It had been her mother's idea to hold the service here. Kyle had never entered before, and the chamber seemed cold and alien. Honey-stone walls rose to meet stained-glass windows depicting scenes quite foreign to Kyle. High above, the ceiling soared into a series of stone-vaulted arcs. The shining pipe organ poured out a colossal amount of sound. The choir stood and sang words Kyle could not understand even when she tried.

Once they were seated, the minister rose and spoke. His voice rolled out in sad tones, more words Kyle didn't bother to hear. She did not know him, so how could he talk about what she was feeling? She sat there, still and silent, going through the motions set in place by her mother, just as she had been doing ever since the doctor had come out and announced to them that her father had slipped away in the night.

A man she recognized from visits to their house, Senator Allenby, walked to the dais. She asked herself against the backdrop of words she would not hear, why, why? Why did it have to happen now? Now, just as her father was beginning to talk with her as an adult. Kyle sat and pretended to be part of the rite, and remembered the last serious conversation she'd had with her father.

It had been three weeks earlier, on the occasion of her seventeenth birthday. By then the tradition had been well established. They had celebrated together, just the two of them, with a lunch in the boardroom. The preparations for yet another of her mother's high-society parties was not even mentioned. That day, as Kyle and her father had been finishing their dessert, she had asked how he had started his insurance business.

"The telling is easier than the deed," Lawrence had replied

with an affectionate smile. "I can't say I started with nothing. My family had enough money to give me a leg up, and the Crawleys helped even more."

"What about Mother?" Kyle already knew her mother's family had been wealthy.

Lawrence shook his head. "They were against it from the start. Abigail's father, once he realized that Abigail had made up her mind that she was marrying me, wanted me to come in and take over his operation—he had no sons. But I saw insurance as the coming thing and wanted to give it a go. And between you and me and the gatepost, Abigail's father had pretty much run the family business into the ground. Her grandfather was quite a businessman, an important wholesaler. But her father . . . anyway, they didn't give me a penny, didn't let me take on any of their own insurance work, not even when it looked like I might go under."

"Did she ask them?"

"Your mother . . ." Lawrence stopped, waving it aside. "Abigail wanted a big house, and they gave us the money for that. They gave us that fancy car, even paid for our first servants. Couldn't see their little girl going without."

"That must have been awful," Kyle said quietly. "Them not helping you with the business, I mean."

"They had their reasons," Lawrence said, cutting off that line of conversation. "In the end I made out all right."

"You sure did," she said, so proud of him she could burst.

He was quiet a long moment. "Beginnings can be terrible times, especially in business. Twenty hours a day, six days a week, living and eating and breathing it, and knowing if it didn't happen, I'd never get another chance."

"But it happened," she offered.

"So slow it was hard to believe I was going anywhere but under," he replied, his normal ruddy features grim with the task of remembering. "To be honest, I don't even know when we actually turned the corner. But one day I forced myself to realize that I didn't need to ask anymore whether we'd make it. Now the question was, how far and how high."

He had looked at her then, a thoughtful, searching gaze. As though he was trying to decide whether to say something or not. Finally Lawrence coughed and told her, "Nobody makes it on their own. You ring up all sorts of debts, and the hardest ones to carry are the ones you can't pay back in coin."

Kyle felt her stomach freeze up. She dreaded what might be coming, more from his tone than his words.

"Your mother has been an asset. She is intelligent and shrewd and knows her way around the upper class. I'm wise enough to know that she has brought a good number of clients to the firm. And I appreciate that. She's been good for me as well. Stimulating. I've not regretted my choice. But there may have been times, especially in the early days of our marriage, when *she* wondered if she had done the right thing."

He seemed so solemn that it made Kyle shiver with fore-boding. But because her father was the one talking, all she said was, "I understand, Daddy."

"Do you?" He smiled then, but his expression was touched with deep sorrow. "Your mother . . ." He stopped, the internal argument working its way across his features. "Well, we both know your mother, don't we?"

Kyle nodded. All her thoughts and fears were a huge ball in her throat. But this was her father. And he needed her help. So she forced herself to say, though it was the hardest thing she had ever done in her entire life, "Tell me what you want me to do, Daddy."

He seemed able to see what she was feeling, because his ruddy features turned solemn. "You'd do it for me, wouldn't you, honey?"

"Anything," Kyle said miserably. "Whatever you want, I'll do for you."

"What I want." The words sighed out with such force that all the breath drained from his body. "What I want."

Kyle waited through the longest moment of her entire life. Even her heart seemed unable to beat, the atmosphere was so heavy with anticipation.

Then Lawrence straightened and drew in a breath that

seemed to bring with it a new resolve. A strong new determination changed his entire demeanor, from somber and resigned to angry and obstinate. "What I want," he said, measuring each word with force, "is for you to be happy."

The pronouncement was so unexpected, Kyle drew back from the table. "Daddy?"

"Happy," he repeated. "Is there anything so strange about that?"

"No, Daddy, if you're sure—"

"I'm sure." And he was. His eyes glowered as he stared through the door, out beyond the hall and the offices and the building, to whatever foe he saw in the invisible distance. "And I'm going to fix things so that you can do just that." Then he abruptly changed direction, giving her a conspiratorial smile, and said, "Since it's your birthday, I wonder if Chef might have another piece of banana cream pie for me?"

When the funeral service was over, and they had started back down the aisle, Kyle spotted Randolf Crawley standing two rows back looking appropriately solemn. Farther on was her father's former protégé, Kenneth Adams. His eyes were held by the coffin, carried by six men just ahead of Kyle and her mother. Grief was etched in his face and expression. Kenneth chose that moment to look at her, and the depths of his gaze caused her to look away. His eyes mirrored all the pain and sorrow she held deep within herself. Nor did she allow herself to even glance toward where the coffin was being carried down the church steps. She could not do that and maintain her control. There would be time enough to give in to her loss once she was no longer on display. Right now, she was grateful for the numbness, the scattered thoughts.

In a strange way, it was reassuring to be thinking of little things, like the way the trees and shrubs looked as their lim-

ousine wound its way through the streets. Or the way a motor-
cade of police motorcycles cleared the road ahead. She concen-
trated on how the sunlight danced between the branches
overhead, or how fresh the grass looked, as though someone had
come out and scrubbed it clean just for them. It was comforting
to have such thoughts, especially after last night.

She had accompanied her mother back from the funeral
home, where Abigail had gone to take care of last-minute details. Kyle had not spoken a word the entire journey. She had
known her mother had said things to her from time to time, but
it had been too hard to even hear the words, let them take shape
in her mind. Kyle had walked in the front door, knowing Maggie
was there and saying something, but again there was nothing but
a blur of sound. She did catch a sense of concern behind Maggie's
words. But she could not even acknowledge her friend's loving
anxiety.

Kyle had climbed the stairs and gone to her room and lain
on the bed with her clothes still on. Her mother had come in
to say something, then she had left. But Kyle had paid no mind.
She had lain there and stared at the ceiling, watching the light
from outside fade until the pale blue walls were a dusky gray,
and then to black. And she had felt as though she had died with
her father, only her body had not realized it yet.

Now, at the cemetery, Kyle allowed herself to be guided into
a chair in the front row. She was grateful for the veil, as it helped
to hide her face and her thoughts from all the prying eyes sur-
rounding them. She kept her attention on the pastor, but only
because it helped to avoid looking at the ugly hole in the ground,
the one ready to take her as well as her father.

Did other people have such thoughts? As she sat and watched
blindly as the ancient ritual concluded, Kyle wondered if she was
the only one in the whole world who felt as though she did not
belong anywhere or to anyone. Was there anyone as alone as she
was? Had anyone ever felt so helpless, so utterly out of place?

CHAPTER EIGHT

SUMMER GAVE WAY TO AUTUMN, and autumn had begun to drift into winter's cold embrace, yet Joel still had not gone to Simon's house for the promised dinner.

Not that he hadn't spent a lot of time at the Millers' home. His reluctance about the meal was not due to the strangeness of some of their ways, although the Miller household was certainly different from anything Joel had ever known. Even so, he felt comfortable with them. But though they had often invited him to share a Sunday dinner, Joel held back.

The Miller household held many mysteries. Everyone was busy all the time, and yet a sense of calm overlay all the activities. Mr. Miller was so sick they had been forced to leave their farm in Pennsylvania and come to live in this strange town near Baltimore, and yet they all seemed happy. He had lost his leg, and sometimes his stump was so sore he could not even strap on the prosthetic limb, and yet he moved about all the time. Even when he was sitting still, he was talking or reading or balancing the baby, or all those things at once.

Mr. Miller did not even seem to realize he was handicapped. He kept up a successful business as a custom cabinet and furniture maker. He moved about the back shed where he kept his tools and wood, deftly carving and shaping and hammering and sawing, supporting himself on one leg and a crutch or a wall or a table, whistling and happy. Yes, *happy*. Not some artificial smile pasted over his sorrows. The man was genuinely happy. The whole family was. And Joel simply could not understand it.

Yet the biggest reason why Joel had not accepted their invitation was that he was afraid to ask his parents. The littlest things could set his father off. The issue of pets, for instance. The second time Joel had dared to ask for a puppy, his father had stayed angry for days, as though the asking itself had been a very bad thing. Joel never could tell what would ignite another bout of anger and shouting. So he chose to remain silent and ask for nothing at all.

But more than Joel's naturally reserved nature was at work here, he knew. Joel felt as though the visit could hold some special significance. Without working out exactly why, Joel sensed that joining them for the meal and the promised talk with Mr. Miller would catapult him into something new. Something alien. And Joel was not sure he was ready for that, or if he ever would be.

A month after his fourteenth birthday, Joel waited as usual for Simon after school. But when his friend appeared, his normally spirited expression was downcast. Joel fidgeted nervously, avoiding Simon's eyes. "What's the matter?"

"Nothing," Simon replied glumly.

"Is it your father?" Mr. Miller had gone through a bad time earlier that summer, something about the doctors not being able to adjust his insulin correctly.

"No, Papa is fine." Simon scuffed along the road, kicking at stones. Finally he said miserably, "A letter from home this morning came. Missy has foaled. And Daisy has another litter. Six this time."

Joel had to think a moment. Daisy was the dog, he knew that much. Simon's sister Sarah talked about little else. That was another amazing thing about this family. They had over two hundred animals, counting the dairy herd. But all of them had names. And the children talked about them as if they were all family. "I forget. Which one is Missy?"

"Papa's horse. He promised me the foal would be mine for raising up myself."

Joel felt a stab of envy. His father would not allow him one small puppy, and the Millers had everything. Four dogs, three cats, cows, four horses, two mules, thirty hens, a bad-tempered rooster, and seven nanny goats. There was even a squirrel that had fallen out of the nest as a baby and Mrs. Miller had bottle fed; she now lived in the tree back of their farmhouse and would come and bring her own family whenever Mrs. Miller called to her. "So, that's great. What's the matter?"

"So now somebody else sees after my foal. Somebody else curries him. Somebody else watches him learn to stand and walk and run." Simon seemed ready to cry. "I want to see him. To do for him myself. I miss home. I miss our farm."

Joel did not know what to say. He had never known another town except Riverdale. His parents had taken him to Washington one afternoon to see the White House and the memorials. But he had never even been to Baltimore. He could not even begin to picture the Millers' Mennonite community outside Lansdale, Pennsylvania. From everything Simon had said, it was an utterly different world from anything Joel had ever known.

They walked the rest of the way to Simon's house in silence. Before they had even climbed the front steps, Joel heard the wails from inside. "Sarah, she makes tears," Simon said forlornly. Sarah was Simon's younger sister. "She wants the puppies. All of them, here with us now. Mama says no, there is not the room. And we could not get them down here to us. So Sarah, she wants to go home. We all want to go home."

Mrs. Miller pushed open the door and tried for a smile, but she could not raise one today. She was dressed, as always, in a dark blouse and printed skirt, with a kerchief tied over her hair. "I am sorry, Choel. Today is not so good."

"Sure, I understand." Mrs. Miller's accent was a little stronger than Simon's, but nothing compared to her husband's. According to Simon, his mother's family was progressive, whatever that meant. "I'll see you later, Simon."

"Perhaps you will come and choin us for worship on Sunday, yah?" The words had been spoken by Mrs. Miller every week since she had met Joel. And every time he had come up with another excuse. The woman did not press. And Joel had never delved into his reasons for delaying.

Today Simon did not even wait for Joel's response. He trudged up the front steps, his shoulders slumped in misery. Joel felt a sudden yearning to do something for his friend, something that would make him happy again. "Sure, Mrs. Miller. I'd love to come."

His unexpected assent astonished them both. Mrs. Miller's anxious expression gave way to a beaming smile. Simon whirled about. "You will? Really?"

Joel was so surprised at the effect of his words that he could only nod.

"That is good." The word off Mrs. Miller's tongue sounded like *goot* to Joel's ears. "Welcome you, we will. Come at ten, and stay you must for the Sunday meal."

"This is very good, Choel," Simon said, and his grin upheld the words.

"Sunday next," Mrs. Miller said and reached forward to pat Joel's head. "It is good to have reason yet to smile today."

Joel walked down the block, turned, and waved back to where Mrs. Miller and Simon stood on the porch watching him. Sunlight and shadow played over the street as a brisk autumn wind sent clouds scuttling overhead. For some reason, he felt lighter than air, able to skip forward, as if just barely tracing his way along the earth.

But the closer Joel got to home, the heavier he became. He tried to sort out in his mind the best way to approach his parents. His first urge was to not talk about it to them at all. Rather he would just do his paper route, then slip over to the Millers'. But much as he hated the thought of conflict, he decided he had to meet this head on. To do otherwise would taint the way this day felt.

As he headed up his street, he concluded that the direct approach would be best. He would simply lay his request before them and hope they would understand.

The next big question was which parent to tackle first. His mother would probably be the most likely to give permission, but his father detested what he considered playing one parent against another. Harry interpreted it as an act of deceit and reacted with denial of the request, no matter how reasonable it might be.

No, Joel decided, it was best to face them both at once and take the consequences. But when? They were so seldom together. Family fellowship was unknown in Joel's household. He had never experienced an atmosphere like that of Simon's home. There the father read near the room's big lamp while the mother tucked up close on the other side of the small table, knitting needles clacking in rapid succession, keeping time with her chattering tongue. And all about the room, children of various sizes hovered over homework while the smaller ones amused themselves with homemade toys. The baby cooed from the cradle, near enough to one parent or the other so that an outstretched foot could continue the steady rocking.

No, Joel's home could not be more different. His father either hid behind his newspaper or *Argosy* magazine or just sat in his corner chair, staring out at the black night. His mother often retired early, giving Joel a quick brush of a kiss and telling him to be sure to finish his homework. Sometimes she would read in bed her dime novels from the corner drugstore. His father called them "your mother's trash" and always tossed them out if he came across them.

No, Joel decided, heading up the front walk, it would have to be at mealtime. Certainly there would be little competition for their attention if he were to voice his request then. Mealtimes were silent at the Grimes home. But the very thought of the coming ordeal made Joel's stomach knot.

Joel did his evening chores and tried to formulate the right words. But every idea he had was met with images of frowns and headshaking. As he trudged into dinner, he resigned himself to the fact that there was no good way to say it. He would just have to blurt it out.

They were halfway through another silent meal before he cleared his throat, swallowed, and dove in. "Simon has invited me to his house for Sunday morning."

Heads did not even lift.

"His folks have a sort of worship every Sunday."

His mother looked up.

"He's invited me to join them," Joel pressed on. His mother's eyes were on him now. He wanted to speak directly to her but feared it would not please his father.

"What do you mean, worship?" Martha asked.

Joel wasn't sure himself but repeated what little he knew from Simon. "They read stories from the Bible and stuff. They sing, too. Together."

His father's head lifted now. "You mean, at home?"

"In their house," Joel confirmed.

"Why? That's what churches are for."

Joel could not recall his folks ever setting foot in a church, but now was not the time to be pointing that out. "They don't have a church here."

"There are churches all over Riverdale."

Joel was skating toward the edge of his knowledge. "Not their kind."

The frown on his father's face deepened. Joel could see he wasn't pleased. "What are they, some kind of weird sect? I don't want any son of mine getting hooked up with a bunch of crazy fanatics."

He sounded so angry. So final. Joel felt his heart sink. He lowered his head.

"I'm sure Simon's family aren't fanatics," he heard his mother saying. "It just doesn't fit."

"They sure dress funny," his father shot back.

"They are Mennonites. That's the way they're supposed to dress."

"It looks goofy."

"You might not like it," Martha replied in her quiet, flat

voice, "but it doesn't mean they are strange."

"So what does it mean?"

"It's a sort of uniform. Like the army."

His father's tone sharpened further. "It's not like the army at all. That's a stupid comparison. The army has a perfect reason—"

"So do they," Martha cut in. "They choose to be identified in such a manner."

Joel listened as the angry words swirled about the small room. He wished he could just take it all back. He had not wanted to cause another argument. He hated these quarrels worse than anything. He should have just stayed silent, as always.

But his father was not finished. "So where did *you* get all this information?"

"I read about them," his mother replied.

"In one of those trashy books of yours, I guess. Well, if that's the kind of folks they are, then it's settled—"

"For your information, I found out about Mennonites in the public library. I looked them up when Joel started keeping company with that young boy." She flung the words like a well-aimed lance at her husband. Joel looked up in surprise. It was a rarity that his mother would stand up to her husband over anything. But Martha was not finished. She tilted her head, a defiant look in her eyes, and said, "At least I am interested in what goes on in Joel's life."

Silence again. Joel's father seemed too angry to even respond. Joel turned back to his half-finished plate. He had to eat all that remained before he could leave the table, but his appetite had vanished. All he wanted was to flee the room.

At length his father stirred slightly and demanded, "What are they asking you to do?"

Joel found himself reluctant even to respond, not wanting to start the whole controversy over again. "They just wanted me to join them for the singing and reading time, then stay for a late lunch. They call it dinner."

Again silence. At long last his father spoke again. "Don't suppose it would hurt anything," he said without even looking up. "Might give us a chance to catch up on some sleep around here, with you out of the house."

Joel let his astonished gaze travel from his father's lowered head to his mother's still-flushed face. She simply nodded.

As an afterthought she added, "Make sure you wash your face and brush your hair before you go. Folks are supposed to look their best for church."

CHAPTER NINE

"MRS. ROTHMORE WILL BE WITH YOU directly, Mr. Crawley," Bertrand announced solemnly, leading him into the library. "She asks that you wait for her here."

"Fine, fine," Randolf replied absently. When the tall double doors closed behind the departing butler, the young man resisted the urge to pace about the room. It was not like him to suffer from nerves when meeting with Abigail. But something about her summons worried him mightily.

When he had taken over his father's position on the Rothmore board, Randolf had discarded many things. One had been the 'Junior' attached to his name. Another had been the deferential attitude he had formerly used around Abigail. The first time he had addressed her as an equal had been in this very room. She had noticed it instantly, of course. Very little escaped Abigail's notice. She had acknowledged the change in his attitude and its intended message with a regal nod.

There was much that remained unspoken between the two of them. Which was fine with Randolf. As far as he was concerned, some of life's most important matters should never be spoken of aloud. Such as the hunger for real power they seemed to share. The kind of power that could be theirs, *would* be theirs, once the reins of Rothmore Insurance were firmly in Randolf's grasp.

Randolf lowered himself into the leather armchair and

glanced about the room. The Rothmore library had always fascinated him. Whenever he saw himself taking over control of the family assets as well as the family company, it was to this room that his daydreams took him. If any chamber of the Rothmore manor spoke of opulence, it was this room. The rich wood of the oiled wall panels, the enclosed shelves heavy with leather-bound volumes, the hunting scenes and the full-length portrait of Abigail that graced the walls, the Oriental carpets strewn across the polished floor—somehow the room managed to be both masculine and elegant, a marvelous combination in his eyes.

His reverie was interrupted by Abigail's entrance. "Ah, Randolf, so good of you to come," she said as she swept toward him. "I hope it wasn't too much of a bother to join me so early on a Saturday morning."

"Not at all." Something about her tone brought a new surge of nerves. Yet Randolf managed to hold to his outward calm and languidly rose to greet her. "Your call sounded rather urgent."

"No, not urgent. Just desirable. With the reading of Lawrence's will set for the day after tomorrow, this could not be put off any longer." Rather than settle upon the sofa opposite where he had been seated, she marched to the other side of the hand-carved cherrywood desk. "Won't you be seated?"

He had no choice but take the high-backed chair across the desk from her. "Thank you."

"I've been doing some thinking." She hesitated, toying with the open ledger on the desk before her. Then she added, "About Kyle." Another long moment of silence before Abigail offered, "She's still very young."

Randolf had the sudden impression that all this was staged. Making him wait, seating herself behind the desk, the hesitation—all of it was simple theatrics. No, not simple. Not with Abigail. Everything had a purpose. Even this. And the implications of where this was headed filled him with foreboding.

"I know I have been pushing you to seek, well, some sort of commitment." She picked up the gold-plated dagger used as a letter opener and rolled it back and forth between her fingers.

The light flickered directly into his eyes. "But recently I have been experiencing second thoughts."

"Second thoughts," he echoed, his mind racing.

"I have been rather demanding at times, I'm afraid." Abigail sighed dramatically. "And this loss of her father has been most difficult for her."

Randolf knew he was expected to respond, but he could not. The words would not come. His one chance to wrest full control of Rothmore Insurance was suddenly slipping through his fingers. And yet he could not fathom why. He studied the woman seated across from him, searching for the purpose behind her actions.

"I've been wondering if we should not push her so," Abigail continued. "Perhaps Kyle should be given more time to grow up."

Randolf resisted the urge to scream, to tear his hair, to leap to his feet and rage from the room. *But what about our plans?* he wanted to shout. *What about all my ambitions?*

He took a breath. Another. Only when a semblance of calm was restored did he say, "But I thought you were concerned that she might . . ." He was uncertain whether he should even mention out loud what had never before been spoken. But with all his dreams going up in smoke, he had no choice. He pressed forward with, "I thought you wanted to be certain that she had no opportunity to . . . to select a husband of her own choosing."

A small smile flickered around the corners of her mouth, though she tried hard to disguise it. "That is not so pressing now. With her father gone . . ."

"Ah." The word was a release of both pent-up tension and hope. It was clear to him now. Bitterness tainted his voice as he demanded, "So you are severing me from any relationship with your daughter?"

"Oh, my dear Randolf." She leaned back in the big desk chair. Her small figure looked dwarfed by its size, yet a new sense of authority gave the impression that she was quite at home there. "Quite the opposite. I would be perfectly thrilled if Kyle were to choose you. But I also feel that we can now allow her a bit more freedom. After all, she *is* little more than a child."

"That scarcely concerned you before," Randolf pointed out acidly. It no longer mattered, though. Nothing would change Abigail's mind. He knew that for certain. She was going to run the company. She would make her own rules.

Abigail studied him carefully for a moment before replying coldly, "Think what you might, Randolf, but the fact is that all I have done for Kyle has been done with her best interests in mind. She is such a child. She thinks the world is made up of sugarplum fairies and doting fathers. I have had to take a firm hand because no one else would."

Randolf hesitated. She sounded so sincere. Perhaps she cared more for the girl than he had realized. "But I care for your daughter as well, Abigail," he ventured. "She is attractive and intelligent, a rare combination. And her sweet sense of innocence is most refreshing. Business was far from my only motive, I hope——"

"Of course I knew that." She waved a dismissive hand. "I would not for one moment have encouraged you if the business had been your only motive." Abigail's gaze held a new quality, a sense of realized power. "Your qualities are well known to me, Randolf. I will continue to require them, both as an ally within the company as well as a suitable gentleman for my daughter."

His shoulders slumped with sudden relief. All was not lost. Not entirely. Just postponed. Perhaps. "You mean——"

"I meant just exactly what I said." She held him with this new, powerful gaze of hers. "I intend to take a firm hand within the company, and I expect another firm hand to take over when I depart. I know full well how quickly fortunes can rise and fall. My grandfather had wealth, as you full know. My father managed to lose almost all of it, not because he was not intelligent, but because he was weak. I cannot permit either this family or this business to fall into weak hands."

Randolf pushed himself to his feet. He felt drained. Trapped. Abigail was so incredibly in control. "So I should still continue to see her."

"Of course, my dear Randolf." She looked directly into his

eyes. "But there is no need to press. Not for the moment, at least."

He nodded mutely and turned to go. He knew the words were his dismissal.

Kyle had begun the habit of rising with the sun. She found it gave her a much-needed respite from her mother, as well as time for quiet reflection. She would dress and walk through the garden, occasionally stopping for a chat with old Jim, but usually preferring solitude. Those winter walks became her refuge, when frost covered the grass with diamond shards and all the world seemed to hold its breath.

Dawn came late and slowly on those mornings, and the sun's arrival formed stark etchings in the frozen yard. Everything was either bathed in frigid shadow or sparkling with a myriad of tiny rainbows. Each of her footsteps whispered through the thawing grass, marking her passage with dark imprints. She carried bread with her, feeding crumbs to every bird she saw. By early December, the birds had come to expect her and would flutter about with quietly drumming wings as she sprinkled the glittering lawn with food.

Afterward, Kyle went into the kitchen and had her breakfast with Bertrand and Maggie. They sat down together, said grace, and ate as they discussed plans for the day. Then Bertrand left to do his morning rounds of the house, and Maggie took out her Bible and read quietly. Several times she offered to read out loud, but Kyle shook her head. She was happy to just sit there and feel the peace as Maggie read to herself.

Kyle avoided the house's big rooms as much as possible. They echoed with her father's absence. There was nothing left to keep the cold, precise emptiness of her mother's style and personality at bay. Whenever Kyle walked through the great hall or the formal chamber or the dining room, with their beautiful paintings and sparkling chandeliers and waxed floors and polished silver-ware, she felt as though she had wandered into a strange and empty museum.

That first Saturday in December, when Maggie rose to begin her chores, Kyle donned an apron and worked alongside her. Maggie protested, "Child, you've got a score of other more important things to do than work here beside me."

"I don't, really," Kyle said, holding to her matter-of-fact tone. "Emily Crawley and some of her friends are coming over for tennis, but not until eleven." Several of the wealthy families had built communal courts, one indoors and another outdoors, at the bottom of their garden. "Besides, I didn't invite them. Mother did."

"Speaking of which," Maggie continued, "if your mother found you in here working she would not be pleased."

Kyle's hands stayed busy washing the greenhouse strawber-ries Bertrand would serve with morning coffee for their guests. "Don't send me away, please, Maggie. I don't have anywhere else to go."

The older woman's tone softened as she asked, "What on earth are you saying?"

Kyle kept her hands busy. It helped her hold to the calm tone. "I don't belong here. I'll never be the proper lady Mother wants me to be."

"Oh, honey, my dear sweet Kyle." Maggie walked over and settled one arm around Kyle's waist. "You are the most wonderful young lady I have ever set eyes on, and that is the truth."

"Not according to Mother," she replied. The sunlight streaming through the back window became a lancing blade, and Kyle had to stop to wipe at her eyes with the back of one hand. "She's been at me nonstop since Daddy . . . since the funeral. Nothing I do is good enough. And she's right."

"No she isn't," Maggie said, her voice quiet yet firm.

"Yes she is."

"Look at me, dear."

Kyle let the berries drop into the plastic strainer and turned to face her friend. The sunlight was revealing as it rested upon the old woman's features. Yet a lifetime of hard work had not dimmed the clarity of those wide-set gray eyes. They regarded her now, the gaze clear and direct and loving. "My dearest child, I love you like you were my own daughter, you know that."

"I know," Kyle whispered.

"Then believe me when I tell you, life will always try to bring you down. If it were not your mother, it would be something else. Do you know why?"

Kyle found herself unable to answer, so she made do with a little shake of her head.

"Because your heart is too big for this world. You hold too much love, too much tenderness. It is clear to anyone with eyes open to the truth." A cloud began tracing its way across the sky overhead, cutting out all the light except for the single ray falling upon Maggie's face. It transformed her gray hair into a shimmering silver crown and made the light in her eyes so strong that they seemed to hold the sun itself. "A heart like yours needs protection, my beloved child. It needs the shield of prayer to keep it from seeking out the shelter of cynicism and hardness. Do you understand what I am saying?"

"I'm not sure," Kyle murmured. She wanted to run away, and she wanted to stay. She wanted Maggie to stop saying these words that left her feeling so vulnerable and shaken, and yet she wanted her to keep talking for all her life long.

"You need to ask the Lord into your life, my beloved little one. You need to have His presence guiding you, showing you the path your feet should be walking." Maggie inspected her with a gaze so penetrating that Kyle felt as though it reached deep into her confused heart.

"I'm not—" Her response was cut off by the sound of the front doorbell. "Who is that?"

Maggie stepped back a pace, bringing her face into the shadows, and once more she became a gray-headed old woman. "I have no idea who that might be. Deliveries always come to the back door."

Kyle listened but did not hear Bertrand's measured tread. "I suppose I'd better go see who it is."

As she turned away, Maggie settled a hand upon her arm. "Here, let me take your apron." After removing it, Kyle handed it over, and the woman said, "Will you think about what I have told you, child?"

"Of course." Yet as she walked through the kitchen door and entered the grand foyer, Kyle felt the words slip from her. Like a cloak left behind after a hard summer shower, she cast them aside. She had no choice. Here in the harsh reality of her beautiful home, as her heels clicked across the polished marble tile, Kyle felt as though the words had no place. Nor the sentiment. She could not survive with an open heart. Not here, not around her mother and her mother's friends. They would grind her down and devour her, unless she somehow could learn to be as hard and as cold as they were.

Kyle stopped in front of the oval mirror and checked her reflection as her mother had trained her to do before answering the door. But she caught herself looking into a pair of sad, hopeless eyes. And she had a fleeting glimpse of a thought: *What if Maggie is right, and they are wrong?*

The doorbell sounded again, bringing her from her reverie. She straightened, turned, and opened the door.

Old Mr. Crawley, Randolf and Emily's father, stood in the entrance. "Hello, Kyle."

"Good morning, sir. Won't you come in?" she invited warmly, remembering this man's years with her beloved father. "Was Mother expecting you?"

"Not exactly. We are planning the reading of your father's will, as you know."

"Of course." It was circled in red in her mother's social calendar and had been for over a month. Abigail's secretary had typed letters to each of the family, inviting them all, as though it was some important social event. Every time Abigail spoke of it, she did so with a spark of barely repressed excitement. It left Kyle reeling to see her father's memory reduced to such crassness. But as always, Kyle had remained silent. And safe. "But isn't that on Monday?"

"It is indeed." For some reason, the old gentleman seemed

nervous. "There's a certain matter . . . well, I thought it best to speak with you two in private."

Bertrand appeared, apologetic at having been caught away from his post. "Miss Kyle, excuse me, I was out back making arrangements with the caterer for Monday's reception, and didn't hear—"

"It's quite all right. See if you can find Mother, won't you?"

"Of course, miss. Right away." He gave Mr. Crawley a stiff bow and turned away.

"Perhaps we'd be more comfortable in the library, Mr. Crawley." She held none of the negative feelings for the older gentleman that she had for his offspring. Mr. Crawley had married late and was a good twenty-five years older than his wife. He possessed the stiff bearing and formal manners of another generation. But he had always treated her with reserved courtesy. There was nothing false about him, nor any of the cold deceit she felt from Randolf Junior. "Can I offer you a cup of tea?"

"No, thank you." He entered the library, took the offered seat, set the bulky briefcase beside his chair, and waited in some inner tension. When steps announced Abigail's passage across the marble foyer, he almost leapt to his feet to greet her.

"Why, Randolf, what an unexpected treat," Abigail said, entering with her hand outstretched. The formal smile said that in truth his arrival was anything but a pleasure. "If you are looking for your son, I'm afraid he's already come and gone."

A fleeting expression of alarm passed over the old man's features. "You're sure he's gone?"

"Yes, of course, I saw him off myself." She allowed herself an instant's curiosity over his attitude, but clearly there were more pressing matters on her mind. "I'm so sorry I can't invite you to join us for lunch, but I really must—"

"I'm not here for a meal," the older gentleman said grimly. "And I know how busy you are. But we really must talk."

Abigail lifted her chin a fraction, so as to give the impression of looking down at the taller man. "Really, what on earth can't wait until our meeting Monday?"

"I have asked myself the same thing, and wondered if I am not breaking your husband's instructions by being here," he responded crisply. "But as you have refused to listen to my entreaties for the first reading of the will to be held in private, I feel I have no choice."

Abigail showed an instant of uncertainty. She gathered herself with an effort and said, "Won't you sit down?"

"Thank you." Stiffly he resumed his seat.

"As I have already told you," Abigail went on, "I can see no reason for agreeing to this odd request of yours. Lawrence has no doubt shown his relatives the same generosity that he has always demonstrated."

"My suggestion had nothing whatsoever to do with how Lawrence has treated the others. What you may not be aware of, Abigail, is that your husband retained me to take care of some very private matters."

This time, the woman's surprise could not be masked. "I beg your pardon?"

"Matters so private," Mr. Crawley persisted, "that not even my son was to know of them. By Lawrence's own instructions I was ordered not to divulge them, not even to you, Abigail, until the reading of the will. But because of your persistence in making this a public event, I felt it necessary to speak to you personally in advance."

There was the sudden focusing of energy so potent that time seemed to slow. Kyle felt as much as saw her mother's tension. Abigail began turning toward her, but the movement seemed to go on forever, and all around them rose the invisible swirling cyclone. "Wait outside, please, Kyle."

"As a matter of fact," Mr. Crawley interjected, "this very much pertains to your daughter."

"I said wait outside." Her mother's voice was so flat it sounded metallic.

"Abigail—"

"You may have affected some secret relationship with my late husband," the agitated woman snapped, the cords in her throat standing out. "But I am still mistress of this house, am I not?"

Mr. Crawley observed her as he would a witness on the stand, then turned away with a brief harrumph and began shuffling papers brought from his briefcase. Kyle rose and left the room in silence. Quietly she closed the tall double doors behind her, glad to be away from the gathering storm.

But she had scarcely made it halfway across the foyer when Abigail shrieked at the top of her voice, *"WHAT?"*

Kyle stopped in her tracks. The kitchen door popped open, and she was joined by Maggie and Bertrand. Together they stood and gaped at the library's closed doors.

There was the low murmur of Mr. Crawley's voice, then a long silence, followed by Abigail's shout, *"You cannot be serious!"*

A further low murmur was cut off by Abigail shrieking, *"I will not stand for this!"* But the murmur persisted, rising slightly, yet remaining too low for them to make out the words. Kyle was not sure whether she was sorry or glad to be unable to understand what the old gentleman was saying.

Suddenly the library doors were flung back with such force they banged upon the side wall, knocking down one of the portraits. Abigail stalked out, her face drawn and white, her lips a thin line. She shot a single furious glance at Kyle, then fled in a staccato beat of her high heels.

Mr. Crawley emerged, wiping his forehead with a white handkerchief. He gave Kyle a look of pure sympathy. Yet all he said was, "I can see myself out."

CHAPTER TEN

THERE WERE MANY THINGS THAT Joel found disconcerting about the Miller household. But they were not why he felt so nervous as he walked up the path and climbed their front steps that Sunday morning. He paused on the porch to adjust his tie and slick down his hair. Before he could raise his hand to knock, Ruthie had already opened the door.

"Hello, Choel," she welcomed in her softly accented brogue. Little Ruthie was what she was called around the house because she had the same name as her mother, but Ruthie was not small. Just an inch shy of Joel's own height, she had the look of a healthy, hearty farm girl. Her height and strength only added to her pleasant attractiveness. As always, she wore the same homespun blouse and long skirt as her mother, but the kerchief in her hair was of a brighter color. She stood straight and tall, her face full of her sweet nature. Ruthie held the screen open for him. "I wish you good Lord's day, Choel," she added formally.

"Thank you," he murmured, uncertain quite how to react. The family became so traditional at certain moments. As he entered, he had a closer look at the sadness in her eyes, and he said, "I'm sorry about . . . about your farm home . . . being so far away, Ruthie."

She rewarded him with a look of such gratitude that it warmed him all the way down. "I am glad you are come, Choel," she replied. "You make happy the whole family with your coming."

"Choel, hello, welcome." Simon approached in his simple clothes and lace-up boots. "It really happened yet. To believe it is hard for me. You have come." Simon's accent was stronger today, and the words came out sounding like *you haff gom.*

Joel allowed himself to be guided into the living room where the family was gathered. They all called a hearty welcome— even the baby cooed a hello. Yet as Joel settled himself into place between Simon and Ruthie, he could feel that sadness still cast a pall over the gathering. He felt his own thoughts sobering. He shuffled and cleared his throat, his eyes passing from one face to another.

He found that Mrs. Miller was watching him from grave, dark eyes. He heard her say, "Such a feel for folks you have, Choel. You come, you sit, and already you know how we ache some more."

Joel was astounded by her words. He stared at the fine-featured woman with her brown hair tucked under a kerchief and wondered how she could know this. He had a lifetime's experience at keeping himself hidden, yet this woman was aware of his thoughts and how he studied others. He lowered his eyes and nodded. "You miss your farm," he said simply.

From her place beside him, Ruthie gave a quiet sigh. Across the room, her younger sister, Sarah, choked back tears.

Mrs. Miller turned to her husband. "Did I not tell you? A tender heart has the young man."

Mr. Miller nodded slowly. He was a big man, his work-hardened hands twice the size of Joel's. His sparse blond hair rose back from a broad face that seemed perpetually sunburned. His beard was reddish brown and cut so it ringed his chin and left his mouth clear. He rumbled in his heavily accented way, "Such a greeting we give to Choel, our honored guest. Such a sadness on the Lord's day."

When Joel first had come to the Miller home, he had found it very difficult to understand what Mr. Miller was saying, since he was missing every other word. But with time Joel had come both to understand him and to feel the same relaxed comfort around the big man as he did around the rest of the family.

The youngest boy, Gerth, whimpered softly, "I want home again, Papa."

"Me too," whispered Sarah.

This was greeted with none of the impatient anger Joel would have found in his own home. Instead, Mr. Miller nodded his head again, the motion slow and measured, the eyes grave. He stroked his long beard a moment. "Yah, yah, this have I heard now many times."

Joel felt his glance drawn to Mr. Miller's right pant leg, which was folded and pinned back above where his knee should have been. The first time Joel had seen the man without his artificial leg, he had felt sick to his stomach. But he had come to pay it as little mind as Mr. Miller did. In truth, the big man moved about his home and carpenter's shed as agilely as any other man would on two legs.

But today seemed to be different, because Mr. Miller bent forward and began massaging the end of his stump. His wife's face instantly showed her concern. "Choseph, something the matter is?"

"Ach, it is chust a little soreness. Nothing. Nothing." But he did not stop his rubbing. Instead, as one great hand massaged his leg, the broad face with its rounded features turned and stared at each of his children in turn. He said nothing, but a sense of growing power seemed to fill the room. A sense of communication on a level far beyond that of words.

"Something to help, Choseph?" Mrs. Miller asked.

"Perhaps my shot should I have early this day," he said.

"Yah. So I think too." Mrs. Miller was up and moving for the kitchen before she finished speaking. The room was silent enough for Joel to hear her open the refrigerator, shut it, and hasten back. "Here now."

"Thank you, wife." Without taking his eyes from his family, he pulled the stopper from the needle, pointed the syringe straight up, tapped the glass base, and pushed the plunger until a little liquid squirted up.

Joel knew from Simon that Mr. Miller had to have these injections several times a day. But when Mr. Miller swabbed a patch of skin, pointed the needle downward, and prepared to plunge it into his arm, Joel had to look away. He turned to his friend. Simon's gaze remained fastened upon his father. His brow was furrowed, as though he was concentrating hard, trying to understand something. Some lesson, some message that he was attempting to grasp.

"Well, now."

Joel allowed his gaze to return to Mr. Miller as he set the syringe on the side table and lifted the big family Bible. "Why do we not show our guest how we like to sing? Ruthie, you choose, why not."

She suggested something that Joel did not understand, and only when they began singing did he realize that the words were in German. But it did not matter. The whole family sang. But it was more than just *singing*. Each took a part of the harmony, even the youngest girl, and made music together with such ease and beauty that Joel could scarcely believe what he was hearing.

He glanced from one face to the next. They sat in a loose circle around the room, some in chairs and some on the floor. There was no accompanying instrument. Some sang with eyes closed, others with eyes gazing unfocused. But there was an effortless calm to each one, a sense of having cast aside all the world and joining with one another in song.

Hymn followed hymn. As the music continued, Joel stared at the bare walls and saw how the lack of pictures and decoration matched the simple majesty of their music. He looked at the plain table and chairs and hook rug and saw in the homemade quality the same strength of spirit and self-sufficiency that he heard in their voices. The home held neither radio nor television. Yet it now seemed complete in a way he could not understand.

Finally the music drifted away, but the calm remained. Mr. Miller adjusted the big Book in his lap and said, "Choel, you speak no Cherman, yah? So I read the Cherman, then another for you to read in English. Who? Ruthie? Yah, you with the lovely voice. Good. We start with Isaiah, chapter fifty-two, verse seven."

Slowly he intoned the unknown language, one that seemed to roll much more comfortably from his tongue. Then Joel listened as Ruthie read carefully from a smaller Bible, " 'How beautiful upon the mountains are the feet of him who bringeth good tidings, who publisheth peace, that bringeth good tidings of good things, that publisheth salvation, that saith unto Zion, "Thy God reigneth!" ' "

"Good, good. And now chust one more, I think, yah." He turned the pages, licking his thumb and tracing one finger down the page. "Here at Matthew, chapter ten, verse thirty-four."

Ruthie waited until he had finished before reading, " 'Think not that I came to send peace on earth. I came not to send peace, but a sword.' "

"Such a dilemma," Mr. Miller said when Ruth had finished. "Such a paradox." He cast an eye to Joel and said, "Such words I understand because they are the same in Cherman. But my English, so bad it is. Can you understand?"

"I understand you fine," Joel said, liking the big man very much.

"Good, good, you listen well, you try, you understand. That is good. So. These verses, do they talk of two men? No, how can it be, for does not Isaiah speak of the one who brings salvation? There is only one who this great thing can do." He smiled down at the little girl at his feet. "And who is that, my sweet Sarah?"

"Jesus, Papa. He can."

"Yah, only Jesus. But He the one is who says He comes with a sword. Such a paradox. How peace and conflict can exist together yet. In one world. In one family. In heaven or on earth? Such a mystery, yah? Such a great problem."

He looked from one face to the next. His expression was somber, yet his eyes were glowing. "So. Let us think. What could this mean? Perhaps it is this. Perhaps peace is not meant to be man's at all."

Ruthie cried out, "But, Papa—"

"Wait, my little one. Chust wait and think. Not man's. *Never* man's. But that does not tell us, peace we can never have. No. It says, peace is only God's. All other peace, it comes, it goes, you cannot hold any more than you hold water with a fork."

He paused a moment, then asked, "So a peace that comes only from what we have, will it stay?"

There was a long pause before Simon quietly responded, "No, Papa."

"And why not, my son?"

Joel was surprised at how Simon seemed embarrassed as he replied, "Because it is earthly peace, not God's."

"Yah!" Mr. Miller cried triumphantly. "Peace to earthly things cannot be tied. Why? Because they come, they go, they are cut from us like with a sharpened sword. We lose this and that, health and puppies and even maybe a farm. But does this mean that saddened we must be?"

Joel watched as one head after another gave a small shake in response.

"But God, peace He has. God says, turn to me, and peace always yours will be. Peace is His to give. A great peace, yah. But also a *dividing* peace." Mr. Miller's eyes continued to search, probe, look from one to the other with a force that seemed to press each to look within, to think, to find the answer for themselves. "God's peace, it is a sword. God's peace says to us, *choose*. Between heaven and earth, we must choose. And those who choose, those who seek, those who for Him live, peace He gives. *His* peace. For us to have. For us to *keep*. For now, for always. Ours, because His we choose to be, and true peace is with Him *only*."

Joel sat at the Millers' big kitchen table, silent and watchful, and waited as dinner was set in place. Here in this noisy family, all was so different from what he was accustomed to in his own home. Mrs. Miller brought her dishes to the table with a beaming pride, as though not just her work but somehow her heart was involved with what she made for dinner. The children, all five of them, chattered and laughed at once, and the father was there in his big chair at the head of the table, inhaling the steam from the dishes and already complimenting his wife.

But it was more than just the words and the smiles. There was something else. Something Joel could not describe, yet he knew was there. The mystery that had seemed to surround their Sunday service was wrapped around them now, even though the solemnness was gone with the sadness, and all was laughter and happy talk.

"All right, now," Mr. Miller said in his funny accent. "Am I forgetting something, maybe? Do we chust eat now? What for is it to do next?"

"The blessing, Papa," Ruthie said as she came over with a huge platter of mashed potatoes, then explained to Joel, "That's a not-funny choke Papa says every dinner."

"All chokes are funny, they chust need good ears to hear them," Mr. Miller said good-naturedly, then motioned for all at the table to bow their heads. Mrs. Miller placed one hand upon her husband's shoulder and closed her eyes. For once, Ruthie was quiet and stood by her chair, her head bowed with the others.

Joel followed their example and listened to the strange words. He strained to understand with Mr. Miller's accent, and he wondered how praying felt so natural in this household.

"Amen," the whole family chorused, and instantly the noise and tumult resumed. Joel looked from one face to the next and could not help but compare it to home. Mother would set the plates down, then take her place across from Father. They would sit there, the three of them, not looking at one another, with rarely a word said among them. Here there was not the slightest hint of discomfort. The baby squalled and was plucked up by Mr. Miller, set on his one good knee, and bounced. The child squealed with delight and tried to catch the fork as it rose and fell. It seemed as though four or five different discussions were going on at once, and everyone seemed genuinely excited about listening and talking and arguing and laughing. Joel ate and watched and wondered. He had never heard so much laughter at one table.

After dinner, Mr. Miller took up his crutches and walked out to the front porch. When Mrs. Miller refused his offer to help clear the table, Joel followed, almost as though he was being drawn by something beyond himself. As he was leaving the kitchen, Ruthie called out, "You're not leaving so soon yet, are you, Choel?"

"I . . ." His voice trailed off. He pointed vaguely in the direction of the front door, not understanding at all the reason.

Ruthie turned from the sink and gave him a smile that seemed to transform her from girl to woman. "Don't leave now—leave next time."

"Sha, child, sha," Mrs. Miller quietly scolded.

Ruthie blushed and suddenly was once again Simon's younger sister.

Even more confused than before, Joel turned and walked toward the front door. He found Mr. Miller seated in the big porch swing. The day had warmed up, so if he sat in the sun, it felt genuinely comfortable. Joel selected the side of the front step that would direct his face toward the sun and eased himself down.

Simon came out for a moment, looked at them, and left. The two of them sat there a long time, looking out at the street. Joel wondered how it was that he could remain alone with the older man and feel so comfortable.

Finally Mr. Miller said, "The things my son tells me, Choel. Things like, your father is not a happy man."

"No, sir." There was no hesitation. The comment seemed to pull an unseen plug deep within his heart, and before long the words were spilling out. How his family was, how his father acted. Mr. Miller sat and rocked and stroked his beard and listened, his craggy features set in somber lines.

Joel talked until he ran out of words. Then he just sat there, not knowing what else to do or say. He felt as though he had suddenly become connected to someone. The emotions he had kept stored up inside for so many years had formed some sort of barrier. Now that they were out, the barrier was gone, and he could think and feel at a different level.

Finally Mr. Miller said, "Hearts of darkness. Hearts of stone." The words were a gentle rumble, like distant summer thunder arching through a clear sky. "Is such confusion, to think they can ever heal, no?"

"Yes," Joel agreed and found himself trying to swallow a sudden lump in his throat.

"Ach, such sorrow one heart of stone can make. Impossible sorrow. Yah, yah, I know. Impossible pain. But one way there is to find healing. One way, for the hurt and the heart both. For the one who moves in blindness, and for the one who cries deep down. The same One way."

Despite the heavy accent, despite the rolling speech, the words seemed etched in the air between them. There was such a power that even Joel's heart could not suppress the surge of hope. "How?"

"Ach, that I cannot say with words. Such words I do not know. Not in English—not even in Cherman." And yet he spoke with a smile. A soft one, but with incredible meaning upon those broad, strong features. "Perhaps there are no words for such a heart, yah? Only that which is *beyond* words. Only that which straight from God comes. Only His healing miracle."

He leaned over close, his voice falling to a murmur. "What to do, I think, is you must speak with the Master. Perhaps if you are healed, then the healing you to others can give, yah?"

"You mean, pray?"

"Ah, my son Simon, he says you are a smart young man. Smart, yah, I can see. You listen. You think. That is the good sign."

"But I don't know how to pray," Joel said, and somehow saying the words were not hard. Not here. Not with this strange, big, comfortable man.

Mr. Miller stopped his rocking and leaned over until he had brought his face down close to Joel's. "Well, well. An honor it would be, such an honor indeed, if would you let me pray the words with you."

CHAPTER ELEVEN

THE READING OF THE WILL was postponed indefinitely. The caterer was canceled. Abigail's secretary was hastily summoned and spent a frantic weekend contacting all the relatives and telling them not to come. From a quiet corner, Kyle watched the racing back and forth. She listened to her mother's voice, sometimes on the verge of panic, commanding everyone within reach. For some reason, her mother never called for her or ordered her about, which was strange. Usually when these storms struck the household, Kyle was treated with the same imperiousness as the servants. But not this time. Her mother did not seek her once. It appeared that Abigail preferred not to have her around.

Winter slowly moved to spring, and still the will was not read. Kyle knew only because there were occasional visits from irate relatives, who would arrive unannounced and demand to see Abigail immediately. They would convene in the library, where soon the voices rose to a pitch that seemed to rattle the house's very foundations. Kyle took long walks down along the yard's perimeter whenever the relatives arrived. She hated those bitter arguments. She hated even worse how her father's study was turned into a battlefield. Those visits sent tremors through her, as though their angry words sullied his memory.

By March, gatherings at the house began to take on an even grimmer tone. Groups of dark-suited men arrived, to be instantly met and taken into the library. They sat behind closed doors for hours, their voices droning on and on, punctuated by Abigail's strident tones. Kyle heard Maggie mutter to Bertrand about how business should be taken care of in the office, not at home. But he always shushed her after a quick glance at Kyle.

Kyle was not the least bit sorry to be excluded from those proceedings. Just as she was glad not to have to go down to the office. She did not want to visit the top floor of Rothmore Insurance and view it without her father. She was glad to not be a part of any of it. The little snippets of words she caught whenever the library doors opened and closed were more than enough—those and the harried glances the dark-suited men cast her way. She did not want to know what was going on. She wanted to keep her father's memory detached from all this friction and scheming. He had been a businessman, yes, a good and honorable one. But he had also been a kind and loving father. Kyle wanted to know nothing that would shake her hold on this remembrance.

There were a number of very nice things about that reluctant spring, and Kyle clung to them. Focusing on them helped to ease her through the worst moments of loss and reestablish some feeling of balance. She would be graduating from St. Albans and had been accepted to Georgetown University. To her surprise, her mother seemed almost relieved at the news. Abigail's concern was apparently not whether Kyle would go to college, but whether she would continue to live at home. Kyle desperately wanted to study at the university. She was willing to continue living at home if that was all it took to avoid a confrontation with her mother.

Another good thing about that winter and spring was that Kyle saw Randolf Crawley almost not at all. For some reason, his visits were now limited to occasional swift meetings with her mother. Whenever Kyle greeted him in his comings and goings, he would glance furtively toward wherever her mother had last been seen.

Emily Crawley had apparently been bitten by the same bug, for she seemed to avoid contact. Yet whenever Kyle saw her at school, Emily cut off conversation and watched her pass, her gaze thoughtful. Could it even be envious? That surprised Kyle as much as anything, for Emily Crawley had never been envious of anyone else in her entire life.

That March, the weather seemed to match Abigail's gale-force moods. Occasionally days would warm up, as though spring was struggling to break free, only to be beaten back by fierce winds and freezing temperatures. The first day of April was marked by a freak snowstorm that brought Chevy Chase and Washington to a shuddering halt. Kyle spent the day building a snow family with Bertrand and Maggie's four grandchildren, whose weekend visit had been extended by impassable roads. They rolled up a portly daddy snowman and a smiling snow-mom, then made eleven snowkids, from a nine-foot basketball player down to a snowbaby only six inches tall.

Kyle was grateful for the company and the reason to stay outdoors, because Abigail paced the front hall and railed against the weather with anger that frightened her. Kyle could not understand what the commotion was about. She knew Abigail was supposed to have gone to court that day. Kyle wondered if all the meetings and arguments of that winter were coming together, focusing down upon this time in court. The delay caused by the snowfall left Abigail almost speechless with rage.

Two days later the snow admitted defeat. But as the days and weeks flowed on toward May and Kyle's graduation, the stormy cold continued to do battle with spring. Mornings remained frosty, the days overcast. Jim joined her for early walks, muttering about how his entire garden was a month and more late. Even the tulips seemed afraid to rise above the earth and face the unseasonably chilly weather.

April began to approach May, and still spring was held at bay. The weather began to make the news, with announcers vying with one another to describe the freakish weather. Kyle continued the ritual begun by her father, joining her mother for the evening news. Secretly she glanced over from time to time and noted that often Abigail seemed not even to be watching. Her mother remained strangely silent. Even at dinner Abigail did not take up her normal criticisms of how Kyle sat or ate or talked. She said almost nothing at all.

Finally, the first week of May, the bitter weather faded so swiftly it was as if it had never existed. Warmth blasted in, and overnight everything blossomed. Kyle's morning walks became explorations of wonder, for the entire garden bloomed at once. Colors were so brilliant that she felt ready to cry aloud with joy.

By this time, the birds knew her so well they awaited her arrival just outside the kitchen door, chirping irritably if she was a few minutes late. Even the shy sparrows would flit in and land on her fingers, accepting bread from her hands. The household staff took to gathering at the kitchen window, sipping their morning coffee and watching as Kyle coaxed everything from cardinals to tiny finches onto her outstretched arms.

On Tuesday afternoon, Kyle had returned from St. Albans and was upstairs changing when she heard Maggie exclaim, "Mrs. Rothmore, are you all right?"

"Where's Kyle?" came her mother's flat reply.

"Upstairs, madam. Should I—"

"No, never mind. Has Randolf arrived?"

"Mr. Crawley? No, madam, there's nobody here except Kyle and the staff."

Something in her mother's voice drew Kyle out of her room and down the stair's sweeping curve. She held back, able to observe while remaining unseen. Her mother had a wild-eyed look about her. "He should be here," her mother said. Abigail's voice sounded rough, hoarse, as though filed with a rasp. "Why hasn't he come?"

"Madam, I don't know. Should I call someone?"

Kyle could scarcely believe her eyes. Her mother, whose whole life seemed built around looking impeccably polished and perfect, was in total disarray. Her eyes scattered glances every direction. Her hair was coming down in sparse strands. Her clothes looked haphazard. "He'll be here. He said he had to stop by the office. But he'll come. He has to. We must plan. This can't be final. It can't be."

"No, madam," Maggie said doubtfully. "Should I call the doctor?"

The question seemed to help Abigail focus. "Don't be silly. I'm perfectly all right. When Randolf arrives, show him out to the back veranda."

Friday Kyle came out of St. Alban's to find the family Rolls parked directly in front of the school's main doors. Bertrand stood beside the open door, his face blank and stony as Kyle hurried over. "I thought you promised——"

"Your mother's express orders, Miss Kyle." Bertrand ignored her unease and the whispered comments of other students who gathered and watched. He walked around, slid behind the wheel, and continued, "She wants you to join her down at the office."

"But it's Friday," she protested, knowing it was a feeble objection but not able to come up with anything else.

Bertrand shared a somber look with her before repeating, "Your mother insisted."

"Well, at least take the long way," Kyle begged.

Bertrand hesitated, then swung the big car around and headed toward the city's center, not the Rothmore building. Kyle settled down with a sigh. "Thank you, Bertie."

They cruised in front of the White House before heading down Constitution Avenue. The Jefferson Memorial and The Mall were surrounded by hundreds of cherry trees, which the Japanese had sent over to symbolize the end of the war. The trees had grown over the ensuing years until many of the branches met overhead. Bertrand slowed so he could turn and look with Kyle, for in the sudden explosion of a delayed spring, all the trees had bloomed together. The walkways were thick with people, all captured by the glory of the moment. The sun was bright and hot overhead, the trees so ephemeral their blossoms belonged more to the clouds than to the earth.

When they finally turned toward the Rothmore building, Kyle became increasingly uncertain and agitated. As Bertrand pulled up in front, he turned to her and said, "It's all going to be fine, Miss Kyle."

"Is it?" She searched the familiar face, saw the genuine concern. But it only seemed to make it worse. "How can you be so sure?"

"Because I know you," he replied. "And I know you will do the right thing."

"I'm so scared, Bertie."

He hesitated a moment, then said, "I find Maggie's wisdom fits such times very well. Perhaps you should try to find comfort in a time of prayer."

Kyle glanced up and through the front windshield. She could feel her mother's presence and all the unanswered questions there waiting for her. "Prayer doesn't belong in this place," she murmured.

"That is not true," he protested. "The Lord saw Daniel out of the lion's den. He could be with you here, if you let Him."

The words tugged at her heart, but the dark shadows reached out from the high unseen floors and grasped at her. "I have to go," she said through wooden lips.

Before Bertrand could come around, Kyle slid from the car. She did not want to wait, to hesitate even a moment. There was too much risk that her nerve would fail and she would not be able to enter at all.

But once inside, the reactions that greeted her were so unexpected she found herself pushed beyond her fears. A pair of secretaries coming out of the ground floor soda fountain stopped to smile and wish her a good morning. She could only vaguely remember having ever seen their faces before. Then the elevator operator tipped his hat to her and kept up a cheerful chatter about the weather. The elevator clanked up the floors, and as others came and went, all of them seemed to have some kind word for her. Kyle had never known such a greeting before. For her father, certainly, all the employees knew him and seemed to have genuinely liked him. But this was directed at *her*.

When she reached the top floor, a passing secretary greeted her with yet another smile and said that she had just seen her mother down in Randolf Crawley's office. Kyle thanked her but found her footsteps turning toward the far end of the corridor.

She did not hesitate, not even when she pushed through the tall outer door and Mrs. Parker, her father's secretary, greeted her by bounding to her feet and giving her the most brilliant smile Kyle had seen that day. Instead, she went into the inner sanctum and closed the door behind her.

She stood still, her hands on the knob behind her, and leaned against the door. This, she knew, she had to do alone.

She turned slowly to look at the long-familiar broad chamber. The office was so much like her father, she could feel his presence surround her again. At each step, her heart collided with her chest. She traced one finger along the edge of his desk. She looked at his high-back leather chair and mentally heard the heavy tread as he walked into the room behind her.

She closed her eyes so as to hear more clearly his booming voice, smell the English Leather cologne that he always used, feel the weighty pressure of his hand on her shoulder. But when Kyle reached up, she felt only emptiness as her hand touched nothing but the fabric of her jacket.

Carefully Kyle checked her compact to obliterate any trace of tears before opening the outer door. Mrs. Parker was still standing by her desk, as though she had not moved. "Your mother came by, Miss Kyle. I . . . well, I told her . . ." she hesitated, "I said I'd send you down . . . as soon as you appeared."

"Thank you," she murmured, avoiding the woman's gaze. This visit to her father's office had shattered her more than she had expected. "Where is she now?"

"Down with Mr. Crawley, I'd imagine. Shall I ring and find out?"

"No, that's all right, Mrs. Parker, I'll go down."

"Miss Kyle," the woman started, then stopped. Mrs. Parker was a professional woman who had been with her father for as long as Kyle could remember. But now the astringent features suddenly softened in genuine concern. "I just wanted to tell you, madam, that all of us here are rooting for you."

"Thank you," Kyle said, but she didn't know what the woman meant. She entered the hallway, returned the greetings of several people she did not recognize, and started toward Randolf's office. But her legs did not want to carry her. Her limbs felt leadened, as though all her strength and focus had been drained away. She felt utterly alone.

Kyle faltered and reached out a hand for the side wall. But instead she touched a door, which pushed inward as she leaned.

"Why, Kyle, hello, how are you?"

She recognized the voice before she remembered the name. Kyle watched her father's former assistant rising from his desk. "Hello, Kenneth."

He walked over, searched her face, and in that moment his own smile slipped away, swallowed by a mirror of what she felt in his own heart. "It's so hard," he said quietly. "I still can't get over the fact that I'll never hear his voice booming out for me again."

The hollowness in her chest was filled with a soft fire. Her tears began again, leaving warm trails across her cheeks. "I miss him so much," she whispered.

"I know you must. He loved you so." He took her arm, guided her inside, and shut the door behind her. "I never heard such happiness in his voice as when he was talking about you."

Each word seemed to unravel another thread of her control. Her shoulders shook with the sorrow that seemed to always hover nearby. She put her hands over her face, trying to push it all back inside, feeling as though her whole body was crumbling.

Kenneth's arms seemed to just appear, wrapping her up in strength and comfort she had not known since her father's passage. She heard the voice murmur in her ear. She felt a hand stroke the hair out of her face, felt the muscles of his arms cradle her with gentle strength.

Gradually she recovered her composure, until she was able to free herself and wipe her eyes with the handkerchief he offered. "I'm so sorry."

"Don't apologize. I think I know how you feel."

She glanced at him, just a quick look. There was too much sincerity in his gaze to hold it for long. But his words seemed to speak directly to her heart. "You miss him too."

"So much. He was a friend as well as my employer. You don't know, you can't know, how rare that is." He guided her over to a chair, seated himself beside her. "He was a genuine man, right down to the core. Every word he spoke, he meant."

She nodded. That was indeed her father. Still she could not look at Kenneth. It was too hard. Those strong features held an immense capacity for compassion. They pulled at her heart, inviting things from her that she tried to keep hidden.

Kyle avoided returning his gaze by looking around his office. She had seen it several times in the past, usually when her father pushed open the door and proudly pointed to his protégé as though he himself had invented the young man. Yet this was the first time she had ever been inside. Then she noticed the plaque set above the door, and it drew her upright.

He noticed the change. "What is it?"

She pointed at the plaque. "Up there."

"The needlepoint? It's very old. My mother's grandmother did it."

The design was intricate and beautiful, a garden trellis supporting wisteria in full bloom. Above shone a four-pointed sun, shaped like a golden cross. And framed by the trellis and the flowers and the streaming light were the words, "My son, give me thine heart."

"That's from the Bible, isn't it?"

"The quote? Yes, from Proverbs."

She turned to him, recalling the conversation they'd had at the dinner table, the only other time she had really talked with

him. It seemed like memories from another lifetime. "You're a
. . . a Christian?"

The surprise in her voice caused him to smile. "I try to be.
No—that's not correct," he quickly went on. "One does not
become a Christian by *trying* to be one. But I do try to live up
to the standards that Christ set."

Kyle could not bring herself to respond. At a moment when
she felt her world so shaken, she was confronted not with mere
words but with a *fact*. Here was a man who cared deeply for her
father. He showed her the caring concern that her own heart
yearned for. He was successful in business; she knew that by the
way her father had often spoken of him.

And he was a Christian. Here. In the heart of the place
where she thought faith did not belong. Especially now.

Kenneth's eyes turned back to the plaque. "Your father used
to come in here sometimes after hours. We'd talk about everything under the sun. Including faith. Toward the end, we began
to study the Bible together."

She could not keep the shock from her voice. "Daddy?"

But he was not seeing her. His eyes and his mind seemed
fastened upon something very far away, maybe very dear. "He
was one of the most open men I've ever met. Most people who
find success are *imprisoned* by it. They refuse to consider anything that might challenge their hold on the good life."

Kyle found herself nodding at the words. This sort of person
she knew all too well.

"Lawrence was totally different. He was interested in everything. He had no time for fools, and could be quite short with
somebody he thought was wasting his time. But he'd sit there
and listen with an openness I found amazing. He told me
once . . ."

Kenneth stopped. Kyle found her eyes drawn to the young
man. His silhouette was a strange mixture of sharp-angled
strength and the softening of deep sorrow. He took a long
breath, held it, let it out slowly.

"It was toward the end, one of the last times we talked together here in private," he said quietly. "I've found myself won-

dering if maybe he knew what was coming. Lawrence told me he'd never met anybody who talked about faith like I did. He said the words seemed to spring naturally from whatever it was I had inside—that was the way he put it. I told him nobody had ever paid me a nicer compliment. That night we prayed together. He received God's gift of salvation. And there was such a wonderful feeling here."

Kenneth turned to her then, the move unexpected, and seemed to catch them both with aching transparency. Kyle stared into his eyes and felt as though heart was speaking directly to heart. Finally he said, "I miss him."

"So do I," she whispered. "So much." After a pause she said, "Thank you for telling me about this."

A sense of need finally stirred within Kyle. As though a thought had been planted inside her mind, Kyle sensed that here was someone she could ask. Someone she could trust.

She sat straighter and asked, "Please tell me. What is going on around here?"

She would think back over that moment many times in the days and weeks to come. For Kenneth did not disengage and withdraw behind an official barrier. Instead, he stayed right there with her, comfortable with the closeness, willing to go wherever she wanted. "What do you mean?"

"Everybody is so nice to me. They've always been kind, but not like this. It's different."

He nodded slowly. "You haven't been back here for some time, have you?"

"Not since the funeral. I just couldn't."

"You wouldn't have heard at home, of course," he went on. "Around here, though, rumors fly faster than the speed of sound."

"What rumors?"

Again, there was no sense of Kenneth playing calculating games. He examined her face, then asked, "Are you sure you want to know?"

In that moment she began to understand. Not just the day, but all the events of the entire winter. Even before the words made things clear, she felt a dawning sense of clarity. As though she had not wanted to search out what had always been there for her to see.

Kyle did not turn away. Not now. She nodded her head, very slowly, her eyes not leaving Kenneth's face.

He sighed his acceptance. He took her hand. It was the act of a friend, one who was giving her an unspoken assurance that she would not be alone. "Your mother has been contesting the will. Do you know what that means?"

"Yes." She was her father's daughter. She knew the words of his world. To contest meant to challenge in court.

"Your father surprised everybody. He set up a trust in your name. He put all of his stock, the controlling interest of Rothmore Insurance and all its subsidiaries, into this trust. For you."

Kyle sat totally still for a moment before rising to stare out the window.

"I understand that you might be shocked, even frightened," he said. She slowly turned back to him. His face was creased with the power of comprehension. "But this is what your *father* wanted, Kyle. Nobody could have structured this so carefully, or so secretly, unless it was something very important."

He motioned to the seat beside him and waited until she had resumed her place before he continued. "The two trustees will vote your stock until you turn twenty-one. Then you have power to do what you will, except that you cannot sell the shares until after your twenty-ninth birthday."

Her mind was a swirling tumult of questions, so many she did not even know what to ask. Kenneth went on, "Your mother has tried to nullify the will. But your father left enough assets to her, things other than the company, that she has no real basis for a suit. None of her own family's money was used in setting up the firm; that is all on record. Last week the court threw out her case. The company is now yours."

"No," she whispered. "I don't want it."

"The head trustee is old Mr. Crawley." Kenneth continued to speak with gentle insistence. Now that he had started, clearly he wanted to tell her everything. But his voice continued to hold to its kindness. "There have been some real battles on that front as well. When Mr. Crawley heard that your mother had tried to enlist Randolf Junior into her challenge, he threatened to cut his own son off without a penny. And he would have. I'm sure of it."

Kyle remembered the hurried visits, always done in secret. She recalled the glances he had thrown her way, the silence, the sense of fear. "I don't—"

The door was flung open with such force that they both jumped. Her mother looked in, saw her, took in the scene at a glance, and seemed electrified with horror. "What are you *doing* here?"

"We were talking." For some reason, her mother's agitation seemed to only make Kyle more calm.

"Come out of here this *instant*." Abigail almost stamped her foot with rage. "I forbid you from ever speaking with this . . . this *meddler*."

Kyle rose from her chair and started to follow her mother from the room. But just as she was moving through the doorway, she turned back and asked "Who is the other trustee?"

"*NOW!*" her mother commanded.

Kenneth Adams stood in the center of his room, untouched by Abigail's rage. His voice remained gentle as he said, "If you are ever in need of anything, anything at all, just give me a call."

CHAPTER TWELVE

THAT SPRING AND SUMMER were the fullest and most memorable Joel had ever known. Throughout those mixed-up seasons with their crazy weather, he was up before dawn delivering papers. The April frosts were the worst—not the coldest, but still the hardest, maybe because he was expecting warmth that did not arrive.

As soon as the school day was over, he met up with Simon. Usually they went back to the Miller home, where he grew accustomed to helping in Mr. Miller's workshop. The broad-shouldered man was a good teacher and introduced Joel to all his carpentry trade. Joel grew as comfortable with the lathe and drill and sander and broad-band saw as he had with the smaller instruments of his modeling days.

At the beginning of summer, Mr. Miller declared the boys ready to begin work on their own furniture. Joel was as delighted as Simon and started on a rocker for his mother. The two worked in a corner of Mr. Miller's shed and learned to move about the cramped space with ease.

When evening shadows lengthened, Joel found it harder and harder to put down his tools and head for home. Toward evening, Mr. Miller would often look at him, his gaze filled with a thoughtful sadness. But he seldom spoke of Joel's homelife, except for their continued discussions after Sunday services. Sometimes Mr. Miller prayed with Joel about a specific need or a particularly bad day at home.

Joel's life at home became more and more a world apart. He found it increasingly difficult to slip into his silent role as he journeyed home. The Miller household was so full of laughter, of talk and life. Ruthie was always in and out of the carpentry shed, bringing lemonade, a word, and a bright smile. Joel found himself increasingly drawn to the shining-faced country girl. And she seemed to save her warmest smiles just for him.

The first day of August, Joel arrived home just in time for the evening news. He had found this the easiest way to slip back into his home. Walter Cronkite supplied the comfortable conversation his parents lacked. That night was a special treat, because the Ed Sullivan Show would be on later. Joel found himself in hopes that the little mouse, Topo Gigio, would make an appearance. The puppet always made his father laugh. It was such a rare occasion that he and his mother shared a smile behind his back.

He parked his bike behind the house, came in through the kitchen door, and kissed his mother as she stood over the stove preparing dinner. He entered the living room in time to see Elvis Presley being shorn like a lamb, while his drill instructor stood and observed. The entire world had watched as Elvis had been inducted into the army. For some reason, it had made his popularity grow even stronger. The day he had left for boot camp, millions of teenagers had written and wished him well.

At his mother's call, Joel rose and went to set the table. He returned to watch as Marines landed on the sands of Beirut. His eyes on the television, Joel's father murmured, "Look at the leathernecks go."

"What are they doing?"

"Ah, some king got shot," he said. "Over in Jordan or someplace."

"Iraq," Joel quietly commented, remembering now having seen it on that morning's front page.

"Wherever." He waved it aside as unimportant. "Boy, do I ever wish I were . . ."

The words were cut off by a loud thump and breaking glass in the kitchen. Joel and his father stiffened, then leaped toward the hallway at the sound of a long moan.

They raced into the kitchen to find Joel's mother on the floor, one leg outstretched, the other trapped back under her. Her face was contorted with pain. "Oh, I slipped. I can't . . ."

With surprising speed his father limped his way through the broken glass to kneel beside his wife. "Where does it hurt?"

"My back," she moaned. One hand pulled feebly at the trapped leg.

With a gentleness Joel would have not thought possible, his father eased the foot free and stretched the leg out straight. Then he turned to his son and said, "Go get Howard. And fast."

Joel accelerated down the hall and out the door, leaped over the front steps, and flew down the street. At the end of the block he skidded through the turn, caught himself on one hand, and sped on. He raced across the street, ignoring a car that screeched on its brakes and blared an angry blast of its horn. He ran up the front steps of the Austin home, tore open the screen door, and found Doc Austin seated in an almost identical position to his father, watching as Cronkite declared that's the way it was, on that first day of August.

"You gotta come," Joel gasped, fighting for breath, his heart pumping so wildly that he felt nauseated. He thought he was going to be sick and fought hard against it as he sucked in air.

Howard Austin drew his focus away from the screen. His tired gaze spoke of having been disturbed by a thousand pressing calls. When his eyes fell on Joel his demeanor quickly changed. "Slow down, take a deep breath. You're pale as a ghost. Are you okay? That's better."

When Joel could catch his breath enough to form words again, he repeated his message with more urgency, "You gotta come quick."

"Easy now," Howard said. "Now, tell me what's the matter."

"It's Mom," Joel managed. "She's fallen and it's bad."

Alarm spread in rapid stages across the middle-aged features. Howard Austin scrambled from his chair. His wife appeared in the hall entrance, her face creased in sudden concern. "Is she all right?"

"Where's my bag?" he said to answer her question.

"Right here on the table where it always is," she said, holding it out to her husband. "I'll put dinner in the oven. Joel, tell her I hope she's all right."

"Thanks, Mrs. Austin."

"Okay, sport, let's take my car."

Doc Austin drove with practiced haste. Joel sat beside him, his heart still pounding erratically, making his breathing rise and fall in funny little flutters. As always, he ignored the stabbing pains in his chest that came with too much exertion. Soon the doctor was pulling up to Joel's house and easing from the car before the motor had stilled. He bounded up the steps, opened the door, and hurried through to the kitchen. In the doorway he stopped so suddenly Joel collided with him. There was a sharp intake of breath, then Doc Austin crossed the room in three quick strides and knelt beside Martha. Joel felt a chill spread through his belly at the sight of blood spread over the linoleum.

"Where are you bleeding, Martha?"

"It's me," Harry replied, holding up a hand wrapped in a dish towel. "She dropped a glass when she slipped and fell. I was trying to pick it up."

"For Pete's sake, I've got enough to do without you going and making more work for me." Howard Austin slipped a hand under Martha's neck and deftly felt around. "Does that hurt?"

"No, farther down," she murmured.

Harry asked, "Want me to lift her up?"

"No, hang on a minute." As gently as he could, the doctor continued his examination until he grunted softly and stopped.

"What's the matter?" Harry's face was a mixture of alarm and fear. Joel found himself staring at his father. He had never seen such emotion on that normally impassive face.

But Howard did not respond. He felt a moment more, then raised up slightly and asked, "Can you move your toes?"

"I think so."

"Don't lift your legs. Good, that's good." He then turned

to Harry and said quietly, "Better go call an ambulance."

Harry stared at his friend for a minute, then rose and moved for the hall phone.

Howard turned back to Martha and asked, "Do you have any tingles running up and down your legs? Any shooting pains? Numb spots?"

"No."

"Good," Howard sighed, his tension obviously easing. "That's good."

Joel's mother chided, "All I did was slip on a puddle by the sink."

Doc Austin looked down and said quietly, "It appears you've injured your spine, Martha. But you can move your feet, so apparently there's no serious damage to the nerves."

Harry slammed the phone back into its cradle and reappeared. "They're on their way."

"We shouldn't move you," Howard said to the prone woman. "But I can slip a pillow under your head. Would that help?"

"I'll get it," Harry said before Martha had a chance to respond. He hurried down the hall and returned with one of the sofa pillows. As Doc Austin lifted her head, Harry knelt and gently slid it into place.

Joel stood by the door, frozen to the spot. He was caught as much by his father's reaction as by his mother's pain. There was such concern on Harry's features, such caring. It was as though Joel was confronted with a totally different person, someone he had never known except maybe in old photographs. A person who felt, who showed, who cared.

In the days after his mother was settled into the hospital, Joel's homelife went through a subtle transformation. Joel spent an hour every afternoon in her hospital room, as much time as he was permitted. His father, however, spent more time there than at work. At home, Harry remained silent and withdrawn as always, but occasionally his face was softened by worried glances at the phone and a milder tone toward Joel.

Joel found himself amazed by it all. Howard Austin continually reported progress, assuring them that Martha was healing nicely. She was responding so well to traction that surgery probably would not be required. Joel's father remained in his new world of concern, one that stripped away his stony mask and left him openly vulnerable.

Yet when Joel was there in the hospital room with the two of them, his parents were still uncommunicative. To Joel's eyes, it seemed they had become so accustomed to their mute roles that they did not know how to break out of them.

In the evenings when Joel was home alone, he liked to look at the pictures from his parents' very early days. Back before he was born, even before the war. Before everything became shadowed by what he saw on their faces now, like the heavy clouds of an overcast day.

Back then, their eyes seemed to shine with excitement and love and hope. His father had a jaunty smile. Joel could see the traces of that smile still today, only now the lines were twisted downward, the face too quick to grimace and sneer. And his mother . . . back then her eyes looked at the camera with such trust and joy. Such happy times. Why couldn't they have lasted? Was it because of him? Was he at fault? Joel would go through the pictures one by one, wishing there was some way he could make things go back to the way they had been.

During those evenings alone, the quietness of his home had a different quality. The stillness acted like a mirror, drawing him to look at himself and his isolation in ways he had never before experienced. He found comfort in the Bible, ashamed by how even the littlest Miller girl knew the Scripture stories better than he did. By the second week of his mother's hospitalization, Joel was reading the Book every night. And though words still came hard when he prayed alone, he tried to talk with God every night before going to bed, asking first for his mother's healing.

But in time, he found the prayers being extended, almost of their own accord, to include an inward healing for his father as well.

Toward the end of that second week, while Joel and his father watched television together, there came a firm rap on the door. The knocking brought a surprised look from his father, who sat slumped in his well-worn chair. He nodded toward the front. "Answer it."

Joel moved to obey. At the door he stopped in surprise. It was Mr. Miller, his huge frame drooped slightly over his crutches and his good-natured smile on his face. Joel was unsure what to do. They had so few visitors, only Doc Austin and his wife. His heart began to beat a nervous rhythm. As he moved to open the door, inwardly he uttered a short, disjointed prayer. "Don't let it be something about Simon. Please."

Mr. Miller stumped through the open door and asked, "Is your father been to home yet, Choel?"

A voice from the back of the house called, "Who is it, boy?"

Joel swallowed hard. He worked his mouth for a moment, but the words were hard to form. "It's . . ."

"Choseph Miller," the big man called back and started down the hall, lightly brushing past the bewildered boy. The crutches made a dull thud, thud, on the bare wooden floor.

Joel followed Mr. Miller down the hall and saw his father push himself upright from the chair's lopsided cushions. He half stood, half leaned on the chair arms, as though uncertain whether or not to raise himself and greet this man who had disturbed his evening.

But Joseph Miller was not an easy man to dismiss. Joel watched as his father stared openly at the big man. The staccato rhythm of the crutches echoed in the still room. His one good leg moved easily in time to the crutches, his other pant leg fastened at the knee. His father watched as the shortened leg swung with each forward thrust of the man's body.

"Sorry to be cutting in on your evening," the man said, ignoring the chattering television. "But the boy here's been saying you have some problem to yourself. The wife to town took herself today and came back saying I was to bring myself by."

His father glanced toward him, then back to the shortened leg. Harry looked bewildered and even a little angry. Joel could feel his slight frame shiver with discomfort. Surely, he cried inwardly, surely his father would not make a scene. The very thought made him want to dash from the room.

But to his relief his father stretched out a hand in greeting. Joel was pleased that his father did not wince as Mr. Miller gave it a hearty shake. "Have a seat," Harry offered, nodding toward a neighboring chair.

"I thank you." Mr. Miller crossed to the chair and seated himself, placing his crutches carefully together and lowering them to the floor. The pleasant expression did not leave his face. He carefully studied Joel's father before saying, "A hard lot it is, when one's wife is wonderful sick. Makes a man know not where to take himself next. My Ruth stopped by the hospital, says the doctor wants your good wife to stay to her bed when home she comes. And quiet she needs as well. 'How can a growing boy live quiet?' I ask. Boys were made for noise yet. So my Ruth, she says, 'You go and tell the poor father that Choel can come make his noise to our house.' He can stay until the Missus be fine on her feet. No hurry to push her back on up. Choel be chust fine."

Joel's breath caught in his throat. Was he hearing Mr. Miller correctly? Was Simon's father really issuing an invitation for him to live with the Miller family? But he couldn't. He was needed at home. He was the one who ran the errands. Who helped with meals and washed up the dishes. Who soothed his mother when she sank down in quiet despair. Who ran to the store for tobacco or cigarette papers when his father's nerves and hands demanded something to do.

Then another thought came to Joel. A longing to be part, just a small part, of that big, bustling, loving household. Where

141

laughter was common, and teasing was done in good-natured fun. Where food was tasty and plentiful, and laid out for hearty appetites to devour at will. Where prayer was offered to a God who was so real that He seemed to be standing in the very room, somewhere just beyond natural vision.

He would never be able to go, Joel thought despondently. There was no use even dreaming.

But Joel's father chose that moment to speak. His voice was deep and unnatural, and his hand fidgeted restlessly with the frayed chair arms. "Well, the doctor's told us about this place upstate. It's a veteran's hospital—they've done all sorts of work with back problems. Howard said it would do her a world of good. I was wondering how we could—"

Mr. Miller smacked his hand loudly on the knee of his good leg. The big smile lit his face again. "There," he exclaimed. "That does it good. You give your Missus a rest to make better the way she is, and we keep Choel with us for this time."

He beamed from father to son and back again. Joel felt himself squirming on the hard-back chair. What would his father say? Would he agree to such an arrangement? He could hardly bear the moment of suspense.

"That's mighty kind of you," his father said and rubbed one thin hand against his shirt sleeve in a nervous gesture. "It would sure help us out, but I understand you already have a lot of mouths to feed. It seems a lot to ask—"

"Yah," said the big man. "Yah, seven we got. Such a household. My Ruth, she says a pack of hounds chasing the chickens not so much noise makes." Mr. Miller gave a hearty laugh, one that started deep in his barrel chest and rumbled forth in joyous ripples.

Joel's father cut in, as though the sound of untempered good humor unnerved him. "So you've already got enough to care for without—"

"So what is one more on top with so many? Besides, Choel is a good helper, already he shows that." He waved a carefree hand. "He chust fit in fine with the rest of all of them. He won't be hardly of notice."

Mr. Miller reached down and retrieved his crutches. "Simon comes to help Choel bring his things to the house over tomorrow. You think nothing of. Chust fix better your good wife."

Joel's father watched Mr. Miller heave himself upright and settle the crutches under his arms. For some reason, the action seemed to silence whatever further protest Harry was planning.

Mr. Miller proceeded across the room. "I not keep you more from the chores that take up your time before bed yet." His crutches thumped toward the front doorway. He swung it open, then turned and nodded, first to Harry and then to Joel. "Good night to you, and God's peace rest on the house and all who live the roof under."

Joel watched, eyes wide and heart pounding, as the big man eased himself out and closed the door softly behind him.

Silence. Dead silence. Joel did not even stir. He was afraid that his father might hear the frantic thumping of his heart, but the man said nothing. He seemed to be in another world as his fingers picked at the threads of the chair arm. His eyes did not appear to be focused, but rather stared off into emptiness. Joel found himself wondering what thoughts were churning around in his father's head.

But when at last his dad did speak, Joel was totally unprepared for his statement. "You didn't tell me the man was missing a leg."

Joel gulped. What should he say?

"Why not?"

"I . . . I never thought of it," Joel managed.

His father's eyes looked angry. Joel found himself mentally scrambling to try and figure out what he had done to upset him once again. He stumbled on in a hurry, "I . . . it, well, just didn't seem important, I guess."

His father swung around in his chair. "A man is without his leg, and you don't think it's important?"

Joel knew he had to respond, yet found it impossible to meet his father's gaze. His head began to dip, until he remembered how much his father hated it when he hid his eyes like that. He had to be a man, his father often said, and learn to face things head on. Joel lifted his chin. "It . . . I mean . . . Mr. Miller, he never says anything about his leg. He just sorta forgets it. I guess, well, I sorta forget it too. Nobody in the family notices it, hardly ever."

He knew it was not a good answer. But it was the best he could do. Joel held his breath, dreading his father's reaction. He was bound to come back with one of his angry blasts. He was sure of that.

But it did not happen. His father pushed himself up from the lumpy chair and limped his way to the small front window. With a sweep of a hand, he flipped back the simple curtain and stood staring silently out at the gathering night.

Joel remained on the edge of his chair, mute and still, stifling even the sound of his breathing.

When his father finally broke the silence, it was with a softer voice. "You'd better go get your things together and get to bed. Tomorrow will be a big day if you're moving over."

Joel's breath came out in a shaky little gasp. He caught his lower lip between his teeth as he rose and left the room. It seemed that the impossible was to happen. He was to be allowed to become a temporary member of the Miller household. He could scarcely wait to see Simon in the morning.

CHAPTER THIRTEEN

COLLEGE WAS FAR MORE EXCITING than Kyle had ever imagined. Her days were filled with a sense of discovery and challenge. College meant an opportunity to broaden, to expand beyond the boundaries of the Rothmore estate and her mother's friends. She took as many business courses as she could fit around her required freshman classes and mostly found them baffling. But she was determined to learn. She owed it to her father and to his legacy for her.

Years of her mother's manipulation and subtle put-downs had tempered her spontaneous spirit, however, and she made few friends. Kyle watched the other students meet and laugh, and she yearned to be a part of their easy life. But she did not know how to react when they tried to speak with her. And with the need to return home as soon as classes were over, she remained separated from the college social scene. The few free hours she had on campus were spent at the edge of things, watching and listening. The other students were drawn from every strata of society, and their conversations were as great an education for Kyle as the classes themselves.

She knew she did not have a natural aptitude for business. Lessons that seemed to come easily to other students took her hours and hours each night to grasp. But her teachers seemed to recognize her as someone who was genuinely trying, and they showed a willingness to help. Besides that, she loved the *challenge* of learning.

That spring, she began appearing at the Rothmore Insurance building once each week. Her Wednesday classes ended at noon, and her mother did not expect her home before four. She enjoyed the place and the feeling that she might someday become a part of her father's work. She began writing down questions before she arrived, then finding people who could answer them. Some employees seemed suspicious or at least perplexed, a few genuinely hostile. But most met her with a smile and kind words of encouragement. She tried hard to ask intelligent questions, to be honest if she did not understand the answer. The majority responded with a real willingness to teach.

For the first month, however, she did not go to the top floor. Earlier that winter, Randolf Crawley had been elected the new chairman and had moved into her father's old office. Kyle did not want to walk down that long hallway, see the big mahogany door at the end, and know that someone else was now sitting behind her father's desk.

But Kyle found her thoughts continually returning to Kenneth Adams, and in early March she gathered her courage and took the elevator straight upstairs. She walked the long hallway, trying not to look at her father's office. Yet when she paused at Kenneth's office, she found her eyes drawn unwillingly to the end door, now bearing another nameplate. She felt the familiar sadness flood over her.

Hurriedly she knocked and pushed open Kenneth's door without waiting for his invitation, as though blocking the scene from her sight might soothe her aching heart.

"Kyle!" The young man's face broke into a delighted smile. He rose from his desk and hurried over. "You didn't tell me you were coming."

"I didn't know it myself until I was downstairs," she admitted. "How are you?"

"Busy," he said, sweeping a hand over his cluttered desk. Forms and reports and correspondence rose in scattered bundles from every free surface. "Sometimes I think our new chairman intends to bury me in work."

"Then I shouldn't disturb you. I just wanted to stop by and say—"

"Nonsense." He grasped her arm and drew her forward, closing the door behind them. "Come, sit down and tell me how you've been."

Conversation was such an easy matter with him. He seemed to draw her out far more than she would ever have expected—or her mother would have called proper. Abigail had continued to keep a tight grip on Kyle's activities, and Kyle was determined not to give her mother any reason to pull her out of school. But here with Kenneth, what her mother thought seemed to matter a lot less. They sat and chatted with the easy manner of old friends. Within minutes it felt as though she had seen him just the week before rather than months earlier.

They discussed everything—Kyle's studies, her work here within the various departments, and the memory of her father.

There came a comfortable pause in the conversation, and Kyle found her attention caught by the *Washington Post* newspaper dropped by the side of Kenneth's desk. She pointed at the headline that she had heard students discussing for several days now. "What's so important about Fidel Castro?"

He glanced around and saw the newspaper. "Are you following this in the news?"

"I try. He's the new leader in Cuba. But it's such a tiny place, I don't see how it can be very important to America."

"It's not Cuba's size," he explained. "It's how close it is to America. Added to that is the fact that nobody knows what to expect of Castro. Will he allow the Soviets to set up a military base? That's what has everybody frightened."

Kyle loved the sense of being able to discuss anything with him, from world politics to her situation at home. "I read about the Shah of Persia taking power. That's another problem like this one, isn't it? Nobody knows what he's going to do. And he could destabilize the whole Middle East."

"You're exactly right," he said, observing her with some surprise. "Your father would be proud of you, Kyle."

She blushed, then asked the question that had been at the back of her mind ever since she had decided to come upstairs. "The last time I was here, you said if there was anything you could do for me, all I needed to do was ask. Do you remember?"

"Very clearly."

"You told me there were two trustees." She took a breath. "You're the other one, aren't you?"

"Yes." Kenneth instantly sobered. "Yes, I am."

"Why didn't you tell me?"

"It is not always correct for . . . for a minor to know who is responsible for managing a trust," he said, choosing his words very carefully.

"But that's not the real reason, is it?"

"No." His voice turned quiet. "After you were here the last time, I was ordered not to call you, not to approach you, not to write you. Since I could not come to you, I hoped you would come to me. The same applies to what has been happening in regard to your trust."

He seemed to wait for her to ask the next question, but suddenly she could not remain in her seat. Kyle rose and crossed to the window. From the executive floor of the Rothmore building, she looked out over the tops of neighboring white stone buildings. In the distance rose the needle-point of the Washington Monument. Below her, the tree-lined streets were brightly decked with spring foliage. People walked back and forth, stopping below burnt orange awnings to peer at window displays. They were free to come and go, live where they pleased, marry whomever they loved. Kyle sighed, wondering if anyone else in the whole world felt as trapped as she did.

"I didn't want Rothmore Insurance," she said quietly. "Not ever. I hate how all these possessions only imprison me tighter and tighter. I feel so . . . so manipulated. And Daddy's memory—they're all so busy twisting things around, turning the goodness he showed me into dollars and cents. I hate it."

There was a long silence, until Kenneth said quietly, "I have been praying for you."

The words were so unexpected that Kyle found herself staring at him before she realized she had even turned around. "What?"

"It is the only thing I know to do for you." His gaze was as steady as his voice. "The only gift I can give."

Kyle struggled to cast off the sudden feeling of having been caught defenseless and vulnerable. Her eye caught sight of the framed needlepoint still hanging over his door. "I remember something about your father being a minister."

"He was. He's retired now."

She found herself still struggling to bring the fact of his faith into perspective. "I suppose it's natural that his beliefs have been passed on to you."

"His beliefs?" Kenneth smiled. "I was raised with Bible knowledge, of course, and am very thankful for my upbringing. But that doesn't mean that God offers us a family savings plan."

Kyle found herself drawn to Kenneth's deep-seated calm. "What do you mean?"

"Salvation is not simply passed down from one generation to the next," Kenneth said. "It is something that each one must find for himself or herself. Just having a pastor as a father is not a guarantee of God's presence and blessing here on earth or a place in heaven. Only belief in Jesus can do that."

Kyle could not keep the bitterness out of her voice as she said, "I can't see much room for God in everything that's happened to me."

"I understand," he said, his voice so mild there was no sense of conflict. "You feel as though your whole life is caught up in random winds. All around you blow storms so great they push you back and forth without any hope of gaining control."

The words held such insight they threatened to draw tears from her eyes. "I don't understand any of this. I don't know why I'm even listening."

"Because your heart hungers for something, and I believe what you are looking for is the Lord's strength and guidance," he replied. "And I pray that you will find it."

In the distance, a church bell chimed the hour. She glanced

at her watch and was startled to see that it was four o'clock. "I have to be going. Thank you."

Kenneth rose to his feet to see her to the door. As she turned to leave, he said quietly, "Whatever you need, whenever you need it."

"I know," she replied. "And again, thank you."

"Miss Kyle!" Mrs. Parker's brisk voice stopped her at the elevator. Her father's former secretary looked both pleased and surprised. "Were we expecting you today?"

"No, I was just . . ." Kyle allowed her voice to trail off. She had heard downstairs that Mrs. Parker was now acting as Randolf Crawley's secretary, and she was not sure whether she should say anything of her visit with Kenneth.

"Of course," Mrs. Parker said, misunderstanding her. "Well, your mother is already in with Mr. Crawley."

Kyle took a step back. She was not sure she had heard correctly. "My mother?"

"Yes, she arrived earlier than expected, but Mr. Crawley canceled an appointment so they could get started." She held up the tray she was carrying with the empty pot. "I was just going to make some fresh coffee, but if you like I could first show you in."

"There's no need," Kyle said weakly. She was trapped. She could not leave now. Her mother would hear about her visit and grill her about what she was doing. No, it was better to simply go straight in. "You go ahead, I know the way."

Mrs. Parker smiled brightly. "Yes, of course you do."

But when she entered the outer office, the raised voices behind the inner door stopped her cold. Kyle stood in the middle of the room and heard her mother say, "I am telling you, Randolf, this situation must be resolved *immediately*."

"First you say, 'Don't rush,' now you insist I do."

"You know things have changed since that foolish will was brought to light!"

"Yes, I most certainly do." His voice carried a tone of strange smugness.

"Don't be difficult, Randolf," Abigail cut in.

"I wasn't being difficult. I'm just frustrated. There are too many people telling me what I can and cannot do."

"It's quite simple. We mustn't dally. Time is of the absolute essence."

"And I am telling you," he lashed back, "that I can do absolutely nothing about it."

Kyle found herself remembering another overheard conversation and all the discomforting questions it raised. She started to turn and leave, but some unseen force seemed to hold her in place.

"What on earth are you talking about?" Abigail was demanding harshly.

"Haven't you heard a word I've been saying?" Rather than his usual forced friendliness, Randolf Crawley's tone had an edge that sounded razor sharp even through the closed door. "My father has forbidden me to have anything to do with Kyle. Do you hear me? I am *forbidden* to even approach her."

They were talking about her. Why was she not surprised? Kyle moved closer to the door. She heard her mother snap, "What utter nonsense."

"Nonsense, is it? How would you like all my shares and voting rights to be returned to my father? Would you care to see him demote me and resume his place on the board? Because that is *exactly* what he has threatened if I so much as call your daughter."

There was a lingering silence. Kyle's gaze flittered around the room. Randolf's absence from her mother's little parties made sense now. Along with how there had been less mention made of him in discussions with Abigail. Instead, Kyle had simply been kept on a short leash, allowed to attend college classes so long as she did not have time or space to make new friends.

"That old fool," Abigail muttered. "I thought his meddling

was only temporary, that he would leave you alone once the business with the will was finished."

"So did I." There was a loud creaking, and Kyle's hand flew to her mouth. She knew that sound. It was her father's chair. Randolf Crawley was leaning back in her father's chair. His cultured voice went on, "His health is not good, you know, and—"

Before she fully realized her intentions, Kyle grasped the doorknob and flung it open. The shock on both their faces was reward enough for her boldness. Her mother had been standing by the side panel, holding a crystal plaque given to her father at some honorary banquet. It fell with a crash and shattered on the hardwood floor. "You!"

"Good afternoon," Kyle said evenly. Seeing Randolf leap to his feet gave her the strength to remain calm and continue. "Excuse me for disturbing you. I was here doing some research for school and heard you were here, Mother. I'm downstairs in the coffee shop whenever you're ready to leave."

She turned and left the room, closing the door quietly behind her. The absolute silence that marked her departure granted her a sense of satisfaction all the way back downstairs.

Abigail sat musing. It was not a pastime that she readily allowed herself. She did not like to reflect. One could get oneself in a state of morbid discontent if one thought too deeply. No—action was more her style. Quick, decisive action that left no room for sentimentality or self-pity.

Not that she had much reason for self-pity, she admitted, as her eyes traveled over the expanse of the elegant library.

But it had not always been so. With a grimace she thought back to the fear she had known in her teen years, when her father's inept business dealings had whittled away at the family fortune. And that had been followed by those tough, struggling years of her early marriage. The scrimping to make last year's wardrobe look fresh for a new season. Even now her face flushed with the humiliation.

Somehow, Lawrence by his sheer will and hard work had pulled them out of that morose state and provided them with more than an adequate lifestyle. Their success had been a matter of great importance to Abigail. She had enjoyed showing off the new wealth in front of her father, the man who had blustered and fumed when she had announced her intention of marrying a man who had little, as far as her father was concerned, and not much chance of changing those circumstances.

Why had she been drawn to Lawrence? Abigail dared for the first time to ask herself that question. Had it simply been to challenge the authority of a weak-willed father? The father who spoke forceful words, prefaced always with, "For your own good," and then followed with demands that indicated only his own desires?

Certainly she had been drawn by how utterly different Lawrence had seemed from her loud and blustering father. There was a gentleness to Lawrence, despite his rough masculinity. There had always remained an underlying sense of strength and genuineness in his hearty manner. One never could have called him weak. He was decisive and firm when the situation called for it. Even her complaining father eventually had been forced to admit that.

Lawrence.

Abigail paused in her reverie, one delicate finger tracing the rim of the gold-edged cup. Lawrence. It seemed so strange without him. She hadn't expected to miss him so much. It wasn't that they had been really close. Yet it was not the same house without his energetic presence. He had always been so generous with his praise, so easy with his encouragement, so much the protector and provider. He had not been one bit like her dark-browed, scowling father. Even his hearty disagreements had added spice to her life, keeping her alert in seeking ways to best him.

She stirred herself and brought her thoughts back to the issue at hand. Kyle.

Kyle was not cooperating. In fact, she was most exasperating. Abigail wondered how much longer she could keep Randolf on a tether. He must be as tired of the delay as she was herself. Perhaps he was even tired of Kyle. And now there was this unwelcome interference by his dotty father.

The very thought made her stir in irritation. What would happen if Randolf now decided that Kyle was not worth the wait? That the company money and position was not worth the effort of trying to win Kyle? Would he give up? But he couldn't. They would both be losers. Dreadful losers. The way the exasperating will was set up, neither Randolf nor Abigail would acquire control of the company that they wanted. It would be horrible. Just horrible. No—even worse. It would be disastrous. There was only one way for Abigail to maintain any control of the company. Kyle had to marry Randolf. She had to. There was no other way to work out the situation.

Abigail stirred again, her hands trembling on the cup between her fingers. She had to find some way to convince the girl—to force her if necessary.

But how? She had tried everything she knew. Was she going to lose it all now? Lose it because of this girl who wasn't even of her own blood—nor Lawrence's? Why had she let him talk her into an adoption? Why? She should have known it would come to no good.

Then a new idea came to her with such clarity that it stiffened her shoulders and lifted her chin. "Ahh," she heard from her own mouth and her eyes took on a new glitter. She wasn't done fighting yet. There were still ways that she hadn't explored.

She set her coffee cup on the marble-topped table with such force that it rang out in sharp protest. But Abigail did not notice. She was done with musing. Now was time for action. She lifted her head and reached for the bell.

When Bertrand appeared, her words were clipped, curt. "Bring round the car immediately. I need to go to the office."

"Very well, madam." He gave a slight bow, but she was already heading for the hall and the long, winding staircase. She would freshen her makeup, grab her handbag, and be off for another session with Randolf.

CHAPTER FOURTEEN

JOEL CLIMBED THE MILLERS' FRONT STEPS, his heart racing in its painful flip-flop fashion. Was it just his sorrow, or was today's wild flutter from some other unknown reason? These bouts, whatever they were, had been coming more often lately and seemed to leave him shorter of breath. Much as he dreaded the thought, maybe he should talk it over with Doc Austin.

Once on the Miller porch, he found himself unprepared to enter and face what waited behind that door. He turned and leaned against the weathered banister. The morning was clear and fairly cool for July. Birds sang from every tree. A lone car slid quietly down the street, one of those new sporty Corvairs. The Corvair had been a hit from the start, a sort of affordable T-Bird. Small, low, and well balanced with its rear engine, all a guy had to do to wow his friends was to claim to have driven one. Joel watched the car roll by and listened as the radio blared out "Smoke Gets in Your Eyes." Joel sighed. The song certainly fit his mood.

Normally Saturdays were great. Ever since he had stayed with the Miller family that previous summer, weekends were spent with them. He would finish his paper route, return for breakfast at his house, then leave for a day of carpentry and fellowship and laughter, returning home only after the Sunday service and meal the next day.

Those weekends, and the three weeks he had lived with

them, were a retreat from a world in which he mostly felt alien-
ated. The Millers were so full of life and hope and fun that his
own home, school, and the rest of the world seemed like a different planet.

Along with watching no television, the Millers never went
to the movies. In a year when Danny and the Juniors took all of
America to the hop, the Millers remained completely untouched
by popular music and its accelerating influence on society. Nor
did the strife and strained silence so familiar to Joel have any
parallel in their joyful, boisterous household. He looked forward
all week to these times of work and laughter and worship.

But today was very, very different.

"Ah, Joel, what do you say, sport." As Doc Austin pushed
his bulk through the front door, Joel was not surprised. It was
not unusual for Doc to be at the Millers'. He checked on his
patient frequently. Doc Austin's tired-looking eyes regarded Joel
with mild interest. "Over for a last visit?"

"Yes, sir." There was no escaping it. Squaring his shoulders,
he turned to face the front door. "I guess I am."

"Never would have expected it, the son of Harry Grimes
becoming friends with the Millers." Doc Austin stuffed a prescription pad in the side pocket of his rumpled jacket. His
clothes looked perpetually slept in, which was kind of strange,
for the doctor's face looked as though he rarely slept at all. His
cheeks were puffy, his eyes lined with dark smudges. Joel's father
said the man was destined to an early grave. "Cheer up, son.
You'll make other friends."

"Not like these," Joel said simply.

"No, perhaps not. The Millers are one of a kind."

It surprised Joel to hear the doctor agree with him. He found
the strength to say what was on his heart. "I feel as though I'm
losing my own family."

Eyes far older than the man's years regarded Joel. "Your
mother tells me you've gotten quite caught up in their religion."

Joel met the doctor's gaze. "It's the most wonderful thing
that has ever happened to me."

"Ach, such a fine parting gift Choel gives the family, to hear

157

how simple faith he values." Joseph Miller pushed open the screen door and stepped carefully out on the front porch. His normally broad smile was tempered with sadness. "You are well, Choel?"

"I guess so." Seeing the sorrow in Mr. Miller's face made his own heart ache even worse. "Well as I can be."

"Yah, yah, a hard day it is for all." Joseph offered the doctor his hand. "To you I owe more thanks than words there are."

"Don't mention it." Doc Austin accepted the hand, yet seemed embarrassed by the man's openhearted tone. "I've been real glad to see you respond so well to this new medicine. I'm thinking about writing up your case, sending it in to the *Journal.*"

"Yah, with patience and skill, years of life you give me. Strength and time to see the farm again. Such a debt we carry back with us. Glad we are to be able to go home again. Now my brudders can care for their own fields and stock and let me take over the work of mine once more. Too long we have kept them over busy. And the children—they miss their cousins, many that they are, and their pets." His somber nods spread his beard down flat across his chest. "This debt to you, we will never be able to pay it still."

"I've already been paid." Doc Austin fumbled with the strap to his black bag. "Not to mention the porch chairs and table you made for me and my wife. The finest things I've ever seen. We're much obliged."

Mr. Miller stumped over and placed a hand on Joel's shoulder. The strength of that grip brought a lump to the boy's throat. Mr. Miller went on, "Prayers we will say. May you hold the gift of life, Doctor Howard Austin. That gift only One can grant, and for that we will pray."

The doctor's nervousness increased. "Never had much time for religion."

"Speak with Choel. Here is one who has found the time. He has learned well."

"Not yet, but I'm trying," Joel mumbled.

"Yah, yah, lessons of faith are there for all our days." The grip tightened. "But salvation is yours. This you know."

"Yes," Joel said, lifting his head to find the doctor's gaze upon him. "That's right. I do."

Doc Austin opened his mouth, closed it, nodded absently to them both, then turned and shuffled down the front walk. Mr. Miller waited until he was around the corner before saying, "Such a man, he does not know his heart cries to the Savior."

"I wish he'd listened to you," Joel agreed.

"Perhaps," Joseph Miller said quietly. "Perhaps it is you who he listen to."

The door opened behind them. A teary-eyed Ruthie appeared, her hands in a tight knot before her. "Mama says come to the table."

"Yah, the first furniture in to come, the last out to go." Mr. Miller turned and moved into the house. "Mama has made the house a home and given our kitchen a heart."

Joel tried to return Ruthie's wobbly smile, but felt as though his face merely twisted into a different shape. He followed the two of them inside. His heart thumped in his chest as he surveyed the empty rooms. Nearly everything was already packed and loaded into the two trucks, even the pallets they had spread out to sleep on last night. Joel had skipped two days of school to help with the loading. Their silent acceptance of his gift had been the finest thanks he had ever known.

The table and few chairs still in the kitchen somehow made the room look even emptier. Mrs. Miller turned from the stove long enough to give him as big a smile as she could manage, but she did not say anything. Joel asked, "Where's Simon?"

"Moping in the shed," Ruthie said. "Sit yourself down, Choel."

But before he could settle himself, Ruthie's younger sister Sarah grabbed his hand and pulled him toward the back door. He did not resist. Together they moved to the back stoop, where Sarah looked up in a silent challenge to him before calling toward the carpentry shed, "Simon, come from your work in, the coffee soup's on the table and Choel's about to et himself done already!"

"Hush yourself," Joel countered, continuing a game that

Sarah had started the day he had moved in with them. At first, he had found their speech among themselves to be utterly baffling. But by the time his three weeks in their boisterous household was drawing to a close, he had picked up quite a few of the phrases himself. "Sarah, go comb yourself wunst, you're all strubbly," he added.

"Am not!" For a brief instant her lively face lit up with the joy of playing a game of her own making. "Talk like that, Choel Grimes, you ain't so fer schnitz pie!"

"And change that terrible schmitzig apron, wunst," Joel said, wondering how it was possible to joke when his heart was cracking.

She pretended to look down at herself. "Been layin' over the dough, got to get my bakin' caught after."

"Then hurry up wunst, and go smear me all over with jam, a piece of fresh-baked bread."

She slapped little hands over her face. The first to giggle lost the game. She gave a little high-pitched laugh, but just as swiftly her sky blue eyes filled with tears, and she turned and fled through the back door. Her forlorn wail sounded through the empty rooms.

Simon walked over, cleaning his hands on a rag. "Never did I think we could be so sad over going back to the farm."

Ruthie pushed the door open, stepped out and stood there, her hands still gripped tightly together. "Mama says come to table now."

Joel looked at her and repeated the words she had said to him after his first meal there, then said again the day he had left to go home the summer before, "Don't leave now. Leave next time."

She swallowed and tried to smile. A single tear traced a lonely path down one cheek. "You must promise to come visit, Choel."

He nodded. "Next summer." It seemed a lifetime away.

When they were all seated and the prayers said, they ate in silence until Mr. Miller finally set down his fork. "Choel, such sadness my family shows because of one thing only. You do not come with."

All eyes turned his way. Joel stopped pretending to eat food he could not taste. "I will miss you. All of you. So much."

Mrs. Miller reached over and rested a work-hardened hand on his. "You are like another son to me, Choel."

Joel could only nod in reply.

"Choel." Mr. Miller waited until he raised his gaze, but then could not seem to find a way to express himself. He glanced at Ruthie, who turned pink and looked at her plate. Joel glanced in confusion at Mrs. Miller, who was smiling gently at her husband. Mr. Miller cleared his throat and tried again. "Choel, at our table a place waits for you."

"Thank you," he managed, unsure exactly what was meant but finding himself blushing just the same. "Thank you very much."

Before the sky had given itself over to night, Joel excused himself and went upstairs. He closed his door to the murmuring television and stretched out on his bed. He missed the Millers with an ache that left him hollow. Their laughter, their smiling concern, their simple acceptance of him. Never before had he felt such a sense of belonging. Now they were gone, and their absence was a ballooning void in his heart, so great he could scarcely draw breath.

He climbed out of bed. There was no use trying to sleep. Lying there in the darkness only made the loss worse. Joel seated himself at his desk and turned on the lamp. He pulled over his Bible and opened it to the Old Testament.

He loved the ancient words. He loved the sense of divine history displayed before him. He loved belonging to something so strong that it had borne the test of time. A long parade of people, marching down through the centuries, had learned from

God and passed on the lessons, step by step, until *he* was able to sit there and read their stories and hear their messages. No matter how hard this moment might be, still they were there in spirit with him, letting him know he was part of a huge and loving family, united by the Spirit of God.

The next day was the first Sunday he had spent without the Miller family in almost two years. Even so, the ache was not as bad as he had expected. After lunch, Joel carried his Bible out on the front porch. He knew he would need to find a church of his own, but not yet. Right now, the Millers' absence remained too strong. But the sense of being surrounded by a comforting presence was there with him still. The best part of the Miller family was a part of him forever, and this knowledge took the edge off his sorrow.

He was so caught up in his reading and his thoughts that he did not hear the door open. Only when a shadow fell over the page did Joel look up to find his father watching him.

"What's going on here?" his father demanded.

For some reason, his father's irritation did not touch him. Not this time. "What do you mean?"

"This religion thing." He flung a hand toward the Bible open in Joel's lap. "Seems like every time I see you, you're all wrapped up in that book."

Joel studied his father. The situation was so similar to all their other arguments. His father's voice held both accusation and anger even before Joel said a word.

Yet there was a difference, too.

This time his father's bluster did not appear backed up by genuine anger. Instead, there was a nervous indecision, as though Harry was not completely sure he wanted to have his question answered at all.

And Joel knew a sense of comforting isolation, of protection, even while encountering his father's ire. He sat calmly before his father and realized he was neither alone nor defenseless.

Joel sent a silent prayer lofting upward and instantly knew what was needed here. "Pop, how many friends do you have?"

"I've got lots of pals." His father's retort lacked his usual heat over being challenged. "Buddies at work, men down at the Veterans' hall, lots of them. Howard, old Doc Austin, he's around here almost too much."

"That's not what I mean," Joel persisted, both thrilled and awed by the sense of guidance. "I mean, a friend you can trust to be there whenever you need him. Someone you can always rely on, through thick and thin."

"That's the problem with kids these days, they got their heads up in the clouds," Harry blustered. "You can't expect too much from people. They'll let you down every time. Just like life."

"But I've found a friend like that."

"Simon?"

"No—not him. None of the Millers. That's not what I mean," Joel countered with quiet confidence. "Another friend. Someone I can trust with everything I am and everything I have. Someone who loves me, who will always be there, who will always guide me. Someone so great and powerful that I can trust my entire life in His hands."

There was a long silence, then Harry asked gruffly, "You're talking about God?"

"Yes, I am," Joel agreed. "I'm talking about the Lord Jesus Christ."

CHAPTER FIFTEEN

KYLE WAS DREADING THE SUMMER.

School let out four weeks before her twentieth birthday, leaving her with no reason to escape from the house. Three long months stretched out before her like an endless void.

Abigail had adamantly refused to grant her permission to take summer classes. Her mother's grip on her life had continued to tighten over the last several months, until now it threatened to choke her. Kyle found herself thinking of running away. The fact that she had no money would not have stopped her, though her mother kept her almost penniless. Abigail measured out just enough to pay for meals at school, refusing to let Kyle take a job, even locking up her jewelry unless she was wearing it. But money was not the problem. Kyle knew she could borrow enough from Maggie for a bus ticket. What kept her back was school. She loved her classes, loved the thrill of learning. She was determined to hold out and earn her degree.

But it was not just the emptiness of a summer without school that so worried Kyle. At the beginning of May, old Mr. Crawley had passed on. Ever since the old man's funeral, Abigail had paced the house like a hungry tiger. Her attitude toward Kyle had sharpened. Kyle could feel something was being planned. Something she knew she would hate.

And Randolf Crawley had been appearing more and more frequently.

The last week of May, Maggie called Kyle in from her early morning time in the garden. When she stepped through the door, Maggie handed her the phone with a curious look. Kyle accepted the receiver and said, "Hello?"

"I'm sorry to be calling you so early," a familiar voice said.

"Kenneth?" She accepted the cup of coffee from Maggie's outstretched hand with a smile. "I thought you weren't supposed to be in contact."

"I'm not supposed to, but I was hoping to catch you before—" he paused, then continued—"before the rest of your house woke up. I haven't seen you around here recently, and we need to talk."

"Mother has ordered me not to come to the office." She made no attempt to keep Maggie and Bertrand from hearing. They already knew all about it. "I don't have school as an excuse for getting out anymore."

There was a long pause, then, "I don't want to get you in trouble, Kyle, but we really do need to talk."

The quiet urgency to Kenneth's tone stilled further questions. "Just a minute." She held the receiver to her shoulder and asked Bertrand, "Can you run me downtown?"

She did not need to finish with *before Mother wakes up*. Bertrand glanced at the wall clock and decided, "We'll need to leave immediately, Miss Kyle."

She raised the phone and said, "I'll come right now."

"Good." Relief rang loud over the line. "I hated the idea of your hearing this from someone else."

"Hearing what?"

"I'll tell you when you get here."

Kyle had Bertrand drop her off a block from the insurance

company. She did not want anyone seeing him and bringing trouble down on his sweet, graying head. The light changed, and Kyle allowed the crowd to almost carry her across the street. The capital city had changed so much in the past few years. Every time she came into Washington, D.C., there seemed to be another huge building going up somewhere near her father's. When she was a child, she had often thought Rothmore Insurance was the biggest building in the whole world. Now it wasn't even the largest on their block.

"Kyle, good, come in." As soon as she appeared in the doorway, Kenneth Adams was up and out of his chair and coming around to usher her into the room. "How have you been?" he asked as he closed the door behind her.

"All right," she said as she sat down. "But I wish I could come down and work."

The words brought a glint of anger to Kenneth's eyes. The muscles in his jaw bunched up tightly. "I asked you here today because I feel you need to know what is going on."

She took a tight grip on her purse to give her hands something to do and gave a little nod.

Kenneth hesitated a moment longer, then said, "Your mother is pushing to have Randolf Crawley named head trustee over your estate."

She felt her whole body clench at the news. "Can they do that?"

"Probably. Old Mr. Crawley apparently left no instructions. I suppose he thought he had more time to take care of those matters." Kenneth sighed. "And your mother's voice carries a lot of weight. After all, she is your sole guardian."

She searched his face. "But you'll still be around, won't you?"

The internal struggle showed on his features. "I have debated for weeks over what I should tell you, Kyle. But to remain silent at this point, I feel, would be terrible. So I have decided to ignore your mother's instructions and the orders of my own chairman."

She could feel a chill grip her heart. "Tell me."

"If Randolf is appointed, or perhaps I should say when," Kenneth said slowly, "he will most likely seek to have me dismissed."

She stared at him. "What?"

"Legally, you have just over a year left before you come into your inheritance," Kenneth persisted grimly. "But I am afraid that if they do manage to have me discharged, they may seek to extend that period. Or change the particulars. Theoretically, anything could happen."

"Can they do that?" she asked again.

"They *shouldn't* do it," he responded. "But they might try. I have no evidence to indicate that it would happen, but I'm afraid—"

"Daddy went to all this trouble for a reason," she said, tension raising her voice a notch. "To change it would be *wrong*. Can you stop them?"

"If you are very sure this is what you want," he said with a slow nod. "But it will mean defying your mother."

The chill crept through her body. Kyle forced herself to rise to her feet. "If what you say is true, then I have to try and stop it. But I need to be sure." Though she dreaded the prospect of confrontation, she declared quietly, "I'll talk to her today."

"Yes." Kenneth rose with her. "Do you want me to come with you?"

She shook her head, wishing he could come, wishing she could rely on his strength, but knowing she needed to do this alone. She was almost at the door when she stopped. "I don't have any money. Can you lend me cab fare, please? I—"

"What?" The question seemed to shock him.

"Mother says there's no use indulging me from her monthly allowance," Kyle said, too burdened by what she had just heard to worry about revealing such news. "She says I'll only just give it away."

"Kyle, don't you know the trust pays you a monthly income?"

It was her turn to be shocked.

"Last month you received—wait, I have the exact figures right here." He leaned over his desk, ran a finger down a list of numbers. "Yes, last month your dividends totaled thirty-four thousand, seven hundred dollars. A check was deposited in your account, just like always."

Kyle managed a weak, "What account?"

He stared at her a moment longer, emotions running across his features. Then he sighed, shook his head, and reached for his wallet. "Here," he said. "I've got, let's see, a hundred and twenty dollars." He handed her all but one of the bills. "Will that do?"

She watched herself reach out and accept more money than she had held at one time in her life. "But this is yours."

"Please take it. We'll work out the money side later."

"Thank you." She seemed to move in a fog of confusion. So much was hitting her all at once. But when her hand touched the doorknob, the world flashed into focus with a startling thought. Again she turned back, this time to ask, "What—why are you helping me, Kenneth?"

The question did not seem to surprise him at all. He replied quietly, "Because of your father. It's what he wanted. . . ." His gaze deepened, until Kyle felt as though she could see into his very soul. "I hope you understand," he said quietly, "I have not done any of this for my own personal gain."

She nodded slowly. It amazed her, how even in all of this confusion, there could be such a moment of clarity. "I trust you," she said softly.

But when the taxi dropped her off at the entrance to her drive, Kyle saw a cream-colored Cadillac convertible in front of her house. The car belonged to Randolf Crawley. Kyle knew she could not face the two of them, not together, not with this. She skirted the house, walked through the gardens, and followed the sound of balls striking rackets. Her steps led her down to the communal tennis courts. The courts were tree-lined and fronted by a slate-tiled veranda. Kyle loved the game, but she still felt out of place and uncomfortable with the players from wealthy families who used these courts.

Emily was playing singles with a man Kyle had met at one of her mother's little soirees. As Kyle approached, Emily left the court and walked over. She flashed Kyle a sardonic smile. "Well, the little princess has decided to join the lowly masses."

"You're the princess," Kyle countered feebly. Emily did look regal. She even had the ability to perspire prettily.

The blond girl patted her face with a towel. "Has your mother found you?"

"I didn't know she was looking for me."

"She's sent the penguin in a tuxedo over twice looking for you." That brought a titter from the lounging girls. "Whatever is his name?"

"Bertrand Ames," Kyle replied and felt ice congeal in her middle.

"Why, Kyle dear. You would think you actually were a friend of the *butler*. I mean, excuse me, but is he not simply one of your help?"

Kyle turned and walked away, certain that something had ended. She crossed the garden toward the waiting figure of Bertrand, thinking, *They are like actors on a stage. They never show what is real, what is important. Not to each other, and not to themselves.* Never again would she put up with their petty, cutting ways.

"Ah, Miss Kyle, Mrs. Rothmore wishes to have a word with you." Bertrand pointed at the veranda where her mother was seated. "I asked down by the club courts, but—"

"Thank you, Bertie." She stopped there beside him and placed a hand on his arm. She didn't care who saw. She stared into his eyes, willing herself to show enough affection to wipe away all the slights and insults he had borne on her account. "You are a dear, dear friend."

"Miss Kyle." He faltered. "Perhaps I should serve tea."

"That would be fine," she said. "And thank you. For everything."

Her mother was seated alone on the veranda, the metal chair turned to face out over the formal gardens. Abigail was dressed in a blue cashmere day suit, with a cream Shantung silk blouse and a single strand of pearls. Kyle noted her mother's customary look of faint disapproval, and something else. As Kyle seated herself across the table, she detected an unaccustomed nervousness. "Where is Randolf?" she asked. "I thought I saw his car . . ."

"He just left. Some emergency at the office." She focused beyond Kyle. "You may bring in the tea service and set it here, Bertrand."

"Very good, madam."

"Kyle, be good enough to serve us."

Kyle did as she was told, carefully handling the silver pot without spilling a drop. Abigail accepted her cup with a hand that seemed as fragile and transparent as the china. Her spoon made a musical tinkling sound as she stirred. "I never thought you would ever manage to properly learn the art of pouring a cup of tea."

Kyle kept her face utterly impassive. She stilled her hands from betraying any impatience by clasping them in her lap.

"Aren't you joining me?" Abigail asked.

"No thank you, Mother. There was something you wanted to talk with me about?"

Abigail shot her daughter a glance. "Obligations, young lady. A word you have had as much trouble with as you did the tea service."

Kyle's calm features and lack of response only seemed to irritate her mother further. "Obligations," Abigail repeated sharply. "They come with the territory, the name, the house.

You are not a free spirit, young lady. You have responsibilities to uphold."

The words were so familiar that Kyle did not even bother to respond.

"Life is full of unexpected change. And responsibility. And the fact is, you shall never be able to live up to your responsibilities alone. You need someone to take care of them for you."

"Mother," Kyle said quietly, gathering herself for what she had planned to say. "What do you and Randolf plan to do about the trust?"

Her mother sat in silence, staring at her. There was no change to her features that Kyle could see. But inwardly Kyle felt as though a choice had been made, a change begun.

"So," Abigail said finally. "Randolf was correct."

"I want to know," Kyle said quietly.

"Yes, I see that you do." Her mother's normal poise seemed exaggerated into a new stiffness. "Kyle, I want you to brace yourself for some very bad news."

She nodded. Apparently Kenneth's suspicions were right. It was hard to say why she was not surprised.

Abigail's features were abnormally stony. "My dear, I am afraid I must inform you that you were adopted."

"I do not want you to change Daddy's . . ." Kyle's voice sank to nothing as her mother's words hit home. "What?"

"Yes. I did not want ever to tell you, but circumstances are such that now the truth has to come out." The words were evenly spaced and spoken with a metallic clip, as though Abigail was reading off an unseen script. "The welfare of your heritage, and that of our family, demands that you know."

Kyle gripped the chair's arms to stop herself from trembling. "What . . . what do you mean?" She could not control the quaver in her voice.

"I could not have children. Your father wanted a daughter. He—that is, we chose you." She glanced over, then away. "But never mind that now. The reason I am telling you is that your inheritance has been brought into question. There are apparently some discrepancies with the adoption documents. Fortunately, Randolf has unearthed them in time. He has offered to take care of everything and make sure that none of this ever comes to light."

Kyle would have risen to her feet, but she could not force her body to move. Tiny tremors shot through her muscles, little electric shocks in time to the ones bombarding her mind.

"Randolf is offering to become your guardian, Kyle. To take care of all your needs. Both in regard to your inheritance and your future. *Our* future. The future and welfare of Rothmore Insurance."

Feebly Kyle raised a hand, silently begging her mother to stop.

"In return," Abigail pressed on doggedly, "you will marry Randolf. He is a most capable young man, quite handsome, an enviable catch. Really, Kyle, I don't see why we should be having this discussion at all. He has courted you quite properly for years. And even though these discrepancies could mean that you would be totally disinherited if brought to a court of law, he still wishes to go through with marriage. You should be grateful."

At Kyle's look of sheer panic, Abigail continued. "You are so exasperating, I am honestly at the end of my rope." She took a deep breath. "You shall marry him, and that is that. Your twentieth birthday is coming up in a month's time. It will make a perfect occasion to announce your betrothal. Then you shall have a year to complete your schooling. On your twenty-first birthday we shall organize a gala event. You shall be wed on the day you receive your inheritance."

Kyle had to leave. She *had* to. Her only hope was to get up and walk away from this terrifying encounter. She focused all her attention on moving her legs, bringing her feet up and under her, readying herself for the effort of trying to stand.

Abigail's hands moved nervously about, touching her hair, her pearls, twisting her gold bracelet. "It's *your* fault it has come to this, I hope you realize. If you had only shown the good sense to realize marrying Randolf was the only *proper* course, that the family *demands* you do this, it would *never* have been necessary to speak of it. But no, you have dillied and dallied, and now I've reached the end of my tether. The *absolute* end, Kyle. I hope you realize what you've put me through . . . Kyle? *Kyle!* Where are you going? Don't you *dare* walk away from me! I'm not through, do you hear me? Come back . . . "

Without knowing where she was going, Kyle walked down the back stairs and away from the veranda. Her feet seemed to know where she needed to go, for her mind could not move beyond the single word. *Adopted.* She had not been born into the Rothmore family, did not belong to Lawrence Rothmore. Not really. Had never been his true daughter. The thought hit her with such solid impact that it left her weak and drained.

Her entire being felt uprooted, torn away from everything she had ever known. She wandered aimlessly down the graveled walk lining the back garden, her frantic thoughts tumbling about in utter confusion.

Suddenly she recalled a storm that had struck many years earlier. She had been only seven or eight. That night the wind had been so fierce that the rain had struck her window with driving fury, fighting to break in. Lightning had blasted from every side, flickering so constantly that everything in her room had come alive and danced with the blinding light. Kyle had been absolutely terrified. She had hidden, whimpering, under her covers until her father had come and taken her in his strong arms, quieting her fears with love and calm words.

The next morning, they had walked outside to a world transformed. The garden, normally so neat and precise, was a jumble of trash and debris. Limbs had fallen from trees, and almost every bush had lost its flowers. Kyle had walked along, her hand tucked safely in her father's, and listened as he had consoled Jim. The gardener had been numbed by the destruction. Together they had walked over to where one of the grand old elms had been uprooted. The tree, almost as tall as the house, had lain there on its side, the bundle of roots sticking up in soil-strewn defeat. Kyle had stared up at the great twisted wreckage for a long time. She had felt as though only her father's strength had protected her from the storm.

But now, when this new storm raged and tossed her about, her father was no longer there. She did not have a father. Had never really had one. Why had he deceived her—the one person she had felt she could trust? Why? Kyle shivered with the loneliness and the fear.

Adopted.

CHAPTER SIXTEEN

THE YEARS HAD NOT TREATED Dr. Howard Austin very well. He did not need a mirror to realize this. Reaching up to his head meant encountering more bald patches than hair. A glance downward meant he was confronted with an expanding paunch. Whenever he caught sight of his reflection, he could not help but see the dark half-moon pouches below his eyes.

I care too much. The thought came unbidden to his mind. But the words had been repeated so often over the years that they no longer held the power to ease his burden. Especially today.

As Joel sat on the edge of the examining table and rebuttoned his shirt, Howard fiddled with the papers in his hand. "I've known you since before you were born," the doctor said, surprising them both.

Joel grinned. "You delivered me. I remember Mom talking about that once."

"That's right." Suddenly tears pressed against the back of Howard's eyes. It was not a giving in to today's sorrow. Rather he felt as though all the loads he carried, all the pains and discomforts and illnesses he had seen, all suddenly crowded up in a mighty wave, hitting him when he least expected. He swallowed hard. "That's right, Joel," he said again. "I was there from the beginning."

"You may as well go ahead and say it," Joel said quietly. And though the voice was only that of a young man, the calmness

Joel showed seemed to Howard Austin to be coming from beyond time. "I can see on your face that the news is not good,"
Joel probed.

A young man cut down in his prime. Howard wondered if perhaps he should put off telling him until Joel's parents could be
summoned. But the young man sat there, his peace and inner
strength so evident that Howard found a calm for his own troubled mind.

Which gave him the strength to say, "The results of your
tests have come back. And this examination verifies the diagnosis."

Joel searched his face. "Not good," he repeated.

"No." The word was a long sigh, drawing all the breath, all
the resistance from his body. Telling the boy was a defeat, both
for Howard and the body of medicine as a whole. "You have a
degenerative heart condition."

Joel gave a slow nod, his eyes suddenly fastened on nothing.
"I knew it had to be something," he said quietly. "I've been feeling so tired lately. And my chest hurts a lot. It's been worse the
last six months."

"*Last six months?* You've had this a long time?"

Joel nodded. "I guess so."

"Why didn't your folks bring you in earlier?"

"I never said anything about it." Joel looked down. "I didn't
know anything was wrong—really. It wasn't until the pain and
weakness got bad that I thought . . ."

The silence hung between them. At last Joel spoke again.
"Would it have made any difference if I'd come earlier?"

"In all honesty, probably not. You have degenerative heart
disease, and your condition is inoperable," he replied. Howard
was flying directly into the face of his normal habit, which was
to give very little information to the patient at all. But this
strength about Joel—a strength that transcended the problems
of his body—was something Howard had recognized whenever
they were brought together. Even here, even now. "I've seen
this before, and I have to tell you that your condition will only
grow worse."

Fathomless eyes looked across the chasm that now separated them, and Joel asked, "How long do I have?"

Why was he doing this? Why had he even started talking about it at all? Despite his desire to cover over with platitudes, Howard continued with his chosen course. "Hard to say, son. Six months, a year, two at the outside."

As though he understood the struggle inside the doctor, Joel said quietly, "It's okay, Doc."

The words were so strange, coming from a young man who had just heard of his own approaching death, Howard felt himself jerk back a step. "What?"

"I really appreciate you being straight with me. It'll give me time to do some things. Prepare as best I can."

The words left Howard feeling indignant. "Doggone it, Joel, I'm the one who's supposed to be consoling *you*."

Joel's grin came and went very quickly. "Mom will be the one who'll need consoling. We'll need to tell her together. And Dad."

"Your father doesn't feel much of anything." The words were out before he could think, and he wished he could take them back.

Slowly Joel shook his head. "I used to think the same thing, but I've decided it's not true. He feels too much. That's his problem. He's never been able to get over his sorrows. He cares too much about things."

Another wave of sadness swept over the doctor. "Here you are, just graduating from high school next week. All your friends will be heading off to college."

"Not so many friends," Joel said without remorse. "I got to be known as Simon Miller's buddy. Most of the kids couldn't understand him. They felt really uncomfortable about his clothes and his attitudes. Even since the Millers left, the other kids still see me as an oddball. I don't really mind. It has helped me to rely more on the Lord."

Howard found himself shocked by the easy manner with which Joel talked about God, as though He was a close personal friend. Howard stared at this young man, seeing him with new eyes. "You've grown, son. So much it makes me feel older than I already am."

"It's the Lord's doing, not mine," Joel said. "I feel like I never really lived before coming to know Him."

In the silence that followed, a shadow of grief passed over Joel's young features. "I've been saving my paper-route money for college," he said quietly. "Plus I want to go see the Millers. It's going to be hard to tell them."

Howard found himself unable to respond. There were so many levels to this young man, such a sense of timeless maturity. He was less than half Howard's age, yet already he had the strength to accept as well as the strength to honestly grieve.

"It doesn't seem fair," Joel said with a sigh. "Why should I be struck down now? Why do I have to suffer from a bad heart?"

Howard stood and watched as the young man sorted through his thoughts and knew Joel was coming to grips with his own death. And doing so with a strength that left the doctor feeling incompetent. All his life he had cared but had run away from caring. Why? Because he did not have the strength required for the responsibilities of caring.

"I hate bringing pain to my family," Joel mumbled. "I hate missing out on all the things I wanted to do. But life isn't fair, is it? That's what Pop's always saying, anyway."

For some reason, the moment held a reflective power for Howard Austin. He observed the young man seated on his examining table, but in truth he was paying more attention to his own mind and heart. He had hidden behind a hopeless yearning for another man's wife, and never given as much as he should to anyone else. Not to his wife, not to his patients, not even to himself. Why? Howard Austin did not need to search for the answer. It rested there directly in front of him, as clearly as though the words were being spoken straight to his very soul. He had run away from caring because he had always cared from an empty heart.

Joel seemed to gather himself. He straightened, and the hollow lines of his face filled with renewed calm. Howard stood there and watched it happen. "As long as I'm prepared to go,"

Joel went on determinedly, "death is nothing to be feared. The Lord has shown me that. I think in a way I've known what you were going to tell me, and He has helped to make me ready."

For the first time in his life, Howard had the feeling that what Joel spoke of was something genuine. In the past he had always used his trained mind to dismiss what could not be seen. But here in the calm strength of this young man, in the shining eyes and wisdom beyond his years, Howard found himself accepting the reality he had always refused to consider before.

Howard felt the young man's gaze rest on him and struggled to find words to fit the moment. "I'm so sorry, Joel. If there's anything at all I can do . . ."

The words drew Joel outward, in a way that spanned the distance caused by Howard's news. "There *is* one thing, Doc."

"What's that?"

"Pray for me." A veil lifted from Joel's eyes. "Pray I'll be strong enough to see this through to the end. And pray that I'll do what the Lord wants with what I've got left."

There was a crumbling inside, a silent acceptance of Howard's own defeat. "All those wasted years," he murmured, not even aware he had spoken.

"Nothing is wasted," Joel replied quietly. "Not if in the end it brings you to your knees."

"You don't know," Howard said, no longer speaking to the boy. He could not be saying these things to someone so young, especially not Martha's son. *Martha*. Howard released a long, aching sigh. The yearning was with him still, for what might have been.

"No," Joel agreed quietly. "But God does."

Howard raised his head. The light in Joel's eyes was as clear as summer sun, a breathless promise of all that his own life had lacked. Mutely he nodded his head. Once. And in the act, he felt another unseen barrier lower, and he found himself looking into the void at the center of his being, the one he had always refused to see, the endless, aching hunger that had consumed him and left him bereft.

"I wish I could pray with you, son. I really wish I could.

But, well, life—your God, if you will—hasn't dealt too kindly with me. I'm afraid there is nothing left inside that can . . . can reach out in prayer . . . even for you."

There in the whitewashed doctor's office, with its smells of disinfectant and iodine, Joel spoke quietly, yet sincerely. "Then *I'll* pray for *you*, Dr. Austin. Every day that I have left."

Martha Grimes paused in the front room and examined herself in the mirror hanging above the scarred table. It was a nice face with pleasing features and clear eyes. Yet there was something missing. Maybe it was the light she had seen for months in her son's face. It had been there even as Joel had sat with Howard Austin and delivered the news. Such a peace and light that even as she had cried over the coming loss of her boy, she had felt the serenity reach out with his hand and gently touch her, easing her sorrow.

But over the hours, the days, that followed, Martha had been tossed to and fro, one minute accepting, the next collapsing in uncontrollable sobs. It couldn't be happening. It couldn't. She would never be able to bear the loss of another child.

Harry did not—could not—help. He had curled his emotions into an even tighter ball. He came home only to eat and sleep. Martha did not know where he went, never dared to ask. Did he just walk the streets, or was he trying to dull his sorrows at the local bar like many of his army buddies? She never smelled liquor on him when he did finally come in. But that didn't prove anything.

In between her bursts of tears and desperation she watched Joel. *He must feel it—this dreadful horror of what the future holds, but he looks so calm. So settled. How can he be this way?* she asked herself over and over. *He has so much to live for. How can he bear the thought of dying?* Martha had no answer.

She lifted her eyes again to the mirror. *What is missing inside* me? she wondered, running her fingertips down her cheek. Whatever it was, she had learned to live without it for so long that she had not given it thought. But now it was here before her. All she had to do was close her eyes to again see the light shining from Joel's face. It seemed as though the light grew stronger with each day. He did not need to say anything. Anyone who looked at him with honest eyes had to see the growing strength from inside even as his body gradually weakened.

Martha glanced down the hall to where her husband sat at the kitchen table. She found herself wondering if he could see the changes in Joel as well. She walked down the hallway, entered the kitchen, and seated herself across from her husband. Martha examined Harry. There was a small scar on his forehead, one he had brought back from the war. The thin line had been joined by a dozen others and now had deepened until she could no longer tell which one was the actual scar. The skin of his face looked gray, as though the silent exertion of keeping so much inside had aged him beyond his years.

She seemed to see him for the first time, as though all the years and all the memories and all the sorrows had been washed away. It only lasted a moment, yet it was long enough for her to observe him with crystal clarity. This was a gift from beyond herself, of that she had no doubt, both the vision and the compassion that filled her heart. He had known such a hard life. Working every day at a job that was as close as he could ever come to his dream. Bringing himself back home, staying here with her, doing the best job he could. It was not all that good, no, but he had tried.

She found herself reaching across the table, taking his hand. The move was so alien that Harry jerked upright and stared down at her hand.

"I think Joel has found something that can help us," Martha quietly told him.

He looked over at her. Instead of the barrier of old disappointments and bitterness, there was only confusion. "You mean, this religion thing?"

She nodded. "I feel as though, well . . ." Martha stopped

and gathered herself, as though just saying the words was enough to push them both over the edge. New beginnings loomed before her, strange pulses ran through her veins. It took a long moment before she realized what she felt was hope.

She took a breath and went on. "I think maybe we could start over, you and I. If we ask God to help us."

There was no cutting response. None of the acrid mockery that normally greeted anything she said. Instead, his gaze dropped back to her hand resting upon his own. He murmured, "I don't know what to do."

"Maybe—" she whispered, her breath catching in her throat, "maybe you could ask Joel to teach us how to pray."

To her surprise, tears formed in Harry's eyes and dropped unheeded onto her hand. He said nothing, just turned his palm upward and enclosed her fingers with his own.

"It seems too much," he said when he was able to speak. "First our baby girl—now this."

For a moment Martha's eyes showed her surprise. Then they too filled with tears.

"You miss her, too?" she asked quietly.

His tears increased. He nodded.

"I never knew. I mean— you never talked about her. I thought I was the only one . . ."

"I visit that upstairs room, too, when no one is around."

Martha was weeping openly now. "I didn't think . . . I mean, you never said—"

"I couldn't. Not without . . . blaming you. You shouldn't have done it, Martha. Shouldn't have given away our little girl. There would have been a way. Some way. My mother . . ."

"I couldn't ask her, Harry. I barely knew her. I couldn't ask. I felt so alone—and scared. All I could think about was that I'd lost you and I couldn't bear to . . . I didn't even want to live."

He reached a hand to her cheek. "You cared that much?"

"Oh, Harry, I thought I'd die with the pain of it. I wished that I'd been in that battlefield. That I'd died, too."

"But when I did come home you were so distant." There was puzzlement in his voice.

"I was numb by then. Dead inside. And you were so changed. I felt I didn't even know you anymore."

"Guess I was numb, too." Ancient pain creased his features. "I'd had a tough time out there in the field hospital. It was really bad, Martha. A lot of pain. Took almost three months before I remembered my own name."

"It should have been different, Harry. We should have clung to each other. Through our sorrow. We could have helped . . ."

He brushed at her tears with a clumsy hand. "This time we will, Martha."

"I'm still hoping, praying that Doc is wrong. That Joel will be all right. He's such a good boy. Surely God . . . Doctors have been wrong before, you know."

Harry shook his head. "I'd like to hang on to that, too, but those x-rays look bad. Doc showed them to me. You don't have to be a doctor to know. He says it's a wonder that we've kept Joel this long. That he could do his paper route and all. He's been hurting for some time, Martha. He must have known."

"Why didn't he tell us?"

Harry cleared his throat and pushed back from the table. He ran a shaking hand through his thinning hair. "Isn't that we've been easy to talk to, Martha. We've both shut ourselves away."

"We need to pray," repeated Martha with a strength of conviction in her words.

Harry walked out to the back porch and seated himself in his customary chair. The afternoon shimmered with the year's first heat wave. Suddenly Harry was consumed by a memory of another time, another place of heat and dust and light. And noise.

He was back in the desert, preparing himself for the first big push. Beside him was a young man who spent his last hours before the battle in prayer. There had been such a sense of peace about him, such a sense of light drawing down and near. Harry had intended to speak with him about it, about the way he spent his time reading the Bible, even when the coarse humor and arguments echoed about him.

But when the young man had been killed in the skirmish, Harry had shrugged it off, thinking that the man's faith had not helped him at all.

Harry shook his head to clear it, and once again he was surrounded by birdsong and his own back garden. But the lingering light from the young man's eyes remained with him, joining with the memory of how his son had been over the past months. The light from both pairs of eyes now touched his heart like gentle fingers prying open the long-closed recesses inside him. Then the light seemed to grow until it surrounded him on all sides, flooding into his mind and heart. And Harry knew that what his wife had said was true. That if he wished, he could start anew. He could be healed within. He could begin again. It was not too late. Not even for him.

Had anyone been watching all they would have seen was a single nod. He would speak with his son.

CHAPTER SEVENTEEN

AS SOON AS THE FAMILIAR VOICE answered on the other end of the line, Kyle felt a tremendous flood of relief. "Kenneth, it's me."

"Kyle." The warmth with which he said her name made her think of her father. "Where are you?"

"At the Economy Inn out by the airport."

"Why on earth did you go there?"

She looked around the shabby room, then waited for an aircraft to pass overhead before replying. "I needed to have some time to think. I had your hundred dollars less the taxi fare, so I came here. I've even got money left over for meals."

"This is crazy," he muttered. "Look, stay right there, and I'll come pick you up."

"Thank you." She did not want to go home, but the money was running out. Calling Maggie and Bertrand meant making them risk their jobs, which she knew they would do for her, but still she did not want to chance it. "Thank you so much."

It was more than relief she felt when she saw him enter the hotel lobby. She stood and watched him cross the room. Unlike Randolf, he was not particularly handsome. Yet an honesty shone from his face, a strong vitality. His direct gaze seemed to reach straight to her heart. "I'm sorry to have dragged you into this."

"Kyle," he said, taking her hands in both of his. "There is nothing I would rather be doing. Nothing at all."

Coming as they did after five lonely days of soul-searching and sorrow, the words were met with a burning behind her eyes. She could not speak around the lump in her throat.

Kenneth seemed to understand. He released one of her hands to pick up her small case, then led her toward the doors. "Come on, let's get out of here."

On the way back across the river, he told her, "I've reserved you a suite at the Mayflower."

She stared at him in alarm. "I can't afford that."

"Yes you can." He stopped at the light by the Fourteenth Street Bridge and turned to smile at her. "You might as well start getting used to it."

"The money is not mine," she protested. "It's Daddy's."

She knew that Kenneth had no idea what the reclaiming of her father's relationship meant to Kyle. She had spent days struggling to sort out who her father really was. Who *she* was. Finally she had come to accept the truth that Lawrence had *chosen* her. Had given her his name and his love. She really did belong to him. Perhaps, she had ventured to think that very morning, perhaps they were bound by even stronger ties than if she had been his blood child. The knowledge had brought tremendous relief and freedom. Adopted? Yes. But she was still her father's daughter.

"It's Daddy's money," she repeated.

"And he left it to you. Just as he had every right to do."

"Kenneth, did you know I was adopted?" It was the first time she had said the word aloud since hearing it from Abigail, and she was almost afraid to see the shock in Kenneth's eyes. But when she looked into his face, she realized before he spoke that he already knew.

"Randolf told me the morning after you disappeared. Probably his attempt to scare me off. But it will take more than that." He handed her a bulky envelope. "Here."

"What is it?"

"As trustee to your estate, I've arranged a small withdrawal from your account. There's a paper in there you need to sign."

She opened the envelope and gasped at the bills. "Small?"

"It's better not to draw attention too often to your account, not until everything is cleared up. Your mother . . ."

When he did not finish the sentence, Kyle said, "She's worried."

"No," he replied slowly. "Abigail left 'worried' behind right after you disappeared. She's crossed the great divide and entered the land of 'frantic.' "

She found it nice to have a reason to smile. It was the first time she had done so in what felt like weeks.

"She's even spoken with me—well, shouted really. She accused me of kidnapping you."

"I've made more trouble for you," she said. "I'm so sorry."

"Abigail has made no secret of how she feels about me." Kenneth turned onto Massachusetts Avenue and asked, "Where would you like to go?"

"To the office, please," she said, steeling herself for what had to come.

He glanced at her. "Are you sure?"

She nodded. "And please cancel the reservation at the Mayflower. That's my mother's kind of place. I want to find something nice, simple, and within walking distance of Rothmore Insurance."

He studied her more closely. "You're not going back home, then."

"When Mother stops fighting against what Daddy wanted us to do," Kyle replied, forcing herself to keep her voice steady, "then I will go back home."

Kenneth did not say anything further until they had stopped in front of the Rothmore building. Once there, however, neither had much desire to leave the car's safety. It was Kyle who finally spoke. "I don't know what I would do without you, Kenneth. You are a true friend."

He lowered his head and stared at where his hands gripped the wheel. It took a long moment before he was able to reply, "I would like to be more than that."

"I know," Kyle said, and found herself not at all surprised by his admission—or her own. It had been there between them for a long while, never said but there just the same.

Suddenly she was very uncertain. Nothing in her past had prepared her for the affection that rose within her. It was so real, so *genuine*. She did not know how to act, what to do or say.

But Kenneth kept his head lowered and did not see the nervous uncertainty that gripped her. He said quietly, "Ever since the first time I walked into your house, and you came over to welcome me, I have been head over heels in love. You were so kind. You tried to hide it and be just like the others, aloof and sophisticated. But I could see it in your eyes and hear it in your voice. You were different than the rest of them. You didn't really fit there."

"No," Kyle agreed softly. "I never belonged."

He looked up then, instantly contrite. "I'm sorry. That's not at all what I meant."

"I know." The need to reassure him gave her the strength to reach over and take his hand. She felt a little thrill run through her as he released the wheel to enfold her fingers. "It's the truth. I've always known I never fit in."

"Perhaps," Kenneth told her, "that is why your father loved you as he did."

It was the perfect thing to say. She pressed his hand tightly, feeling that she could tell him anything, ask him whatever was on her mind. "Why have we waited so long to talk like this?"

"Your mother has been against me from the first day we met," Kenneth said. "It was frightening to see how strong her reaction was."

"I know."

He went on, "And I wanted to be sure you understood that what you possessed, or what your name was, had nothing to do with how I felt."

My name, she reflected, and felt the hollow sorrow bloom again within her chest as it had done over and over those past few days. Her father's love was not enough to erase the questions from her mind. *My name. What is my name? Who am I really?*

But Kenneth was not finished. "There was something else." Kenneth regarded her a moment longer before saying, "At times like this, I have to keep in mind what is most vital in my life."

"You mean, your religion?"

"My faith, yes." He searched her face, as though looking for something, yearning to find it. "It is something which I absolutely must share with, well . . ."

For once, the words did not unsettle her. In accepting him, she was coming to accept what made him the man he was. "I would like it very much," she said quietly, "if you would teach me."

His face seemed to crumple in relief and joy. "Thank you. From the bottom of my heart, thank you."

"Kyle!" As soon as she stepped from the elevators onto the executive floor, Randolf Crawley hurried down the hall toward her. "Thank goodness you're all right!"

"Hello, Randolf." She squared her shoulders, and with only a brief backward glance to where Kenneth stood, she allowed Randolf to lead her toward his office. She needed to get this over with, and she needed to do it in private.

"Miss Kyle!" Mrs. Parker sprang to her feet, relief written over her features. "We've been so worried."

"Call Abigail," Randolf barked, not slowing down.

"No." Kyle shook off his hand so abruptly that he continued on another step before coming to a halt. She said to Mrs. Parker, "I will call her myself in a few minutes."

Mrs. Parker looked from one face to the other, then made her decision. "Very well, Miss Kyle."

"Thank you," she said, then passed before an astonished Randolf and entered her father's old office. She seated herself across from the desk and felt the familiar pang as she stared at its massive polished surface.

Cautiously Randolf circled the desk and took his place. Clearly her actions and attitude were not what he had expected.

"Has Adams had anything to do with your disappearance? Because I am seriously thinking—"

"Kenneth has done nothing but what I asked him to do, which was to bring me here," Kyle said sharply. "And I consider him to be not only a dear friend, but a highly valued associate. Just as my father did."

"Of course, of course," he agreed warily. "It is only that we have been so concerned for your welfare."

"I am fine. I merely had some things to think over."

"Yes, your mother informed me of your discussion." His handsome features creased into an expression of sorrow. "It is so unfortunate that you were ever forced to find these things out. However, I want you to know that I have everything under—"

"I want to find my parents," Kyle stated flatly.

"Your . . .?"

"My birth parents."

"My dear Kyle, that doesn't matter. Whoever they might have been makes no difference to you now." He presented her with one of his professional smiles. "Or to us."

"It matters to me. Very much."

The pronouncement drew him up sharp. "Why? You are doing fine as you are."

"No, I'm not. I'm all alone in the world."

"Of course you're not." His refined manner made the words sound as though he listened to them first in his mind before saying them aloud. "Why, your mother and I are very much here with you, you know that."

"I want to know, Randolf."

The words came more slowly. "Whatever the reason behind their giving you up for adoption, you can be certain it wasn't a happy one. Don't you think such sadness should be left alone?"

"No, not at this point in my life—or theirs."

"You disappear without a word for five days, then return and start making these astonishing demands." He turned quite patronizing. "Really, Kyle. Your mother has always said you were a trial, unwilling to listen to a thing she said."

"Which means," Kyle said, "you are not going to help me."

He spread his arms. "There is actually very little I can do. Your adoption papers are sealed."

"What does that mean?"

"Your parents gave you over to the state. Your records are sealed by law." He talked with pedantic superiority. "They cannot be opened."

She struggled to keep her voice calm. "Mother told me you knew enough to take care of some 'unsettled' matter. Which means you also know enough to give me something to start on."

Her persistence finally rattled his composure. "Really, Kyle. I have heard about enough of this. Let it go. They have their life, whoever they are. You have yours."

She rose to her feet. "I decided I had to give you one last chance, Randolf. This was it."

He rose with her. "What on earth are you talking about now?"

Kyle turned toward the door. "This conversation is over."

She walked into Kenneth's office, as tired as she had ever been in her entire life. She shut the door and said in a voice ragged with weariness, "I've just gotten off the phone with Mother. She said basically the same thing as Randolf. They won't help."

She crossed to the window behind his desk. "I've known people like them all my life," Kyle began. "They're powerful and they have money and they have all the wonderful things of life. They are focused on power, and they are ready to leap at whatever opportunity comes their way. They're in control."

She glanced back at the closed door and went on, "But they're lacking something. They seem empty inside. All that hardness, all that brilliance and drive, is wrapped around . . . around an empty void. They would never understand that outside their fancy houses and their boardrooms is a wonderful world full of sunsets and trees and people. People with needs and cares and concerns." She looked back at him and smiled ruefully. "Sorry for the lecture."

"Not at all, Kyle." Kenneth's voice was as reassuring as his words. "You are talking about something very important. About that empty place inside everyone—rich, poor, greedy, generous. Any person who doesn't know God's love."

There was a sense of moving in harmony with him, of feeling a comfort and closeness she had not known since her father died. "I want to know that love," she said quietly. She looked at him, reveling in the quiet strength she found there.

"There is nothing I want more than to introduce you to Him," Kenneth said. "Is there anything else I can do for you, Kyle?"

She took a breath and replied, "Help me find my parents."

CHAPTER EIGHTEEN

BUT FINDING A PLACE TO START the search proved much harder than Kyle had imagined. Summer slipped into autumn, then winter had begun spreading its cold blanket over Washington, and still Kenneth could come up with no information as to who had given her up for adoption. Any tiny lead quickly turned into another disappointing dead end.

As the weeks changed to months, Kyle found it best to avoid even thinking about the lack of progress. Impatience too easily led to bitter frustration. Thankfully, there were many things to occupy her mind. An overwhelming amount of newness flooded into her life with each passing day. Learning to live one pace at a time was crucial to making it through this period of change.

The week after her confrontation with Randolf, Kyle had signed up for the final term of summer school and moved into a dormitory room. Arriving in the middle of summer had been good, for the dorm had been almost empty, thus granting her a way to experience this transition in gradual stages.

Since then, days were split between school and the company. She became increasingly comfortable around the work and the terms used in the insurance business. Yet her interest did not grow as she had hoped. When she lay awake in her little room at night and listened to the laughter and music ringing up and down the dorm's hallway, Kyle knew that she would make an adequate businesswoman. But the spark of enthusiasm, of interest, that had made her father so special in his field was missing. And try as she might, this was not something she could learn.

Throughout all this time, her mother and Randolf remained strangely quiet. Kenneth assured her that there had been no direct action taken against the trust. Kyle was not sure how she felt about their silence. Her emotions were so confused and tumultuous, she found it easier not to think about that at all.

Twice there had been attempts within the boardroom to have Kenneth Adams dismissed. The first time, Randolf had tried a frontal assault, accusing him of gross negligence in his duties. To Randolf's surprise, every other working executive had spoken up in Kenneth's defense. When Kenneth had told her about it the next day, his voice had been full of emotion and awe at the compliment paid him.

Then in November Randolf had tried a more indirect approach, proposing that the board take the cost-saving measure of eradicating Kenneth's entire department.

Kenneth called her that night to break the news. "Randolf was at his most persuasive, painting pictures of enormous profits to our stockholders. The vote was put off a month, pending a report from the accountants."

Kyle found herself as concerned about him as she was about the action. "You sound exhausted."

He did not deny it. "Things have not been very pleasant around here for me."

"But all this is going to work out, isn't it?" When he did not reply, Kyle pleaded, "Kenneth, tell me you're not leaving."

"I have been offered a directorship with another company," he replied slowly.

She fought down rising terror. "You'd leave me all alone?"

"Kyle, I never want to leave you. But . . ." He hesitated a long moment, then continued, "You've been so quiet, I haven't been sure how you feel."

It was true. She could not deny it. She had kept her distance from him, building walls to keep him at arm's length ever since their talk in the car.

"There's been so much happening," she replied, knowing it

was inadequate even as she said it. A girl she vaguely knew came down the hall and gave her a knowing little smile. Kyle grimaced in reply, then rested her forehead on the wall beside the phone. It was as much privacy as the dormitory's hall phone could offer. "I feel as if I'm just barely holding on as it is."

"I understand," his voice was sympathetic. "And I've tried to be patient. I really have. But, well, I feel as though I've spent most of my adult years waiting for you to decide."

Kyle opened her mouth, but the words were not there. In truth, she did not know how she felt. And she could not shake the honesty between them by pretending otherwise. "Kenneth, I . . ."

"I would still be there for you. But not inside Rothmore Insurance." He sighed. "There's something else. I'm pretty sure all this cost-saving hokum is merely a smoke screen. Randolf thinks if he can get rid of me, you will be more . . . well, amenable to his plans. He's very shrewd, make no mistake. He knows I'm concerned about all my staff losing their jobs. So he's bargaining. If I went to him and offered to leave, he'd probably be willing to drop the whole thing and leave the other employees in place."

She found herself so weak with pending loss that her knees threatened to give way. "What will you do?"

"I don't know," he breathed. "Pray. That's all I know to do."

"I . . . I've wanted to tell you." She had to take another breath to steady her voice. "I've been going to church with Maggie and Bertrand."

"Kyle, that's wonderful." Enthusiasm rang in his voice. "How was it?"

"Good, I think." A tear escaped to trickle down her cheek. He was so happy for her. He had done so much, given her such warmth and kindness and friendship and strength. Why could she not respond? "Please don't leave me, Kenneth. I need you."

There was a long silence. Then, "Do you?"

"Yes." But even this admission seemed wrenched from her. She had to change it. She could not leave it without further explanation. "The company does." It sounded lame even to her.

"I see." The tired flatness returned. "I have to travel to some of our other offices these next few days. I'll think things over and speak with you when I return."

Kyle replaced the receiver and staggered back to her room. From the open door of her neighbor's room came the tinny sound of a little phonograph. "Somewhere beyond the sea, my lover waits for me," the voices sang. Kyle felt as though the music was heckling her. She closed her door and sank down onto the floor.

Kenneth was going to leave. She could see it happening with absolute clarity. What reason had she given him to stay?

She covered her face with her hands and suddenly found herself recalling a conversation she'd had with Maggie after church the Sunday before. As they had left the vestibule, Maggie had busied herself with her Sunday gloves, then commented, "I notice you don't bow your head when the pastor invites us to join in prayer."

"I'm trying to be honest," Kyle had replied.

Maggie had stopped, waving Bertrand to continue on without them. "Honest? Or are you trying to hold on to your independence?"

The woman's quiet perception had rocked her. "I don't know what you mean."

"I think you do." Maggie chose her words carefully. "You have had to fight hard to reach a point where you could think and act for yourself. And I am proud of you. But this does not mean you can go through life by yourself. Not with any sense of real peace or real success. You think upon what I have said."

Kyle remained curled up on the floor of her little dorm room, her face hidden behind her hands. Gradually her breathing slowed, and the words seemed to form of their own accord. *Help me*, she said, and felt something inside flowing out from behind the self-made barriers, reaching out and into the unknown. *Please help me.*

She stopped. There was more to be said. She could feel the thoughts hovering about her mind and heart, waiting for her to open further and accept. But she could not. It was suddenly all too much. She sighed herself up from the floor, only to sprawl upon her bed and close her eyes to the world.

She was awakened the next morning by a knock on her door. "Kyle?" The voice outside her door sounded both sleepy and irritated. "There's a call for you. A Kenneth Adams, I think that was his name."

She raced down the hall, grabbed up the receiver from where it swung upside down, and stammered, "Hello?"

"Success!" Triumph rang in his voice. "At least, a little bit. The first step, and they say that's always the hardest."

Kyle focused upon the wall clock. It was a quarter past six. "Where are you?"

"The office. I've got to get some things done before I leave town. And lucky thing, too. There was a message on my desk from a contact in the state government. Do you have a pencil?"

"No, wait, I don't . . ." Kyle tried to force her fuzzy mind awake. She fumbled in her pockets, came up with a lipstick holder. "Okay, yes."

"Riverdale. That's a little town just over the Maryland border." He seemed a half-breath away from laughter. "The fellow had time for only a brief glimpse at the notes related to your case. They contained an enquiry made a year or so after your adoption. The man claimed to have been the doctor attending your birth. The notes were in pencil and so smudged my friend could not make out either the doctor's name or street. But the town was definitely Riverdale."

"Oh, Kenneth." Electricity seemed to zing through her system, and her heart took wings. "Are you sure?"

"This guy has never failed me yet. I'm sorry it's not more."

"It's a start," she breathed. Finally. "How can I ever thank you?"

"Say you'll come out to dinner with me."

He had asked many times over the months, and almost before she could think, the standard denial was there on the tip of her tongue. That she wasn't ready. That it wouldn't be right until she was sure of what she wanted and who she was. But she stifled the impulse and instead said weakly, "Yes, please, let's do that."

"What?"

"I said yes."

This time the laugh broke through. "Do I have the right Kyle Rothmore on the line here?"

"Thank you," she said again. "With all my heart. Thank you."

"You're welcome," he said softly. "With all my heart."

The instant she set down the phone, Kyle knew it wasn't enough. She hurried back to her room, dressed in haste, and rushed to call a taxi. Impatiently she waited in the chill misting rain until the cab arrived. She flung open the door and said, "The Rothmore Insurance building, please. Massachusetts Avenue."

She was out the door before the cab rolled to a halt. The elevator seemed to crawl up between floors. As soon as they opened upon the executive floor, Kyle was out and running down the hall. She almost collided with Kenneth as he came out of his door, overcoat in one arm, briefcase in the other. He stared at her in astonishment. "What are you doing here?"

"I had . . . I had to speak with you," Kyle puffed.

"Wait and catch your breath." The smile broke out again. "Maybe it really was you I spoke with this morning."

She took one step inside his office, impatient to speak, to

get out what was pushing up from deep inside. "I wanted to say thank you, Kenneth. For everything."

"You're welcome," he said, the smile still tracing through his voice and eyes.

But she was not done. "All my life, I've hidden myself away. I've never even realized how much time and effort I've spent holding myself apart from everything and everybody."

The smile faded as he searched her face. "You have had as much reason to do it as anybody I've ever known."

"But not now," she said, rushing on. Fearful that if she stopped her courage would drain away and she would not be able to start anew. "Not with you."

"No," he said quietly. "You don't need barriers with me. Not ever."

"I know that now. It's just that, after all this time, it's so hard—"

"Kyle! How wonderful it is to see you again." Randolf Crawley pressed his elegantly dressed form through the doorway. "Could you join me in my office, please?"

"No I cannot," she replied. She pushed down her irritation and said evenly, "I have no intention whatsoever of going anywhere with you."

The firmness of her tone and manner shocked them both. Randolf tried to dredge up a pasty smile. "Kyle, you don't mean that."

"Yes I do. And right now Kenneth and I are having a conversation," she responded. "A private one."

Randolf gave Kenneth a very hard look, then turned back and pulled his face into more polite lines. "Don't tell me you are intending to continue with your silly pursuit."

"Searching for my parents is silliness?"

"Your *mother* is very concerned about your welfare. As I am." Randolf strained to hold to his smile. "I really must urge you. Don't take this dangerous course."

She inspected him carefully. "How is it dangerous?" she asked finally. "Are you afraid to find out who I really am? If so—why? What could it possibly mean to you?"

The false smile slipped away, revealing a coldness in his eyes. He retreated, pausing at the door long enough to shoot Kenneth a venemous look.

Kyle stared at the space Randolf had vacated for a long moment. Part of her mind wondered where she had found the strength to stand up to him. Perhaps it was the knowledge that her back was to the wall, that she could retreat no further.

She turned back to Kenneth and found him watching her with that same patient regard she had seen so often before. "Oh," she said dispiritedly. "That special moment, it's gone now."

"No it's not," he said quietly. "It won't ever be, not if you want it back."

"Help me," she pleaded. "Show me what to do."

"You don't know," he softly replied, "how often I've dreamed of hearing those words."

She placed both hands on his arm, feeling the softness of his overcoat and the strength of his shoulders. Her heart beating like a hummingbird's wings, she raised up on tiptoes. He stood stock still as she drew nearer and gave him the softest of kisses. "Hurry back," she whispered.

His breath a lingering sigh against her cheek, he put his arms around her and held her for a long moment.

CHAPTER NINETEEN

KYLE WAS FRIGHTENED, YES, but she was also determined. She felt as though she had been forced to shed one skin, only to discover something utterly different underneath.

She prepared as best she could. Leaving the office, she went straight to Woodie's, Washington's oldest and most popular department store. It was the first time she had been shopping since all this had begun.

Her mother had always taken her to Garfinkel's, a woman's shop that catered to Washington's upper crust. Kyle had always sought out dark-colored clothes, feeling that they helped her escape attention. A two-piece suit of navy blue or dark forest green would allow her to drift more easily along the edge of things, observing but remaining as isolated and unnoticed as possible.

But not today. She found herself choosing a two-piece outfit in dark gray, with an ivory blouse and simple gray pumps. Things were changing. It was time she changed with them.

As she studied her reflection in the mirror, she wondered if perhaps she ought to smile more. Smiles had always seemed part of the falseness that she had hated so. But she had always loved Kenneth's smile. It warmed her, even the memory of it when he was so far away. Yes, she decided, an honest smile would be a nice gift to share.

"Turn signal, Miss Kyle. There on your left."

"I know where the signal is."

"Then use it, please." Bertrand's tone was sharp, and she turned her head to stare at him in surprise. "That car up ahead is going to stop," he said, tension raising his voice from its usual somber tones. "Please watch the road, not me."

"Well, of course," she told him, turning back to the task at hand. "I can see the stop sign."

"Then you must prepare now. Take your foot off the gas and begin pressing the brake."

"I've already done that." After turning the corner, she said, "Maybe this wasn't such a good idea after all."

"I am quite happy to give you driving lessons," Bertrand said stiffly.

"No, you're not. You're scared silly I'm going to scratch your precious Rolls."

"Don't even speak of such a thing." Nervously Bertrand pulled a handkerchief from his pocket and mopped his brow. "Besides which, it is your car."

"No, it's Mother's. I wouldn't dream of owning such a thing."

"Stoplight, Miss Kyle."

"It's half a block away," she complained. "Give me a chance to see these things for myself. And stop calling me 'Miss.' Please."

"But . . ." Bertrand struggled a moment, then gave a little smile. "I suppose it would be all right, wouldn't it?"

"Of course it would. And calm down. You're making me more nervous than I already am."

"All right, I'll try." He settled back and crossed his arms determinedly. But at every intersection, she could see his foot pressing on the floorboards, reaching for pedals that were not there.

To take his mind off her driving, she asked, "When did you

and Maggie start working for Daddy? It was after I was . . . after I was born, wasn't it?"

"You had just celebrated your first birthday." Bertrand smiled at the memory. "You looked like such a little angel. You stole our hearts the first time we saw you." He hesitated, then said quietly, "I was so distressed to hear of, well, everything. And shocked. It came as a complete surprise to both of us. But it changes nothing as far as we are concerned."

"Thank you."

"The house is so quiet without you. So empty." He glanced over. "Is there any chance you might reconsider and move back?"

"If Mother agrees to leave things as Daddy wanted," Kyle said, but in her heart she wondered if that was still true. After all that had happened, she was no longer sure she could ever have any place there again. The thought left her empty.

"Yes. I understand," he said, as though he could read her thoughts. He turned to watch the Riverdale city limits sign sweep by, then asked, "What exactly are we looking for?"

"I don't know. Maybe nothing. Kenneth will try to find out something more when he returns. But that could take months. I just thought . . ." She sighed. Now that she was here, the task seemed impossible. "I don't know what I thought."

"You're driving very well, Miss . . ." Bertrand stopped himself and smiled. "That will be one difficult habit to break."

Kyle turned long enough to give him a fleeting smile, then resumed her search of the Riverdale streets. The town did not look old, yet already the houses seemed tired and defeated. There was a weary sameness to the little white clapboard houses, many in dire need of paint and repairs. She drove down street after street, unable to find an area that felt like a center, some place from which to begin her search.

Kyle sighed, pushing at her growing tension and frustration. Her stomach felt tied in knots. She stopped at a traffic light and found herself repeating the brief prayer, *Help me.*

On impulse Kyle pulled into the parking lot of a Hot Shoppe restaurant. She cut the motor, then sat looking at the entrance until Bertrand asked, "Are you hungry?"

"Not at all." She'd had nothing to eat all day and it was now past the noon hour, but she did not feel like eating. Steeling herself, she opened her door. "Would you wait here for me, please?"

"Of course," Bertrand said, giving the restaurant a doubtful glance.

She walked in and seated herself at the counter. To give herself something to do, she picked up the menu but could not concentrate on the words. What was she doing here?

The waitress walked over, a sturdy woman with an expression that said she'd seen it all and heard even more. "Ready to order?"

"Just coffee." Kyle waited until the cup was filled and placed in front of her, then asked, "Do you know everyone in this town?"

"Know more than I'd ever want to, honey." The waitress turned away. "But that don't make me a talker."

"Wait. Please. I'm looking for someone."

"Sorry. Can't help you."

"They're my parents." Just like that. Blurted out.

The waitress turned back, took a step toward Kyle, inspected her with eyes the color of gray marbles. "You don't say."

"No, really. I was put up for adoption. I just learned about it." A quick breath. "I don't even know their names. Just that some document has placed them here in this town. At least, they used to live here." She looked down at the cup, feeling the desolate futility swamp her.

The waitress set the coffeepot back on the burner. "I've traveled about a million miles since the last time somebody caught me flat-footed." Another careful inspection. "You eaten today?"

Kyle shook her head. "I'm not hungry."

"You look hungry. All wore out to boot. I'll have Jimmy fix you a plate."

"Really, I couldn't eat a thing."

"Wait 'til it's sitting there in front of you and tell me that." She pointed behind them. "Go have a seat in that booth by the window. And lay off the coffee. Your nerves are already so tight I can hear them humming."

Kyle did as she was told, then motioned through the window for Bertrand to join her. Her offer was declined with a shake of his head.

The woman brought over a steaming plate. Kyle started again to protest, but as soon as she smelled the food, she felt faint with hunger. The woman watched her eat with satisfaction. "There, what did I tell you?"

"This is delicious."

"Slow down, honey. It ain't going nowhere." She glanced out the window, then stared harder. "That battleship on wheels out there belong to you?"

Kyle glanced over, saw her staring at the Rolls. "My mother—yes, yes it does."

"Well, if this don't beat all." The waitress observed her a moment longer. "You say you don't even know what your last name was?"

"No."

"That's tough." She mulled it over, then pulled out her order book and scribbled a moment. She tore out the sheet and laid it beside the plate. "You could try talking to this fellow. He might be able to help."

Kyle turned the slip of paper around and read aloud, "Dr. Howard Austin."

"Been here even longer than me, knows almost every secret there is. His office is halfway down the next block. Might as well leave the barge here, keep from holding up traffic."

Kyle read the woman's name tag. "Thank you, Stella. From the bottom of my heart."

The waitress offered her first smile, and the years dropped away. "What's your name, honey?"

Kyle hesitated, then gave the only name she knew. "Kyle. Kyle Rothmore."

"Well, I sure hope you like what you find. Think maybe you could stop by, let me know what happens?"

Kyle set down her napkin, slid from the booth, and offered Stella her hand. "I promise."

Kyle sat in the corner of the doctor's office for hours. She leafed nervously through magazines whose pages had been wrinkled and torn by countless hands before her. People of every sort and description came and went. Most seemed to know one another, especially the mothers with infants. They sat and dangled the children, or let them play with the blocks scattered across the floor, and gossiped. Kyle, isolated by her nerves and her purpose, wondered what it would be like to feel as though she belonged so clearly to a place and a group of people that she did not even need to think about it.

"Miss, ah, Rothmore?" The nurse was a heavyset woman with strands of graying hair falling out of her starched white cap. "Did I get that right?"

"Yes." Kyle had to use both arms to push herself up, she had been seated so long. "Yes, you did."

"The doctor can see you now," the nurse said doubtfully. Her expression said volumes about what she thought of strange young women who appeared and asked for an appointment, then refused to give any reason. "But he's extremely busy and can only give you a minute."

Kyle tried to ignore the questioning glances from the other people filling the waiting room. "I understand."

"This way, please."

Kyle followed her down the hall and into the office, where a man with a tired face and heavy paunch sat writing in a file. The nurse pointed her toward the examining table, but Kyle stood nervously in the center of the room. She was positive they could both hear her wildly beating heart.

Finally the doctor folded the file shut, put it on the counter beside him, and said, "Yes?"

Kyle glanced to where the nurse stood. In response, she crossed her arms and set her jaw. Clearly the woman was going nowhere.

The doctor looked Kyle over. His eyes were rimmed with great dark circles, yet his gaze was as kind as his tone. "Are you pregnant, young lady?"

"What?" Kyle took an involuntary step back. "N-no, that's not it at all."

"Well, you're obviously not here representing a drug company." He motioned toward the table. "Wouldn't you be more comfortable over here?"

"No . . . no thank you." She swallowed, then stammered, "M-my name, it's . . ."

When she could not continue, the doctor reached a hand to where the nurse was standing. She passed over the single sheet of paper and said irritably, "Like I told you, she just gave her name and address. Refused to fill in the history."

"I see," the doctor said doubtfully. He looked at the page, said, "Well, Miss Rothmore . . ."

He stopped, looked up, and stared at Kyle. "Rothmore," he said softly.

The nurse started forward. "Doctor, is anything—?"

"No," he said, his eyes not leaving Kyle's face. "Leave us a moment, will you, Miss Grant?"

"Doctor, I'm not supposed . . ."

"It's fine." The doctor tore his gaze away from Kyle long enough to say as reassuringly as he could manage, "It's all right, Miss Grant. I won't be long."

The nurse paused long enough to give Kyle a final hard look, then left. When the door had closed behind her, the doctor turned back and said quietly, "How did you find me?"

CHAPTER TWENTY

WEAKNESS FLOODED THROUGH KYLE in a sudden shocking wave. *It's really happening.*

"Hang on," Dr. Austin said, reaching out with alacrity. "Okay, steady now, just come on over here, that's it."

Kyle felt gentle arms guide her over to the examining table and settle her down. The doctor turned away and came back with a cup of water. Gratefully she accepted it and sipped. He watched her with a startled, kindly gaze. "Now, feel like maybe telling me how you got here?"

In bits and pieces she explained how she had come to be in his office. The doctor's amiable questions drew her further and further, until she was revealing more than she had ever expected. About her father's death, and the trust, and how she had found out about the adoption. Even bringing Kenneth into the discussion, and what a help he had been.

Finally the doctor was satisfied, at least enough to step back and regard her with a bemused expression. At length he said, "If you had come in here a year ago, I would have clammed up and sent you on your way. What's done is done—that would have been my reaction. No use in digging up the past."

She found herself tensing once more. So close. But there was no way she could rush things. "And now?"

"Now, well," Dr. Austin let out a noisy sigh. "I'm beginning to find the Lord's hand at work in more and more things these days. Do you have any idea what I mean?"

"Yes," she said, and her answer made her look deep inside and find it was true. "Yes, I think I do."

"Well, it's all still a big mystery to me. But these days the strangest things just seem to be worked out before my eyes." He offered her a small smile. "I still don't understand much of anything. Once I would have dismissed it as mumbo-jumbo. Now I'm not sure *what* is touched by God."

She tried to answer his smile with one of her own, but it was hard. "Can . . . can you tell me something about them? My family, I mean." It sounded so strange, saying those words. Her *family*.

"I'm not sure," he replied slowly. "To tell the truth, I don't exactly know what my role in all this should be."

She gripped the starched sheet covering the table's padding. But she remained silent. Something told her now was not the time to press.

He rubbed one hand up and down his cheek, pondering a moment longer. Then he lifted his gaze and said quietly, "I need some time to sort this through. Could you come back tomorrow and—"

"I . . . I . . ." Kyle started to agree, then stammered quickly, "No, I . . . I can't."

He seemed taken aback by her response. "Why not?"

"Because," she replied slowly, "I broke rules to come today. Bertrand brought me. Mother would be furious if she ever found out. I can't take that risk again, not so soon. It could cost him and his wife their jobs."

He nodded his head thoughtfully, then reached for his prescription pad. "Tell you what. Give me a while to think this over. Call me at home this evening. That's my number."

"Thank you." She accepted the paper with numb fingers.

Dr. Austin hesitated a long moment, then looked down at his hands and said, "It so happens that I do know your parents. They have not forgotten you. The sorrow of losing you nearly ruined their lives. I'm just not sure that bringing you back into their lives is the right thing to do."

There was an awful instant when she felt certain he was going to refuse her then and there. Instead, he remained as he was, his head bowed so that she stared at his bald spot, and murmured more to himself than to her, "Then again, they sure could use some good news right now, what with Joel . . ."

When his voice trailed off and it appeared that he would not go on, she quietly pressed, "Who?"

He raised his gaze and shook his head at her question. "I promise to give it careful thought. Perhaps it wouldn't do too much harm, after all." He offered her his hand. "Nice to know you've grown up and turned out so well."

She walked back down the hall and reentered the waiting room. She did not feel as though she had turned out well at all. She felt lost and utterly alone. Suddenly she was filled with an overpowering need to contact Kenneth, feel his strength, and hear his wisdom make sense of the tumult in her mind and heart. She turned to where the nurse was regarding her from behind the receptionist's counter. "May I use your phone, please?"

"I suppose so." Her tone was disapproving.

"Thank you." Kyle dialed the office, then asked for Kenneth's secretary. When the woman came on the line, she said, "This is Kyle Rothmore. Do you happen to have a number where I can reach Mr. Adams?"

"Miss Kyle, why, yes, hello." The woman seemed tremendously flustered. "I was just trying to reach you at the dorm."

"Why, what's wrong?" The alarm in her voice brought the nurse back around.

"Nothing, that is . . . Mr. Adams is back here. He's in with Mr. Crawley." There was a moment's hesitation, then, "And Mrs. Rothmore has just arrived."

Alarm bells jangled along every inch of her body. "Slip him a note," she said, not trying to hide her apprehension. "Tell him I'm coming. Tell him I'm hurrying just as fast as I can."

The journey downtown seemed to last forever but in truth took less than an hour. Bertrand took the wheel himself and expertly maneuvered the big car through the city traffic. His normal caution was cast aside in answer to her urgent pleadings for speed.

At the Rothmore building, Kyle was out of the car before Bertrand even had his door open. Barely controlling her impatience up the elevator to the executive floor, she flew down the hallway and flung back the door to her father's former office. She took one look at Kenneth's face and exclaimed, "Don't let them do it!"

"Really, Kyle," her mother said peevishly. "What on earth are you thinking? Rushing in here and spouting off nonsense. Honestly, it's just too much."

Kyle glanced at her mother. It was the first time they had seen each other since the start of the school term. She turned back to Kenneth and pleaded, "Don't let them push you into anything."

He turned to her, the entreaty clear in his eyes. "They say they'll keep my entire staff in place, if I—"

She could not let him say the words. "No! I will not allow it."

"Oh, stop it. Stop it right now!" Her mother slapped the arm of her chair. "Sit down and behave yourself."

Kenneth kept his gaze upon her. "That's almost two hundred jobs we're talking about, Kyle."

"Really, Kyle. This is nothing you need concern yourself with." Randolf Crawley was at his most polished. He moved swiftly around the desk, walked over, took her arm, and said, "Here, why don't you—"

She pulled her arm free. To Kenneth she pleaded, "There must be something we can do to stop them!"

"Oh, do be quiet," her mother snapped. "I won't allow you to interfere in something you know absolutely nothing about, do you hear me? I forbid it!"

"I suppose we could challenge the act in court," Kenneth mused aloud. "After all, I am still a trustee."

"But a secondary one," Randolf said, not returning to his seat. His poise slipped a notch. "Really, I must warn you—"

"Please," Kyle said to Kenneth, "please do that. I'll help any way I can."

"*You'll* help?" Abigail gave a shrill laugh. "Oh, this is just too much."

Kenneth turned his attention to Abigail. "Kyle is less than six months from coming into her full inheritance. This includes, as you know, voting rights for over sixty percent of the stock. I would imagine the least we could do is have a holding order placed upon such a decision until she reaches her majority."

Abigail stiffened as though slapped. She glared at Kyle. "You wouldn't *dare*."

Kyle forced herself to remain fully erect. "There's a lot I've been daring to do, Mother."

"Whatever is that supposed to mean?"

"I've just come from Riverdale," Kyle replied. "Where I met with Dr. Howard Austin."

Her mother's face turned absolutely white. "I'll not have you inherit my company just to turn around and hand it over to a family of *peasants*."

"It is not your company, Mother," Kyle said, glad that her voice did not betray her turmoil. "It was Daddy's, and as far as I'm concerned, it still is." She paused, then said, "What do you know about my birth parents, Mother?"

"Nothing." Her voice was a lash. "I had no interest whatsoever in knowing anything at all. Why should I mix with rabble?"

"I am that rabble," Kyle said softly.

"All that is behind you," Randolf said, heading off Abigail's retort. But his soothing tone was marred by nervousness. "Really, Kyle, don't you think we would all be better off if you trusted us to look after your best interests?"

Firmly Kyle shook her head. "I think it's time I started trusting myself."

Abigail leaped to her feet. She snapped at Randolf, "I *knew* it was a mistake to try your roundabout maneuvers. I've had all of this I can stand." She wheeled around to face Kyle. "Young lady, I am *ordering* you to stop this nonsense *immediately*."

Kyle stood with shoulders squared. She felt as though an immense distance was separating them, at the same time hurting her but also sheltering her. "I'm sorry, Mother. But I can't do that."

"Then I will have the courts declare you incompetent," Abigail ground out. She spun away and started for the door. "Come along, Randolf. We have work to do."

When they were alone, Kyle felt her strength and resolve drain away. She sank into a chair.

"I think they are going to find that very hard going," Kenneth mused aloud. "The first time they contested the will and the trust, the courts rebuked them for even trying. Not only that, you're attending college and doing well in your studies. You are six months from your majority, you have been spending time here in . . ." He noticed her expression. "What's the matter?"

"I feel ill." Standing up to her mother had drained the energy from every fiber of her body.

"Do you want something?"

"A glass of water, please." Gratefully she accepted the glass, took a sip, and felt slightly better. "That was dreadful."

"I hate arguments," he agreed. "But you handled it very well."

"Do you think so?"

"I was so proud of you," he said quietly.

She reached over, took his hand, and said, "I could not have done it without you."

"I didn't do anything."

"You were here. That was the most important thing." She felt strength flow through his grasp, up her arm, and warm her chest. "Don't ever leave, Kenneth. Not ever."

He leaned closer and said, "I want nothing more than to be here for you."

CHAPTER TWENTY-ONE

JOEL LAY IN THE BARN LOFT'S snug room and listened to the noisy tumult of another dawn. Whoever thought living on a farm was quiet had never been near one. Dogs and roosters and cows and horses were all competing to make the most racket. He had never known a place as noisy as this—or as pleasant.

The Millers had offered him a place in the big house, but he had declined. He required so much sleep these days, he needed a place to come and shut the door on the family noise and the activity. His chest hurt almost all the time, a dull ache that had become as familiar to him as breathing. A constant reminder of what lay ahead.

Joel shifted restlessly, making the rusty springs of his ancient bed squeak and complain. The room had last belonged to a farm-hand, brought in back when the Miller children had been too small to take on many of the chores. The little room's dresser lacked the two middle drawers, the mirror was cracked and held together with masking tape, and the bed was twice his own age. Yet Joel had never felt as much at home as he did here. Which made his impending departure even harder to bear.

Two days a week, he did light chores around the Miller farm. It was the only payment the family would accept for his room and board. The rest of the time was spent working with a youth mission connected to a Lansdale church. Lansdale was the nearest thing to a city the Pennsylvanian Dutch region could boast.

In recent years, it had gained a reputation as a stopping place for kids on the move. And there were so many of them these days. Runaways, college kids taking a semester off, or kids just roaming around. The Lansdale church work had given Joel an opportunity to give, to share, to love. He had never known such a feeling of completeness. Even when it made him so tired.

For some of the young people he was meeting, he represented their only chance of knowing love. Not the love of the streets, where they bartered their bodies for what they so desperately yearned to have—a sense of belonging. Joel had found he could reach to them on a deeper level, giving from the peace and joy in his own heart, and speak of One who would grant them unconditional love. *Real* love.

Joel had discovered an ability to share that love. He knew this was his gift, his calling, as clearly as he knew his own name. He could not explain why he had been chosen to serve in this manner. He did not understand how someone like him had been selected from a world of believers to have the glory of such a mission. Except for perhaps having come from circumstances with a similar lack of love and acceptance.

Joel heard the farmhouse door slam and took it as a signal to roll from his bed. Today was a chore day, and he had promised Ruthie to hitch up the buggy and take her to town. As he slipped into his clothes, he gave thanks anew for this gift of understanding, the gift of renewal, the gift of purpose.

If only there was some way he could give a little longer.

Normally Joel enjoyed urging the horse and buggy to a brisk pace. The animal was a trotter and loved to run. Joel usually gave him the freedom to do so, as he loved to feel the energy of a racing thoroughbred passing through the leather reins. But today he deliberately slowed him to a gentler gait. There was no need to hurry. They had not managed to leave the farm until late afternoon, what with one chore after another keeping them busy. Ruthie had delivered the cartons of eggs to the local merchant and purchased the few supplies from her list, and now they were headed home.

The afternoon drive seemed a perfect time for slowing life's busy pace. A time for reflection. For enjoying a little leisure, a rare commodity for people who worked so steadily. Even the horse sensed it and settled into a slow, even trot, so different from his normal pull against the reins. Joel relaxed, his arms resting lightly on his knees. The cool breeze gently played with his uncovered hair. The day was warm for fall, and his dark cap lay on the seat beside him.

Ruthie, close at his side in the buggy's confines, leaned back with a gentle smile playing about her lips. Clearly she meant to enjoy every moment of the rare respite from her household responsibilities.

On the road toward them moved another buggy, the horse traveling much faster than their own. Little puffs of dust lifted with each clip-clop of hoof and spin of buggy wheel. Joel pointed and spoke with a smile. "Someone's in too much of a hurry for such a fine day."

Ruthie peered ahead, then replied, "It's the Enns' black. He must be forgetting something up to town."

Joel nodded. Just as some folks knew cars, Ruthie seemed to know every horse in the entire neighborhood. They continued to watch the distance close between their two buggies. There was no other traffic on this road, and the sound of the horses' hoofs fell into a pleasant rhythm in the crisp autumn air.

Ruthie was right. It was indeed Henry Enns, a neighbor to the Millers. He nodded in their direction and called out with a broad grin, "Strange time of day to be courting out!"

Joel frowned. He knew the words were good-natured teasing, but he wondered if there was more to them than that. Yes. Henry likely meant his words. Joel stole a sideways look at Ruthie. What he saw made him stir with uneasiness.

He had grown to know her well over the months, and he could see that the girl's thoughts were taking her in the same direction as Henry's. She blushed and smiled, then shifted slightly on the leather seat. Her arm brushed up against Joel's sleeve. He felt the color rise in his cheeks.

He had to do something. Say something. But what? What could he possibly say without hurting the one he had come to care for so much? He worked his dry mouth and tried to formulate some words. Nothing reasonable came to mind.

Ruthie stirred again. He heard a little sigh escape her lips. She seemed so totally at peace with herself and with their relationship. But maybe she was thinking that the relationship held more promises than Joel was prepared or able to make.

Again he fought for some way to broach the subject. At last he straightened and turned slightly. "Do they really think we're courting?"

The smile on Ruthie's face was a little embarrassed, but she nodded.

"Why is that?" The question sounded much too abrupt, he knew as soon as the words were out.

Her smile wavered, but her eyes did not fall before his. "Because, Joel, we are together much. And we enjoy our times together. This all can see."

"Yes, but . . ." Joel could not deny the fact that he spent a good deal of time with the young girl. Nor would he have tried to deny the fact that he enjoyed her company. But to court her? His sigh seemed to come from the bottom of his soul. No. Courting was a privilege of young men with a future. Men with promise. He had nothing to offer Ruthie, not even time.

"What is it, Joel?"

"You know that . . . that I can't . . ."

The girl's eyes clouded. "You do not enjoy?" Ruthie asked frankly.

"You know I do. It's just . . . you know my circumstances. I'm not well, Ruthie." He glanced at her with painful appeal. "I don't even know how long I have."

Timidly Ruthie slipped a hand over his. Joel could feel her press close to his side. He dared not look at her again. "I know about your heart that makes you sick," she said her voice clear, confident. "I know, and I pray."

"But, Ruthie—"

"Wait, Joel. No one knows the time of parting. The hours, or the days, those are God's to give. We are not to know. Just to live, and thanks to give to Him our Maker. To make good what we have."

The words and the feelings began tumbling out. "But they wouldn't be good, can't you see that? At any time I could—be gone. I can't promise you anything, Ruthie. Not even to live long enough to marry. To build a home. To raise children. I wouldn't do that to you, Ruthie. I wouldn't do that to anyone. I will not make promises that would only be broken."

"Have I asked for promises yet?"

"No, but—"

"And I will not do. But we can dream and plan, Joel. Plans can change—without being broken. And if God wills . . ."

But Joel was shaking his head. The agitation that filled his whole body transferred down the reins he was holding. The horse threw up his head and quickened his gait. Joel had to give quick attention to his driving, but he welcomed the change of pace. Suddenly he wished to have the ride over. To be freed from his difficult position. He straightened and lifted his hands to control the horse that now had broken into a full run. Ruthie's hand withdrew and joined the other in her lap.

"I cannot make plans," Joel declared with a firmness that sounded almost cold. "I have no tomorrows to share. I will not unload this on anyone else."

A quick glance showed him the tears in Ruthie's eyes. Her chin was lifted, her jaw set. "You are a stubborn man, Joel Grimes. Do you not leave room still for love—or miracles?"

"No," he said, and immediately realized he was proving her statement to be true. Maybe he was stubborn but he repeated, "No, I don't expect miracles. And you'd be wise not to be looking for one either."

Kyle's heart soared and plunged a dozen times during her second drive back to Riverdale. What if they did not want to meet her? What if they did not like her at all? Why had they given her up for adoption in the first place? What if the reason was a bad one? Could she survive the news?

Finally Kenneth stopped on a street very much like others they had traversed and pointed to a house ahead of them. "Up there, the second on the right."

Kyle's breath came in quick little gasps. She looked up at the small home. "You're sure this is it?"

"If the address the doctor gave you is right, it is." He stared through the front windshield. "I don't see anyone."

"No." She pressed a hand against her rib cage, willing her heart to slow its frantic pace. She looked up at the house, trying to gather a feeling for who lived there. The narrow yard fell in three grassy steps to the sidewalk. Shrubs colored by late autumn frosts formed a neat border. A picket fence held it all together. "I'm so scared."

"I understand." He reached over for her hand. "Are you sure you're ready for this?"

"I think so." She looked at him. She hesitated, then asked, "Would you . . . would you pray with me? Please?"

"You don't know," he said, still holding her hand, "how often I have dreamed you would say those words to me."

She bowed her head and heard him say, "Heavenly Father, we are so grateful for this moment. Grateful that we are sharing it together, and sharing it with you. Be with Kyle, precious Lord, as she steps into this new part of her life. Guide her, shield her, comfort her. In Jesus' name we pray. Amen."

"Amen," Kyle murmured and raised her head. The first thing she saw when she opened her eyes was a slight, dark-haired woman standing on the house's front porch. The woman held the door with one hand, as though fearful to let it go and step away. She stared down at the car. Kyle whispered, "Oh, Kenneth."

Suddenly her fingers were unable to work the door handle.

Kenneth reached across her and pushed it open. "God will go with you, sweetheart."

The words gave her strength to stand. At her appearance, the woman on the porch raised one hand to her mouth and started down the steps. Kyle took a tentative step forward.

The woman made it down the steps, walked hesitantly forward, and finally whispered, "Katherine?"

Kyle felt her heart twist painfully at the sound of that name. "Mrs. Grimes?"

"Oh, Katie . . ." The woman ran forward, then halted, her arms halfway raised, tears streaming down her face. She reached one trembling hand out, uncertain, helpless to go farther. Kyle found herself unable to see the woman's features any longer for the tears in her own eyes. She took another tentative step, and suddenly the two of them were hugging, and the woman was stroking Kyle's hair and her back and crying over and over, "Katie, oh my little Katherine."

And suddenly Kyle was crying, too. Partly because the search was finally over, partly for all the sadness that had brought her to this place, partly because she had never even known that her name had once been Katherine.

"So this is your young man," Martha Grimes said for the fifth or sixth time. "How nice. You make such a handsome couple."

"Thank you. It's all very new to us," Kyle admitted with a flush to her cheeks. She shifted, flustered and shy over her discovery of love. While getting her feelings back under control, she let her glance travel about the room. Everything in it spoke of age and hard use. The covers to the sagging furniture were worn, the coffee table scarred. The bookshelves were almost bare, the television an older model with a huge cabinet supporting a small corner screen.

"And you brought him for us to meet." Martha beamed at

Kenneth. "I am so happy for you both."

"It is an honor to meet you, Mrs. Grimes."

"Call me Martha, please. What do you do?"

"I work in Kyle's company. Rothmore Insurance."

"How nice. It's wonderful to have things you can share, isn't it, Harry?"

"Absolutely," her husband agreed.

Kyle looked from one to the other. It was remarkable, how little interest they seemed to have in the Rothmore wealth. Despite their obvious lack, they listened to her speak about her family, her growing-up years, her experience as the daughter of a successful businessman, with interest only because it was *her* they were happy for. They looked incredibly satisfied with what they had.

She turned back to the woman seated beside her. Martha had not released her hand since embracing her outside. Not even the room's dimness could disguise the light that shone from the woman's face. And from that of her husband. Kyle glanced over at the silent man, saw the same gentle light as she had found in the woman's gaze. "You both look so happy."

For some reason, her words caused Martha and Harry to exchange a long glance. Harry finally replied with, "Yes. We are. Finally."

"At long last," Martha agreed.

Harry turned to Kyle and explained, "It was all Joel's doing."

"It was God's doing," his wife corrected quietly.

"True, true." There was another shared glance. "But it was Joel who showed us the way."

"You're believers," Kenneth said. "This is wonderful."

But Kyle's mind was still back grappling with the previous statement. "I'm sorry," she stammered. "Who is Joel?"

The question brought fresh tears to Martha's eyes. "Oh, my dear, sweet child. You don't know."

"How could she?" Harry murmured.

"No, of course." Martha sniffed loudly and tried to collect herself.

Kyle demanded weakly, "Know what?"

"You have a brother," Martha said softly. "His name is Joel."

"A brother?" The word rocked Kyle. A brother? She had always longed for a brother. Had begged for a brother, and now she was discovering she had a brother that she did not even know. It was all so overwhelming. "Where is he?" she finally managed.

"Oh, he's not here," hurried Martha. "I know he'd be as excited as we are if he only . . ."

When Martha's voice dropped off, Kyle had to take several breaths before she found the strength to whisper, "Doesn't he know about me?"

Martha's head lowered and she fiddled with the hankie in her lap. "No," she said and there was anguish in her voice. "No . . . we never told him."

"But why . . ." Kyle could not finish her question.

Even so, the words brought a fresh rush of tears from Martha's eyes. "Losing you was too painful to even talk about."

"Even between us," Harry added quietly. Lines like jagged furrows etched his face as he sadly observed his wife. "All those wasted years," he murmured.

"We could not even talk to each other . . . until . . . recently." Martha wept as she said the words. "And only after Joel brought us face to face with our need. After the doctor . . ." She could not go on. Sobs shook her shoulders.

Harry crossed to her and put a protective arm about her, comforting her with clumsy yet gentle pats. He looked over at Kyle and said, "It truly is God's doing, bringing you here now."

Kyle could sense that something was wrong, something more than the emotion of all the lost years. There was an underlying current of sadness in the home, even amid the evident feeling of peace and the joy of reunion.

"Oh, Harry, must we speak about that now?" Martha said, trying to stop the flowing tears.

"I think so, but if you'd rather . . ."

Martha hesitated, then dropped her eyes and sighed, "No, no, I suppose she should know it all."

Kyle felt a chill. "Know what?"

"Your brother," Harry Grimes replied quietly. "He's not well."

"His heart," Martha said and wiped her face anew. "The doctors—they say there's nothing they can do." The last part of her sentence was spoken so softly Kyle wondered if she had heard correctly.

No. No. Kyle fought against the fact of finding a brother and then losing him in nearly the same breath.

"Is he in the hospital?" she heard Kenneth ask on her behalf.

"No, he's . . ." began Martha.

"Honey—I think we need to start at the beginning and tell her everything."

Kyle sat and heard the full story. The meeting of two young people just as the country was going to war. The marriage and their few short but happy weeks together. The war. The injury and loss of Harry's ID. The anguish of a young mother, seemingly widowed, giving up the baby she wanted and loved. Harry's return to an empty cradle and a grieving wife, suffering through the loss of his health and his profession and the daughter he never knew. The arrival of Joel, whose presence in the home was unable to heal the deep rift that had driven them apart. Martha's accident and the gradual breaking down of some of the unseen walls. Joel's friendship with the Millers. His finding a faith that he shared with his parents when they needed it the most. The doctor's diagnosis had been cruel, crippling, yet with God's help they were somehow managing to bear it. Now Kyle—their little Katherine—had been brought back into their life. Surely it was God's doing.

Kyle wiped away tears as she listened to the story. Why had it happened? Why the strange circumstances and twists of fate that had ripped them all apart? And brought them together?

And a brother. A younger brother. As the story wound its way toward her presence here in this room, Kyle found she could hear no more. She simply could not emotionally face anything further. She rose to her feet, shaking her head as if that would help to put things into some kind of focus. "I . . . I need to be going," she stammered.

"Oh, must you?" Martha rose with her, holding Kyle's hand as though not wishing to ever let her go. But there was no conviction behind Martha's protest. Clearly they all felt overwhelmed by the day's events.

Harry's wounded leg was giving him trouble as he pushed himself erect. "When will we see you again?"

"Soon," Kyle promised. She would be back. Just as soon as she could catch her breath and sort things out. But she had to see Joel. Her brother. She had to. "Where will I find Joel?"

Martha looked to her husband for guidance and stammered, "Oh, Harry, might this be too much for his poor heart?"

But Harry was shaking his head. "Emotionally he's the strongest man I've ever met. He wouldn't be able to do what he's doing if he wasn't. He'll be all right."

Kyle's attention was caught and held by a single word. *Man.* Harry had called the baby brother she had never known a man. Again she felt overwhelmed. "I really must be going." Kenneth held her arm protectively.

The Grimes led the two out to the front porch. Harry's slight limp continued to pull at Kyle's attention, as though that leg contained the mystery of the missing years. Kenneth walked alongside her. He did not speak, just remained close enough for her to draw from his steady strength.

"He's been staying on a farm in Mennonite country, north of Philadelphia," Harry explained. "He and a fellow from the family, they do charity work together, I guess you'd call it."

"Joel's such a wonderful boy," Martha said proudly. "I'll show you his letters next time you come. They're so full of love and warmth they just make you want to weep."

"Last time we talked, Joel said he's found needs he didn't even know existed." Harry leaned against the pillar by the front steps, one strong arm around his wife's shoulders. "Joel came home for a while, but he couldn't settle back in here. Kept on about the needs out there and something he wanted to do before—while he still could."

"A mission, he said it was," Martha added. "A calling from

God. His last letter said he felt he had discovered what life was really all about."

"They work with some group that helps all these kids piling into the cities," Harry said. Clearly he was troubled by the thought. "Runaways and the like."

Kenneth spoke for the first time. "My church has become involved in that as well. It's a growing problem down here in Washington."

Martha was still unwilling to let go of Kyle's hand. "I miss my boy," she confessed quietly.

"He's doing God's work," Harry intoned quietly. "You can't read his letters and doubt that for a second. But it's hard on both of us, him being gone when we don't know how long . . ."

"Here." Martha reached into her cardigan and brought out a pencil and a scrap of paper. She released Kyle's hand long enough to scribble hastily, then hand over the paper. "This is the address for the Millers' farm. They don't have a phone. I'll be sending him a letter today, telling him everything, but why don't you write to Joel yourself?"

"Thank you," Kyle said, accepting the slip, yet knowing she could not wait for an exchange of letters.

"I know how busy you folks must be," Martha said. "But do you think we could invite you back for a meal next week?"

Kyle saw the entreaty in the woman's eyes and knew she could refuse her nothing. "Whenever you like," she said, squeezing the small hand. "That would be wonderful."

The trip back to Washington was made in nearly absolute silence. Kyle had so much to absorb, she felt as though she could not hold on to any thought for more than an instant. The impressions and feelings and images whirled through her mind as she leaned her head against the back of the seat.

Kenneth obviously felt her need for quiet. Every once in a

while he would reach over and pat her hand, not speaking, just reminding her that he was there. Each time, she felt her mind and her spirit calmed by his understanding and care.

Gradually, a single thread began to run more clearly through her thoughts. Over and over she returned to how faith had such impact in the lives around her—in her father, Lawrence, in her adored Bertie and Maggie, even when she didn't recognize it. In Kenneth, and now in the Grimes family. . . .

Strange how she would think of this now. Or perhaps not, she reflected, staring out at the city. The power of God had been reflected in so much that day—the way Harry and Martha described the change in their relationship, for one. She did not doubt for a moment that what they had told her was true.

This power of faith also was evident in Kenneth's peace, his silent understanding, his patience. All of these were offerings in a way. She had never thought of them in that sense, but it was true. He offered to her what he had learned through faith.

As they drove beneath trees dressed in the final flecks of autumn gold, she decided it was time she offered him something in return. But what? She looked over at Kenneth, this dear man who had seen her through so much, and wondered what on earth she and this fragile faith of hers had to give.

As Kenneth pulled up in front of her dormitory and cut off the motor, he said, "You're not going to wait and write Joel, are you?"

His ability to understand her thoughts and direction were another precious gift, especially now. "I can't."

"It won't be possible for me to take another day from work this week," he said apologetically. "I have to meet with the lawyers first thing tomorrow. The best way to halt Randolf and Abigail is to be there first. I must—"

"I understand," she said quickly. No matter how urgent those matters were, she did not want to discuss them. Not now. "I can take the train."

Kenneth did not object. "When do you want to go?"

"Tomorrow," she said, without hesitation. *A brother.*

"Perhaps it would be best after all," he said slowly, "for you to go up there alone."

She tried to echo what her awakening heart was feeling. "You will be there with me," she said quietly. "In my heart, where it counts most."

His gaze into her eyes offered her a glimpse to the depths of his spirit. "With all that you've gone through, what a wonderful thing to say," he said. "Thank you."

And she knew she had been able to offer a small gift of her own. "It's a lesson you taught me." She reached across and took his hand, felt the strength and the warmth and the spirit. Here was a truly good man. "Would you pray with me now?"

CHAPTER TWENTY-TWO

"IT'S VERY KIND OF YOU TO INVITE me in like this," Kyle said. She was seated at the Millers' kitchen table, feeling out of place but very welcomed.

"Choel's sister," Mr. Miller repeated and shook his head once more. "Never did I think such a shock could be such a happiness."

Mrs. Miller rose and reached for Kyle's plate. "Here, let me some more pie bring."

"No, really, I couldn't." Kyle glanced around, taking in the big, bare-walled kitchen with its finely crafted table and chairs, and the people with their curious dress and speech. Despite the strangeness of the setting, Kyle could not help but feel the peace that permeated the room. And something more. The same light shone from their faces as had from Martha and Harry Grimes.

She had taken a train up to Philadelphia, then to Lansdale, not sorry that pressing issues in the company had forced Kenneth to stay in Washington. It was good to be alone for this journey of discovery. The time of travel and solitude gave her an opportunity to sort through her thoughts and emotions. So much was happening and so fast.

As the train had clattered on, Kyle had found herself praying. It had come with the quiet naturalness of a thought about Kenneth, seeing his smile and his strength and his concern for her, feeling the closeness even when every minute of her journey took her farther away. She had closed her eyes, pressing her forehead against the train window, and heard the words drift into her mind. *Help me, Father*, she had prayed, and this time she had felt the words fill her being, running into those that she had earlier pushed away, yet which now stood out as if written in light before her mind's eye. *Help me to come to know you. Help me to understand. Help me to know the life and the joy and the light that I see in other believers' eyes. Help me to understand what salvation truly means.*

The lingering peace had stayed with her, through the remainder of the journey and the long taxi ride out to the Miller farm. She could not call ahead since they did not have a telephone. But it had not mattered, for they had accepted her with hugs and cries of delight, and drawn her into the kitchen for coffee and fresh pie and talk and smiles. They had explained that Joel was not there right then but was doing mission work in town.

The young man named Simon rose to his feet. "Perhaps you would like to walk the farm now."

"Yes, thank you." She returned their openhearted smiles; only the young woman called Ruthie remained quietly sad at the table's other end, watching her with an unreadable expression. "You've all been so kind."

Simon walked with her toward the paddock. "I stayed home from the mission church to help with the chores this day," he said to her unasked question. "Papa, he has good days and bad days. Today is not so good."

The late autumn sun turned the pasture a glistening gold. The horses spotted their approach and came trotting over to the fence. The most persistent was a chestnut mare whose nose was flecked with the gray of age. "This is Missy. My father bought her the year before I was born. She is old now. We let her be lazy. She no longer works on the farm."

The mare seemed to realize they were talking about her, for she tossed her mane and snorted before walking up and resting her chest on the top post. She muzzled into Simon's open hand, then turned her attention toward Kyle.

Kyle lifted both hands to the great head and stroked the neck. The horse nuzzled gently against her shoulder. "She's wonderful."

Simon watched in mild surprise. "She looks for sugar. It is a game we play. Never did I see her do this with a stranger. Can you ride?"

"I used to. I haven't in years."

"Sometimes I think horses, they understand things better than people. Dogs too. They have such a simple way of living, as though we could look at them and remember things we have forgotten. Or maybe never really learned."

"You have held to a lot of the simple things in life."

"Yes." He watched as she lay her cheek against the horse and was rewarded with a soft whinny. "You share your brother's way with animals. They must see a good heart in you."

She turned to face Simon. The horse, disappointed by her movement, shoved at her gently. She reached out again to stroke her and asked, "Where is my brother, Simon? I must see him."

"He went to the mission church in Lansdale without me today." He nodded slowly. "I think it is very good that he sees you. Joel needs us all to help him at this time. He is very brave—but he hurts within, more than from the heart that does not beat right."

He stared out to where the fields joined with low-slung hills. Kyle shifted from one foot to the other. She had the feeling that Simon wanted to say more about her brother, but she didn't feel she could press him.

At length he sighed. With a nod back toward the house he went on. "Our Ruthie—she loves your Joel. It is no secret. She cannot hide it. And Joel, he returns the love. Only Joel asks me, what can one give with so few days left? 'Love,' I say. 'For as long as God allows.' But that is not good enough answer for him. So Joel, he has not only a bad heart—but a broken one."

Kyle felt the tears rise in her eyes. Tears for the brother she did not know. "I wish I could do something for him," she said, her voice little more than a whisper.

"That sounds just like what our Joel would say." Simon smiled with surprising sweetness for such a hearty-looking face. "He is quite the man, your brother. He can say more in silence than most folk can with a year of words." He turned to stare out over the paddock. "He understands these people, the wanderers. He knows their distrust of voices. But still he speaks to them. Heart speaks to heart. And their own hearts, they listen."

Kyle felt as though she were reaching through the mists of lost time, struggling to understand a man she had never met. Her brother. "Why do you think he can do this?"

Simon was a long time in answering. "Because," he finally replied, "Joel is an orphan of the storm—the storm of this life—just like them. It has left him alone too much and too long. He understands their sadness, and he speaks to their need."

"I—" Kyle stopped as she saw Ruthie approaching. She had a new appreciation, a new empathy, for the young girl. She wished she could reach out to her, ease the pain of the heart that loved—and sorrowed.

The young woman walked over, stopped in front of Kyle, and in her lilting English asked, "You go to Joel?"

"Yes," replied Kyle with a slight nod.

"Would you give him a message for me?"

"Of course," Kyle responded, but she heard her voice crack on the simple words.

Sadness turned her smile crooked. "Tell him, don't leave now, leave next time."

Kyle wasn't sure she had heard correctly. "But he's already in town."

"He'll understand." Abruptly Ruthie reached out, hugged Kyle fiercely, then released her and turned away, but not before Kyle caught sight of the tears. "And give that for him from me yet."

Kyle stood and watched Ruthie return to the house, saw her hand reach up to brush at her cheeks. Kyle could not stop her own tears from flowing.

Late that afternoon, Joel braved the brisk wind to help with what the church folk had come to call the street patrol. In the early morning and again just before dark, they searched out new faces huddled under blankets or sleeping inside the limping vehicles that had brought them to town.

Lansdale was often called the gateway to the Pennsylvania Dutch country. It was a picturesque place of Revolutionary War–era buildings and grand, tree-lined avenues. Young people headed into New York, Boston, or Washington—or just moving—often stopped here. A few days or weeks—or months. "Beatniks" had for years been the word to describe such young people. Joel shared the feeling of the other church folk that something needed to be done for these lost ones.

Shadows were lengthening and the night was drawing its cold cover over the town when Joel's eye was caught by a lumpy form huddled in a doorway. He crossed the street and identified three bodies shivering under a shared blanket.

He made as much noise as he could in approaching. One of the heads popped into sight, then another. A trio of young girls, the oldest no more than sixteen, stared at him with sleepy eyes. Fear seemed to have been etched permanently into their young faces, a sign he had come to know well. It meant they had been on the road long enough to sample the harshness of life alone.

"Good evening," he said, giving them a gentle word and a wave, but no smile. By now they would have learned that smiles could mask danger and deception. People often lied as easily with a smile as their voices.

The girls watched him with eyes that were swiftly clearing of sleep. Their bodies tensed, ready to flee if he made a sudden move. "My name is Joel. Have any of you heard of the Lansdale Mennonite Church?"

There was a long pause before the middle girl gave a little shiver of a headshake.

"We run a local mission outreach. There's hot soup there. Have you eaten recently?"

The hollowness of their cheeks told him everything. Joel did not wait for them to respond. "Everything's cool," he said, using the language of the street, but knowing it was more important they feel his concern than hear his words. "You can stay as long as you like, have a shower and a bed for a while if you need it. Hot food, there's a doctor, too. If you want, we'll let your folks know you're okay, but we won't say where you are unless you want us to."

Joel waited a moment, long enough to give a silent, open-eyed prayer that the Lord would speak to their hearts. Then he offered them his hand. "It's so cold this evening the streets are white. Feels like it might even snow later. Wouldn't you like to come in and get warm?"

Joel set up rows of chairs, preparing for their evening service. The church was on the outskirts of town, and the mission occupied the ground floor of a neighboring building. They had left the floor open and set the worship area in one corner. They had discovered early on that few of these wary young people would accept the word of God outright. These kids first needed to observe from a distance. They could sit in the lounge area, or help in the kitchen, or talk among themselves. It never ceased to give Joel a thrill of pleasure the first time one of the newcomers would hesitantly walk over, after a few days of careful observing, and sit down and listen to the Word.

A flicker of movement caught Joel's eye, and he stopped to turn and stare with the rest of the room.

Not that the girl was beautiful. No, the features were too definite, the shoulders too square, the bearing too erect. But this was certainly not a person who had come looking for shelter.

She stood there and searched the faces turned her way. Joel

walked toward her. The young lady was definitely not a social worker, not the way she was dressed. She wore a winter suit of palest yellow, with matching pumps and purse. Her hair was brushed to a warm glow, and her skin was smooth as peaches and cream.

Obviously she was looking for a runaway. It happened from time to time, but usually the searcher was someone older. As he approached, he wondered if there wasn't something about her. Something oddly familiar. Something that raised the hair on his arms and brought a shiver up his spine.

"Can I help you?"

She just stared at him, her eyes big and glowing. "Joel?" There was a faint tremor to her voice. "Are you Joel Grimes?"

For some reason he found himself unable to answer. The shiver grew stronger, until his whole body seemed to quiver. He gave her a rather abrupt nod.

She tried for a smile, showing the same trembling nerves that he himself felt. "Is there some place we can talk?"

Joel shook his head. "I can't believe this. . . . Why was I never told?"

"I asked the same question. They said it was all too painful. That they couldn't even talk about it between themselves."

They sat in the mission's upstairs office, as bare and rundown as the rest of the center. Thankfully, they had the place to themselves. When they first came to the room, Joel had seated her by the window, offered her coffee, and started with a few practiced questions—until he realized that Kyle was not there looking for a runaway.

Kyle gave Joel silent space to grow accustomed to the idea of a sister. She spent time inspecting his face. There was the same shape to his eyes, his forehead, and his chin, as she saw when she looked in her mirror. On him it looked good, she decided.

He was a nice-looking young man. A bit too thin and pale, but nonetheless attractive—and pleasant, especially his eyes.

"You're sure?" he said at last.

"Yes. I'm sure."

Silence. Absolute silence. He picked up his spoon and began to stir his coffee. Round and round—his eyes staring into a past only he could see. "The guest room," he murmured as though answering a question.

Kyle frowned. "Pardon?"

But Joel did not explain. He lifted his head and studied her closely. At length he nodded. "I guess it explains a lot of things. Sort of." The spoon continued round and round. "My sister. I can't get over this."

"Dr. Austin delivered us both."

"You're kidding."

"No. . . . He's the tie that got me to your—*our* parents." Kyle watched a range of expressions cross her brother's face.

"So where have you been hiding?"

"A family in D.C. adopted me."

He appraised her. "And they are well-off, by the looks of things."

Kyle nodded. There was no use denying it.

"Did the folks decide to look for you?"

"No, I began to look for them."

"And you found them. How?"

"It wasn't easy. I've had a friend looking for months. The adoption records were sealed. We had to gather hints here and there. I finally found Dr. Austin. He decided to break some rules and contacted . . . contacted Martha."

"Why didn't Mom tell me?"

"She just found out, and she's writing you a letter. They said it's not possible to contact you by phone. I suppose you could call them, though . . ."

"Already she's trying to boss me around," he said to the world at large, and they both laughed. "I *have* been busy."

"Well, they sure would love to hear from you, especially with—"

His gaze swung around to her. "With what?"

"You know." She paused for a breath. "They just miss you, that's all," she finished lamely.

But he understood her deeper meaning. "So you've been told everything, is that what I'm hearing?"

"I'm your sister, Joel. They felt—they thought I should know."

Joel looked away. Clearly, having a stranger know about his illness had unsettled him. Kyle wondered if she should have first warned him. Maybe a letter would have been better. Perhaps he could not understand her longing for family. Maybe she would never be able to explain.

But she had to try. She needed to be open and honest and risk his rejection. "I want to know my family. I really do," she began slowly.

He raised his eyebrows, a small smile tilting the corners of his mouth. "Was there ever anything you wanted in your entire life that you couldn't have?"

She stared at him, wondering if he was dismissing her as merely frivolous and empty-headed. How could she explain her life in just a few words? Kyle was tempted to give up the attempt with some pleasantries and hope for a better opportunity in the future.

But something in his eyes made her take a deep breath and speak the truth. "I used to wish to be accepted . . . loved for who I was. Spoken with, rather than *ordered* to sit up straighter or hold my teacup properly. My father . . . he loved me . . . just as I was, but he's—I lost him. Mother . . ." There was no use trying to explain to him about her mother. "I was lonely," she finished in a whisper.

It took a moment for her halting words to sink in. She watched it happen, watched as her simple explanation settled down deep, wiping away his doubts.

A sense of rightness came between them, and Joel nodded slowly and said, "Then we have a lot in common, after all. More than I thought."

And to her surprise he reached across to take her hand and

give it a little squeeze. He looked at her evenly, the questions now gone from his eyes and replaced by a soft, genuine smile. "I'm very glad you were determined enough—brave enough—to find us. To come find me. I really am."

CHAPTER TWENTY-THREE

THAT EVENING, SHE CALLED KENNETH. "I miss you more than I thought could be possible."

He was silent long enough for her to wonder if she should have spoken. Then he murmured, "Oh, Kyle."

"Everything I see, all that's happening, I want to tell you about, describe to you," she said in a rush. The doors that had been opened in their last conversation were not to be shut again. Not ever. "I wish you were with me."

"Your words sound," he said quietly "as though you had looked right inside my mind and knew what I longed to hear."

"I have so much else I want to tell you," she confessed. "I need your perspective and experience, Kenneth."

"How are things going?"

"Good, I think." She recounted the events, her visit with the Millers, and the meeting with her brother. She finished with, "Now I feel, well, I feel like we're all just beginning to know each other, learning how to communicate. I look into Joel's face, which seems so *familiar* to me. And yet it's so strange to *feel* like we know each other, yet really to know so little—we have so many years to catch up on. . . ."

"Give it time," Kenneth assured her after a moment. "Remember, he's not even known about you, and you've been searching for months. All of you need time to adjust to this discovery."

"Yes," she said, still sounding pensive.

"Where are you now?"

"I've taken a room in the Lansdale Hotel." She gripped the phone tightly. "I wish I could see you."

"Would you like me to come up?"

"Could you? Oh, Kenneth, that would be wonderful. But I thought—"

"Things have changed around here," he said, a chuckle in his voice. "I have some news of my own."

"What is it?"

"Randolf and Abigail," he announced, "are dropping the court case."

"What?" She leapt to her feet.

"Apparently their lawyers have advised them against attempting to disinherit you. That is what our own people think. Bad publicity, risking loss of whatever clout they still have, and a case they don't have a hope of winning—whatever the reasons, the case has been dropped, Kyle."

"You mean, it's over? Really and truly finished?"

"We will have to work out a number of details, but you can leave those to me. Yes, if you want my opinion, I would say we are home free."

"Dear Kenneth," she said softly. "Thank you. Thank you for helping me."

"I would like to keep doing that," he said, his tone matching her own. "For the rest of my life."

The next morning, Joel once again rode the bus to Lansdale alone. Simon was still busy helping his father with farm work. Joel found himself glad for the chance to travel in solitude. The day before had left him very unsettled. All night he had relived the encounter with his sister, trying to come to grips with what it all meant.

He stared out the bus window at the bright blue sky of a country autumn morning, and all around him the world was painted in colors of fire. Each bend and rise brought a new scene into view, but Joel scarcely noticed. He reflected that it was not just this newfound sister that had left him so unnerved.

As the bus wound its way into Lansdale, Joel felt a tugging at his heart, as though his parents were reaching out across the distance through Kyle. He stepped from the bus, waved to the driver, and started down the street to the mission. He spotted Kyle walking toward him, leading a tall young man by the hand. Joel had a pang of envy over the man's obvious strength and vitality.

Kyle halted in front of him and said shyly, "Joel, I'd like you to meet Kenneth Adams. This is my brother, Joel."

Kenneth shook his hand, a calm, compassionate light in his eyes. "This is a true honor, Joel. You are doing great work here."

"Thanks." Joel heard the warmth and concern in the young man's voice and immediately felt ashamed at his first response. "Why do you say that?"

"Because of what your parents told us. I think we're seeing just the beginning here." Kenneth's voice held the same quiet power as his face and his grip. "Everywhere I go these days, I'm hearing about a new restlessness among young people. New challenges to the established order of things. We may not be able to stop or redirect the rebellion, yet someone needs to remind them that the ultimate authority is God. But that His is an authority based on love."

The three walked into the building, and Kyle said, "I'll let you two get acquainted." She backed away and asked, "How about coffee?"

At Joel's nod, Kenneth said, "Make that two, please." He then motioned toward nearby chairs. "Do you want to sit down?"

Gratefully Joel accepted the invitation and moved toward a seat. "It sounds like you're a Christian."

"Yes." Kenneth looked around the vast hall. "When I come to a place like this, it challenges me to make my faith a living, breathing part of everything I am, everything I do."

The honest humility touched Joel, and he sank into the chair with a long sigh. When he looked up, Kenneth was watching him with an expression of grave concern. "Kyle tells me you are not well."

"It's a heart condition," Joel admitted.

"Kyle told me. I'm sorry." The silence fell between them for several minutes before Kenneth spoke again. "Kyle and I both wonder if perhaps there is something more that can be done. There are some amazing discoveries about the heart recently—but I'm sure you are aware of this."

"I've lost count of all the tests I've had. If there had been something—anything—that could be done, I'm sure Doc Austin would have seen to it."

"Would you—and your doctor—be willing to undergo further testing?"

"I'm not sure." Joel offered a small smile, not just to the question, but also to the fact that he was talking so comfortably with a stranger. "Maybe I'm just a coward," he admitted slowly. "Any thought—any faint hope—and I'm afraid I would grasp at it."

"That's natural. God created us to fight for survival."

"It's not just for me. Though I've had hopes and dreams that I would love to see fulfilled. It's more than that. It's my work here. I feel that with these young people I am finally doing something important. Something *lasting*. And the irony is that it's about to end."

Both pairs of eyes drifted over the room where ministry for body and soul took place daily. "Sometimes it seems so unfair," Joel said.

Kenneth nodded slowly. "I understand."

The bonding between the two young men was something beyond the mere words they were exchanging. Joel realized this was no stranger. Kenneth was a *brother*. A brother in *heart*. "Sometimes, when I'm alone, I feel like death is standing in the corner of my room, watching and waiting—taunting me." He lowered his head and his voice. "There's so much I want to do. So much left to learn."

Kenneth was quiet for a long moment. His gaze filled with a sorrow that mirrored the anguish spilling from Joel's heart. "The Lord's hand is truly at work in your life, Joel. Whatever happens, He is still at work."

Joel nodded slowly. He already knew this, but had not wanted to accept it. He now realized that the reason he had fought against the truth of God's hand, even in this, was because he had seen it as a defeat. Yet who was he to question God? His love, His will, or His timing.

At Joel's slow nod, Kenneth continued, the warmth in his voice removing any hint of a lecture. "Perhaps you have been seeing this as *your* ministry. Not *His* ministry. If it is truly His— and truly important—don't you think He will care for it? Perhaps the Lord is asking you to prepare yourself for handing over your responsibilities here to someone else." He stopped and searched Joel's face. "But I can't say that for certain. I'm not sure I should be saying anything at all."

Joel struggled to find words. "I feel like you are saying what my heart has been trying to tell me for weeks."

"Then I'm glad I spoke," Kenneth replied quietly.

Joel straightened his shoulders and looked directly at Kenneth. For the first time in a long while he felt at peace. "I'm afraid I have been taking myself far too seriously. It is God's program, after all, isn't it?"

Light footsteps signaled Kyle's return. Joel raised his head to see Kyle a few paces away, steaming coffees in both hands. She glanced from one face to the other. "I'm sorry, am I interrupting?"

The two smiled at each other. "No," Joel said. "Not at all."

Kyle handed over the coffees and settled onto a chair. She hesitated a long moment, then said, "I called your home this morning. They said to tell you . . ." There was a hesitancy, as though she was uncertain how to continue. "They miss you, Joel."

He nodded, both at the words and at what was unsaid. That

he was nearing his own end, and his parents needed time with him. "I need to go home," he acknowledged. "But I don't like the thought of leaving here"—he looked around—"and the Millers. They have been such a strength to me."

"That reminds me." Kyle hesitated, then said carefully, "Ruthie said to tell you, 'Don't leave now, leave next time.' "

"Yeah," Joel said quietly. "If only I could."

Kenneth quietly offered, "You know, you could take your mission work home with you."

Joel looked up, his question unspoken.

"My own church has an outreach program, trying to help young runaways in the Washington area," Kenneth went on. "They could always use experienced help."

Joel felt a newfound surge of hope. "You really think so?"

"I'll take you over and introduce you myself." Kenneth set aside his coffee cup, looked for a moment at Joel, then said, "I would consider it an honor if we could pray together."

Joel found hope rising still, a gift that gave strength he could not receive through words. He nodded his acceptance and said quietly, "I'm so glad my sister found you."

Kyle did not miss the words. Tears formed in her eyes at the acceptance and the open affection they carried. "So am I," she agreed, reaching for Kenneth's hand, then Joel's. "So am I."

That night Kyle lay in her hotel bed and thought back over the events of the last few days. She had never felt so happy, so filled with a sense of anticipation. *God is at work*, she exulted. She felt His very presence with her, deep in her heart. She never wanted to lose this, not ever. She wanted it to grow inside her, getting bigger and stronger every single day. *Please, God, stay with me and let this . . . this feeling of knowing you are here never leave me. Not ever.*

She reached out to touch the wall between her room and

Kenneth's. He was part of all this—God's plan for her life, she realized. He had somehow brought peace and a new sense of direction to Joel. Joel had even agreed to further medical opinion. Perhaps the diagnosis would be the same. They all had to face that fact. But at least they would have the comfort of knowing they had done all they could. It was important for her to do anything that she could, anything that her resources could arrange for, to ease their parents' hearts.

She no longer had to worry about the will that her father had left, about repercussions from those who had tried to contest it. Kenneth possessed the business expertise to give direction to the company; his faith would help her mold Rothmore Insurance into an organization operating in a way that honored God. He shared her sense of calling—to God, to her father's wishes, and now to her new family.

In the search for her roots, she had knocked on many doors. She had been searching for herself and began to realize it really was a search for God. For the first time in her life, she was coming to see who she truly was. Not the proper society lady Abigial wanted. Not even the girl Lawrence had loved. No, it was something far deeper, far richer than that. She was a child of God. And the realization was another door through which she would enter and continue traveling.

Nor would she go through this journey alone. She *knew* it. No matter that her beloved father had died or that Joel might leave her just as she was coming to know and love him. There was a new vision that calmed her heart and filled the void of loneliness that had been so much a part of her life.

For her earthly family—families—had been joined to an eternal one. The heavenly family was a part of her now. Nothing could ever take that away. She *belonged*.

Martha held Joel for a long time when he first arrived home.

Joel could feel the tremble of her body as she fought against tears, but bravely she tried for a smile as she pushed back and placed her hands on his arms. "I think you've put on some weight," she said. "Maybe you like Mrs. Miller's cooking better than your mother's." Joel could tell she was teasing, and they both laughed.

It was Harry's turn then. Joel had never been hugged by his dad before, as far as he could remember. Mr. Miller gave him an occasional bear hug, but this was different. Harry drew him close and held him snug against his chest. "We've missed you, son," he said with a husky voice that hinted at all the lost years.

Kyle had traveled with Joel and was welcomed by loving embraces, too, and soon the bittersweet emotions turned to joyous reunion. Almost without realizing it they fell into easy conversation.

"I made your favorite dessert, apple crisp," Martha informed Joel as she led them to the little kitchen where the table had been carefully set with the best they had. She turned to Kyle. "Had I known your favorite, dear, I would have made it, too." The words touched Kyle's heart in a strange but warm way.

"I'm sure your apple crisp will quickly become my favorite," she said. The two looked at each other without speaking, but the message that passed between them brought joy to both.

"Well, now," Martha said finally, "let's get supper on the table."

In a very few minutes the four were gathered for the meal. Harry said, "Take your usual place, son, and, Kyle, you sit here in this spot that has been vacant for too many years."

Kyle accepted the seat and looked around her at her family. *Her family.* Harry reached out his hands, one to his daughter, one to his son, and Martha took their hands on the other side.

"I think we need to thank God for far more than our food today," said Harry. "He has blessed us beyond our dreams. Our son"—he gave Joel's hand a squeeze—"and our daughter"—he turned to Kyle—"are both here at our table." His voice sounded husky. Kyle wondered if he would be able to continue. "Our family. Our *whole* family—together at last."

Kyle could hear Martha sniffing. She choked back her own tears.

"Let's thank God. Then let's make the most of this very special day," said Harry.

As Kyle bent her head to join in the prayer she felt a little nudge against her foot. She looked up to meet Joel's eyes, misty but filled with joy. "Thanks, my sister," he mouthed to her across the table. Kyle's heart had never felt lighter.

CHAPTER TWENTY-FOUR

KYLE STEPPED FROM THE TAXI, paid the fare, then stopped a moment to gaze down the long drive. Taking her time, she strolled through the gate, examining the lawns and the house with a fresh new eye. The day held a surprising warmth, as though trying to make up for the previous week's hard frost. As Kyle approached the house, happy childhood memories flooded back. There had been some good times here. Her father's love. The devoted care of the Ameses and the rest of the household staff. Even the training of her mother, though often misplaced and exaggerated, had not been wasted. In her mother's own way, perhaps she had cared.

Not even the cloud of apprehension about what was coming could take away Kyle's feeling of rightness, of renewal.

"Miss Kyle!" Her reverie was interrupted as a familiar figure took a long moment to rise from his work at the flower bed. "If you aren't a sight for sore eyes!"

"Hello, Jim." She hurried over and embraced the bent old man. "How are you?"

"Better, after that hug." The old gardener cackled. "They keep thinking I'm gonna give up the ghost, and I keep surprising them."

"Don't you dare." She took a step back, looked around her, and said, "The place looks wonderful—better than ever!"

"Yep, that's the sign of a good garden. Tend it well and let it kinda grow into itself." The lined face had grime worked deep into the folds, but the eyes were clear and the grin genuine. "You're looking pretty good yourself."

"Thank you," she replied. "I'm doing just fine."

"Glad to hear it. Been awful quiet around here without you."

She glanced toward the house. The high stone edifice looked as regal and imposing as it had when she had been a small child.

"When you gonna bring that young feller of yours around?"

"Soon. I promise."

The front door of the house was flung open and a portly lady in a faded kitchen apron hurried down the stairs. Jim cackled again. "Look at them old bones move, will you."

"Kyle, oh, my baby, it's been so long!" Maggie enfolded her in a warm embrace.

"Hello, Maggie. I'm sorry I didn't call ahead, but—"

"This is your home, child. Why on earth would you need to call?" She held Kyle back at arm's length. "You look absolutely marvelous."

Kyle inspected the dear, familiar lines of her face, and the lump in her throat returned. "So do you, Maggie."

"Oh, look at what I've done." Maggie began brushing her off. "I've gotten flour on your beautiful jacket."

"I'll let you two get on with it. I'm sure I'd not get a word in edgewise," Jim said with a twinkle, tipping his battered cap to the pair of them. "Come on out and chat with me 'fore you leave."

"Come inside," Maggie said, pulling her toward the door. "Bertrand has gone to the shops, but he won't be long. How *are* you? Tell me all about your new family. I can't wait to find out *everything*."

"All right." Kyle couldn't help but smile at Maggie's enthusiasm.

She entered the vast front foyer, looked around, and felt all the old memories surging up. But now she was able to push aside the old anxieties. She was not alone.

Maggie pointed toward the kitchen. "Come join me for a cup of tea."

"Not just now, Maggie." Kyle knew the purpose of her visit could be put off no longer. "How is Mother?"

The woman faltered a moment before replying, "She's out on the veranda."

"How is she, Maggie?"

The woman's forehead creased. "It's nothing I can put my finger on. But the past few days, it seems like all the starch has gone out of her."

"Let me go talk with her. I'll come in after and we can have a nice long chat."

Maggie reached up and patted Kyle's cheek. "You always were a good girl, a good daughter."

Kyle felt a flutter around her heart. "Pray for me, Maggie. And pray for her."

"I always have, child," she replied, her eyes shining. "And I always will."

"Kyle!" Abigail half rose from her seat, light springing into her eyes as one hand reached out toward the girl. Quickly she checked herself and settled back in the chair with an uneasy clearing of her throat. "Well, I was not expecting you," she said in her usual controlled manner.

Kyle longed to rush to her mother, throw her arms around her as freely as she did with Martha, and sob out the long years of loneliness and hurt. But her mother's return to formality kept her from it. "Hello, Mother."

"I suppose you've come back to crow over me in triumph."

"Oh, Mother." Kyle mourned as she walked out on the veranda and pulled one of the heavy metal chairs up closer. "How are you?"

"How do you think?" Abigail answered sharply. "I am faced with watching everything I have spent my life trying to build be reduced to ashes."

"Please, Mother. Nothing is going to be destroyed." Kyle folded her hands in her lap, took a deep breath, and nestled within the gift of calm. Not even her racing heart could overwhelm her sense of being sheltered and guided. "I have not come here to gloat—or to argue."

Her mother took the reading glasses off her nose and put them and her magazine on the table at her side. "Soon it's all yours. All of it. I suppose you're going to bring vengeance on us all."

"Neither Kenneth nor I want vengeance in any way, Mother. He is an honorable, God-fearing man, and he will be directing the company. He will do what is right for us all."

Her daughter's calm seemed to leave Abigail even more rattled. "I hope you aren't expecting me to crawl and beg. The house is mine. Mine, I tell you. Lawrence—"

"Of course it's yours. I wouldn't dream of trying to take anything from you. Most especially your home."

Abigail's gaze scattered across the back garden, and her finger nervously picked up her glasses, then laid them down again. "Well, you had better not have come down here expecting an apology. What I tried to do was the best thing for the company. And for you. You have no idea how to run a company."

"No I don't," Kyle agreed. "But Kenneth does."

"My own daughter," Abigail interrupted. "Turning against me."

"I haven't turned against you, Mother. I've come to see you and find out how you are."

"I thought you had gone to your *other* family," Abigail retorted. "They have no money, no family heritage. But I guess you found that out for yourself. I told Randolf that you'd be back. I told him that you'd soon discover that they couldn't give you anything you didn't already have."

"But they did. The most worthwhile things that life can offer. Love. Acceptance. Family. I haven't turned from them, Mother. I love them dearly and expect to spend a good deal of time with them in the future. I have come back because of you."

"Me?"

"I've come here to say that I love you and I don't hold anything against you."

For once Abigail was brought to an astonished silence.

"If you want it, Mother, I forgive you."

Abigail finally managed, "Forgive?"

"For everything." The surge of love that flooded Kyle's being was like a light descending from above, a power so strong it *demanded* that it be shared.

Kyle reached across the emotional chasm that had separated her from Abigail all their lives, even as her hand reached across the table and took the slim, trembling hand of her mother in her own. "I have discovered salvation, Mother, and the wonderful gift of forgiveness. God has forgiven me and expects me to hold no bitterness toward others. It is *His* gift, a gift of love that I want to share with you. I do love you, Mother. I truly do. God has filled my heart with a love that I cannot even explain. Please don't turn it away. We have so much to share with each other. So much."

There were no words forthcoming from Abigail. Kyle might have wondered if her offering was received had she not felt the clasp on her hand undeniably tighten.

Abigail was looking at her with a strange expression on her face. She gave a tight nod, then quickly said, "Well, don't expect miracles."

Kyle smiled softly and quietly replied, "Oh, but I do."